To: Jaze
Thank All the support

DA HOOD MAKES
FRESH WATER

much love always

Jordan
8-6-09

To all my beautiful people out there or anyone that has read my book. Abuse, sex, money and drugs will only lead to destruction. Whatever Higher Power you believe in, keep that faith first and everything else will fall into place.

On February 25, 2005, BET Nightly News, announced that in the past decade, AIDS among African Americans has risen, but amongst Caucasians, it stayed the same.

So I say to you: Have faith, play safe and stay true to self.

Thank you!

      Much Love!

            Peace Out!

Cover design by Jernell McLane
blackphyrproductions@gmail.com

All rights reserved. No part of this book may be reproduced or transmitted in any form or by any means, electronic or mechanical, including photocopy, recording, or any information storage retrieval system, without permission in writing from the publisher.

Copyright © 2009 DaNeana Ulmer
First printing 2009

978-0-9820870-1-5

Library of Congress Control Number: 2008943901

Published by

NELYMESHA Corp.
P.O BOX 65804
St.Paul Mn 55165.

Ms. Leona

Dedications:
First and Foremost, I want to thank the Lord Jesus
Christ my Savior… without YOU there would be no me!!!
Ms. Leona McCoy (December 11, 1938 – January 22, 2007)
Mommy, thank you for your positive influence
and encouragement in my life!

Chapter 1

Worry

"Roxane, wake up now! Wake up! Wake up!" Slap, slap, right upside of Rox's head.

"Mom, I'm up dang. Why you got to hit me? I heard you."

"Then act like it girl, get in there and meet the brush, towel and sink, before you leave out of this house! Okay Rox?"

"She makes me sick, always gotta yell and shit! Damn"

"I heard you little girl! You better watch that mouth! You ain't grown! At fourteen, your butt needs to still be playin with dolls! Instead, your butt is around here missing your period!"

Oh shit.

"Mom."

"Yeah, you thought your little friends didn't tell me? Well, I just want you to know, I heard y'all whispering in your room!"

"No Mom, it wasn't me. Please listen!"

"Yes it was Rox. It was you, Darlene, Angie and Monique. Y'all all still virgins remember?"

"Huh?"

"Girl, just get ready for school, this will be the last time you will see your friends anyway."

"Why are you saying that Mommy? I'm not going to disappoint you like Lili did."

"Whatever. Just get it together for school."

Rox was in the bathroom, washing her face, when she looked up at the calendar on the wall, it was May 3rd. She was about 3 months shy, of turning 15 and didn't need no baby. Her period was suppose to come and it didn't. She prayed that this would never happen at her age because Rox's older sister, Lili, was a prescription pill popper, with seven kids, by five different men. Lili was short for Lynete Renea Adams. Lili did what she had to do, to get that loot. She was for poppin' tags, turnin' tricks, and curb servin', every now and then.

She loved to pop tags, because she felt it was the easiest way to get that bread. She would go in the department stores and pick all the Levi's, Guess, and DKNY jeans she wanted, then goes to the kid's department and get the tags off and put them on the high price clothes that she had in her hand.

Lili's closet was filled with all the latest fashion. Rox was so pissed, that Lili would always make her pay for her clothes, that she later sold. She would tell Rox, "Oh, I got all color Guess in your size Rox, and I'm gonna save them for you." Then when Rox would get off of work, Lili would already have sold them, to one of her friends, to piss Rox off. Lili would only go in the store with like $100 or $150 dollars, and come home with 20 outfits. She would sell them for half price, to people she did not like, but a third to people that she did like. You know Rox fell in the I-don't-careabout-her category. That meant, when Lili did sell her something, it was for half price.

Lili was jealous of Rox. Rox was a pretty, light skinned 14 year old, that was stacked like "Pam Grier." Rox had a 36-26-36 shape, with "DD" full tits. Lili's boyfriends always watched her and called her "the young cutie with the big booty". It never went to Rox's head, but she kept it in mind because she would use that to her advantage later in life.

"Rox! Rox!"

"Yes Mommy?"

"Mommy huh? Come on girl, I'm gonna drop you off at the bus stop, on my way to work."

"Okay." Rox and her mother walked out to their truck. Rox got in the truck, and so did her mother. Ms. Rovon Victoria Adams a.k.a. Ms. Vickie.

"Mom, you didn't tell me why you said it would be the last time I see any of my friends."

"Because I've met someone, and we are planning to move to south Minneapolis, real soon."

"Just like that Mom? I have not even met the buster."

"What! Watch your mouth little girl. I've told you about that now." "Mom, when am I gonna meet this I'm-moving-over-south man?" "You have already."

"What! When! At what time? I must of been blind or deaf."

"No, it's the nice man that took me out to lunch, for the past year. The one that has been paying for you to go roller skating, with your friends, and paying our rent in this apartment, the insurance on this car for me and you..." "What you mean?"

"Oh, and gives you an allowance."

"Oh Mom, your trippin me out this morning."

"Well is that enough to convince you that Howard Davis is good enough to be your step dad?"

"Mom stop right there."

"Why?"

"This is the entrance to the school."

"Whoa!"

"Mom! You almost hit that boy!"

"It's okay Rox, just get out right here okay?"

"Okay Mom. I need some money."

"For what girl?"

"To eat and hang out after school."

"Hang out? Where and with who?"

"Me and Monique are going to Oxford, to watch the Elks drill team practice." "Okay, I want you home before 9:00 pm, and not 9:05. You hear me?" "Yes Mommy."

"Oh, and just because you're in the 9th grade, and go to St. Paul Central High School, doesn't mean that you are grown, little girl."

"Mom, I got to go, and I know."

"And one more thing, you haven't had your period. We will be discussing that too!"

"Okay, I'm out of here. Mom I heard you."

"Love you." Smooch.

"Love you too." Smooch.

Rox walks up the three flights of steps, to the front entrance of her high school. The only thing I can do, is tell mom the truth. I did two dudes in one day. One is not my man, and the other is the school's football star. Oh God, please, I pray that you make this better for me. I pray that you save me, and make my period come down. Please! Please! Oh God!

"Rox! Rox wake up! Snap out of it Rox!"

"Oh, I'm sorry, what's happening Monique?"

"Your my sis, I told you to call me Mo."

"Sorry Mo."

"What are you thinking so hard about? Girl you are in a trans."

"Oh, I got to get to first hour. Umm my mom was sweatin me about bloody Mary not coming, and I was thinking about what she was saying."

"Mary hasn't come yet?"

"No, and I need to see Carl, before I get out today."

"Oh, if I see him before lunch, I'll tell him to meet us at lunch."

Rox proceeded her way to class, and had nothing on her mind except the events that happened three weeks ago. One Friday night Rox had a date with her man Carl. Carl was a dark skinned, bowlegged 5'10 in height, with round eyes and nice voluptuous lips. Carl was Central High's football star. Every girl in school wanted and dreamed of having Carl. This never bothered Rox. She never worried about Carl cheating on her, because he knew she was young and feisty. She wasn't taking any shit.

She often warned Carl, that if she ever caught him doing anything, such as talking on the phone to broads, chopping it up with them in class, or giving anyone a ride home, under no circumstances, it was not to happen. Rox walked right out of her third hour biology class, and bumped right into her baby daddy, Carl.

"What's up baby? How's my favorite girl doing?"

"Fine Boo, but I'm...."

"What? What's wrong?"

"Nothing, I just can't disappoint my mom."

"What Rox baby, tell me what you're talking about?"

"I will, but not now."

"Yes, you will tell me, now."

"Let go of my arm boy!" Rox steps back, and slaps Carl's hand off of her arm.

"Damn girl! What's up? What did I do? You've had a real attitude lately."

"Look, I'm not gonna make a scene."

"Now Rox, to my car!" Carl pointed in the direction of the door.

"No, I told Monique that I'm going to eat with her, plus we only have a 20 minute lunch today."

"Bullshit girl. I told yo ass, I ain't gonna be playing no games. I want to know now!"

Rox didn't want to make no scene, so she did as her man said, and proceeded her way to the car. As she approached his all black Cadillac, Rox was about to step in the passenger side, And got a tap on the shoulder...

"What I told..."

"Oh shit", Rox yelled as she looked around.

"Um Uh Um. What's up? Where the hell you been and why you ain't call me back?"

"Oh...oh I have, but...."

"Get in the fucking car girl damn."

"Um Terrance, I'll call you okay?"

Carl stood up out of the car "Hey who the fuck are you?" Terrance never looked back, and walked away. Rox then sat down, in the car, while Carl was still standing in the doorway of the car, tryin to make out the back of Terrance's blue jean jacket.

"Hey! Turn around boy, I need to talk to you! I'm gonna catch you! Don't you ever approach my woman, you hear me!"

Terrance just continued to walk, out the schools parking lot, and crossed the street, to get in his own beige impala SS, with tinted windows. Carl kept that thought and kept the look of Terrance's car, in his mind. Carl finally sat down in the car.

"Rox! Who the fuck was that? Huh?"

"It was this dude in my creative writing class, that was helping me..."

Slap! Slap!

"What are you doing C?"

"You keep playing me girl!"

"Hold up, don't start slapping on me bitch!"

Slap!

Rox slapped the piss out of Carl, while he tried to reach and choke her.

"Oh! You hitting back now are you?"

"Yeah punk ass mother fucker! You think you can hit me and I'm not gonna hit back?"

"Who you calling a punk?" Carl continued to grab Rox by her shirt, and pull her hair.

"Let go of my hair bitch, now!"

Slap! Punch! Kick!

"Ouch! Damn hoe!"

"You called me a hoe? You must be mistaken me, for Denise huh?"

"What? Bullshit! You just tryin to get out of what we came here for."

"Nah, punk!"

Slap! Slap!

"Don't try and change the subject. You just messed my ponytail up bitch, and you gonna pay for this!"

"Okay! I ain't tryin to change shit, but I ain't gonna keep fighting you in this damn car!"

"I'm about to go."

"No you ain't! Tell me what you was thinking about earlier."

"No. I got to fix my hair."

"Fuck yo hair girl. Who you getting cute for anyway? I'm right here and you look good as hell."

"Don't play C. I'm fucked up, and you know it. I've messed up my Nike sweat shirt, and my mom just got my hair done this weekend. She's gonna be pissed off that it didn't last a week!"

"I'll get your hair done over. Tell me now!" Carl slid into the passenger seat with Rox, so he could look her right in the face.

"Move C, so I can get out okay? We can talk."

Carl started to grab Rox by the waist, and started kissing her softly on the side of her face.

"Stop C...I got to get back to class, please.." Rox started to move around in her seat, and tried to lift her hips up. When Rox lifted up, she bumped right up in C's brick hard dick.

"Yeah, see I thought you would give in."

Rox didn't say a word. She couldn't resist- her body was feeling warm and tingly. Her pussy instantly got wet, with just the touch of C's hands and soft lips, against her earlobe.

"C, baby, please....we can't....in this car.... please... don't do it baby." C grabbed Rox's hands, and lifted them to the ceiling. He then took his mouth, and covered hers, with his lips. Sucking in and out, he then took his hands, and slowly rubbed Rox's double D's. Rox moaned and started moving her hips, in a grinding motion. C started grinding back and stopped kissing her. He slowly started putting wet kisses on her neck, making his way to Rox's protruding titties. As C sucked Rox's titties, Rox prayed in her mind: "Oh God, this feels so good, but please, if I'm not pregnant, don't let me get pregnant, and please just give me the words to say to C, and if it's not...forgive me, for what I'm gonna do."

"Rox, pull them pants down to your knees."

"Okay baby...just keep sucking my titties baby." C continued to suck Rox's titties, and slid his finger in and out of her hot and wet pussy. Rox was lovin it, rollin her hips and telling C to put it in.

"Baby...put it in please..."

"Wait, do you love me?"

"Yes boo, I love you."

"And what else?"

"I'll do anything for you."

"What else?"

"And I'll never cheat on you, never."

"Oh, then lift yo pussy up, so I can see if you been fuckin, cause I know that nigga was talkin to you for something."

"Baby just put it in!"

C didn't stick his wide and full 10 inch dick in just yet. He took Rox by the waist, and lifted her butt up, so he could see her whole pussy. He pulled it close to his face, took his long tongue, and licked right in between her lips. Rox screamed out pure pleasure. By C being 3 years older than her, he was very mature, and knew just what to do to Rox, to make her do whatever he wanted her to do. C then took his face, and sunk it into her pussy deep, and moved his head up and down, then licked around in a circular motion. Rox's legs began to shake out of control, while she grabbed C's head with her right hand, and held on to the arm rest, with the other.

"Stop C. Stop Boo. What is this?" Rox's legs shook more. "Oh boo please! I'm gonna pee on myself! Please! See it's coming out..please!"

C didn't stop at all. The sounds of him turning my young ass out turned him on. C held Rox with his left arm and licked up and down. He slid his tongue in and out of her pussy hole, then he took his index finger and stuck it in her ass. Rox wasn't ready for this at all. Her body was shaking in a way she had never felt. She didn't know if she was going to pee, cum or shit. She screamed out "C..please...it's coming out! Stop." C didn't listen, he just handled his business. When all of a sudden, "oh shit girl!" C let go of Rox's hips.

"What the fuck?" C had never seen nothing like it in his life, even though he had ate pussy once before, to a well experienced Rose. Rose is a n older woman, in her 30's. Rose turned C out at 14, but never told him what could happen after the fact. Rose was so experienced, that she could control her pussy muscles and any other muscles, for that matter.

"Don't you know how to hold that shit in girl?" Rox was so embarrassed, she had cum mixed with piss and a shit ball, on the seat of C's car.

"Oh goodness! I'm sorry, I couldn't help it."

"Put your damn clothes on, shit."

"Hold on punk, you got my pussy in your mouth, sucking the shit out of it, and now you gonna yell and tell me to put my shit on? You're the weakest nigga in Minnesota right now."

"Well I ain't know yo dumb ass was gonna shit in my car!"

"Bitch I ain't never had no freaky shit like this happen to me, punk ass bitch...."

C slapped the shit out of her, and started beating her ass. Slap! Slap!

"Didn't I tell yo young ass to stop calling me a punk bitch, huh?"

"Oh my God! Boy stop! Stop, I'm about to piss again!" C kept slapping, punching and pulling Rox's hair, when she just bust out

"Please baby!...I'm sorry....I won't..." C kept punching her in her mouth. "I might be pregnant! I missed my period. Please!" C stopped instantly.

"What hoe?"

"Yes and I might of lost it now." C couldn't do anything, but go into a rage in the car.

"No you ain't hoe! You just now telling me and you could of told me earlier? You hear me!" C started to shake the shit out of Rox, while he cried. He slowly stopped and looked at Rox, while she cried hysterically.

"Baby...let me out the car. I can't breathe."

"You ain't going nowhere. I love you girl!"

"Okay, but I got to clean myself up, please." C looked around to see piss shit and white stains, all over the seat, with blood all over his shirt.

"Where did that blood come from?"

"My nose stupid. You only been beatin the shit out of me for the past 5 minutes!"

"I'm sorry baby. You just tell me some shit like this after a fight, a pussy suck and now another fight? Damn that's a lot for me in one day."

"Well yeah, you're the one that decided to do all of this in one day." Rox said sarcastically.

"Okay, don't start getting smart again."

"Just help me boy." C took Rox and helped her out of the car. He went in his trunk and gave her a new shirt he had in his gym bag. Then he had her get in the back seat, and change her shirt.

"Okay, what about my panties and hair? I also stink and you know I ain't going back into class smelling like shit." C started to laugh and handed her a pair of his boxers and his gym pants.

"What am I gonna do with these big ass pants?"

"Girl go in the bathroom and take you a wash up. Wash your hair and you'll be okay."

"Damn, you sure know what I should do. You done this shit before or something?"

"No! But, I know how to wash my own ass when accidents happen, so I know it shouldn't be that hard for you!"

"Oh well, what am I gonna do with your clothes later?"

"What you mean? Dummy, wash them and bring them to the crib later!"

"What? I ain't..."

"Get your ass back there and change! Shit, you already missed 4th hour, and the hall monitors will be out here checking the parking lot." Rox started playing with Carl.

"Go head girl!" Kiss. Kiss. "Go on, call me later."

"Okay." Rox looked at C and asked "Do you love me?"

C yelled out "Yes! Yes! Yes! Boo, now go on!" Rox went back into the school. She wondered where Carl was going but she never turned around to ask him.

Rox made her way to the bathroom, right across from the lunch room. As she walked in, a girl named Denise saw her and was right on her heels, and followed her. Rox had enough time to wet her towel and grab a new bar of soap that was laying on the sink counter. Rox wouldn't dare use a used bar of soap, that was laying in germ infested water, and been passed through so many hands. Right when Rox stepped in the bathroom stall:

"Hey Roxane. I saw you." Rox thought in her mind, who in the hell is that and what did this hoe see me doing what?

"Excuse me?" Rox yelled

"You heard me hoe." Denise started kicking the door to the bathroom stall, while Rox stood there with a soaped up pussy and a towel with blood, cum and pubic hair all over it.

Rox had to think fast. Normally she would of bust through that damn door and stole on anybody that had addressed her, but, under these circumstances she had to think this situation out, without looking like a punk.

"Um...why are you calling me out? I don't even know you?" Rox tried real hard to look through the crack on the door of the stall she was in.

"Yeah hoe, like I said, hater, you know me cause I've been doing things to yo man, that you can't do!"

"Oh yeah? And what is that?"

"Oh, wouldn't you like to know you fake ass bitch. I won't let you trick me into snitching on yo man, but I will tell you that if you keep sneaking around like nobody don't know, then I'll be the first to tell and he will be mines."

Rox stood there for about 30 seconds, with thoughts running through her mind of 'What the hell is she talking about? Why is this old hoe addressing me? She knows Carl will beat the shit out of her for steppin to me.'

"Oh..ah Denise, I'm gonna tell you like this, I ain't worried about no hoe telling my man shit cause he's mine and our bond can't ever be broken, unless we choose to break it. So...say what cha' wanna say. My man ain't gonna believe shit you say about me."

Rox didn't know that Denise had her tape recorder in her hand, and was recording the whole conversation. Normally kid's can't bring anything electronic to the school, because of all the fights it had caused over someone stealing somebody's walkman, flat irons, cds and dvd players. Denise had an excuse for having a hand held recorder, because she was a senior and almost out of school. Denise had to record her lectures for Chemistry. She knew by recording over her lesson, it might hurt her later, but she didn't care. She had to get Carl's ass if he was the last man on earth.

See, Denise was Carl's former girl. She was with Carl in the 9th grade, just like Rox was now. Rox was young, and not dumb by any means, but you couldn't tell Denise that.

"So you can cheat on C and think that he won't find out and then you dumb enough to do it with somebody in the same school? Yeah Rox, I think your pimpin stinks and you will be exposed."

"Bitch! Like I said...you need to go mind your own business and worry about your own man, cause mine's ain't believing shit you say! I don't care how many nigga's I fuck!" Ooops! Oh shit! Did I say that? Oh damn, she heard me.

Denise eyes blew up wide with a smile from St. Paul to Minneapolis. Denise proceeded to turn around, with the recorder in her hand. As Rox peeked through the door to see Denise heading for the door, skipping and jumping, she noticed something in her hand.

"Hey! What's that in your hand?" Denise didn't answer, she just busted out laughing.

"Hey! Hey! Where you going? I thought we were talking?"

"My job is done here hoe, and just so you know, I remember everything you said." Rox thought quick before Denise disappeared out the door, so she had to say something.

"Yeah, I got something on you too bitch!" Denise continued to laugh. Walking out the door, she opened the door back and said "Just wash that nasty shit off you hoe, cause you stunk up the bathroom." Denise then walked on about her business.

Rox was so pissed off that she couldn't whoop the shit out of Denise.

She had to laugh at Denise on her last comment, as she looked around at herself and she did look a mess. She could smell the stank smell that was coming from her clothes. Rox stood at the sink and prayed to God, that no one would come in. She was having a bad day and just needed to have some peace at this time.

She cleaned herself and wet up the whole bathroom floor. She put on her deodorant and sprayed on a little bit of body spray, that she had in her purse. She then disposed of her whole Nike suit, because a dime such as herself, couldn't wash that out and wear it again. Plus, it had too many memories of a bad day. Before Rox walked out of the bathroom, she prayed "Oh God, thank you for making it better for me, but God, please help me. I need my period to come so I won't disappoint my mom. God I want to make her proud of me, and I'm gonna graduate with honors and become a successful entrepreneur, 'cause God, only you know that I can't work for no one but you."

Rox made her way to her 6th hour class. It was Phy. Ed. She made it in on time, so she was the first to get her special jump rope. "Hi Mr. Erickson."

"Hello Roxane, we will be having open class today, so you can do whatever you want for the hour okay?"

"Thanks Mr. Erickson, I needed it today."

"Oh, why? Is something wrong? Any problems you want to talk about?"

"No! I'm fine, just wanted to relax."

"Okay, well you know I'm here, if you want to ever talk okay?"

"Thank you." Rox did her workout. Jumping rope, running, and 500 crunches.

People didn't understand Rox and she knew it. Her goal was to keep herself in shape, until she was 80 years old. Shit, she felt her mother had done such a great job, at 29 years old, she was stacked like Janet Jackson, Diana Ross and Pam Grier in their prime.

Rox was taught by her Aunt Judy, how to keep herself together. Aunt Judy was a track star for Central High school in 1982. She was her mom's youngest sister out of 8 children. She was real close in age with Rox. When Rox was a little girl, she use to copy everything her Aunt Judy would do. She wanted to dress, look and act, just like her. When Judy left, to go to college to study law she basically had to leave Rox to fend for herself.

Rox finished up her workout, And hit the shower in the locker room, she noticed that she had a change of clothes in there as well.

As she finished in the shower, she put on her red DKNY jeans, DKNY tee shirt, and all white air force ones. She noticed that she had a note in her pocket. Rox always checked her pockets, because one of her cousins got set up back in the day. She was never told the whole story, but she was very observant and would always listen to what grown people had to say. She overheard one of her uncles and Judy, discussing how her cousin Kane, was set up, when one of his friends put some heroin in his pocket while they were playing pool at the game room.

The "Pop Shop," was a local game room, where everyone in St. Paul would hang out at after school including the dropouts. It was located on Selby Avenue, and there was never any supervision around there. The old heads were either too high or drunk to pay attention to any of the under age people that hung out there. Even though cousin Kane was 17 when he got caught, he had to stay locked up, until he was 25.

Rox knew that by ear hustlin in grown folks business would gain her a lot of knowledge. Rox pulled out the paper and damn. (Oh my goodness! This is the paper....damn....oh...shit!)

Rox continued to think to herself about the events that happened three weeks ago. One night when her mother was at work and Carl had a late practice, Terrance called to ask for Rox' assistance with his homework. Terrance was in the 11th grade, And school wasn't his priority. But that mighty dollar bill was. Terrance grew up in a shifted family, between his grandma, aunt and mother. Though he preferred to stay at his grandma's because she always made him feel comfortable even when she had a house full. Terrance called Rox and asked her to meet him at his aunt's house for help on his S.A.T. test. It was real important to Rox and Terrance, that he pass this test, because if he didn't, he would have to do the 11th grade all over again.

Rox remembered going over to Terrance's house, but she got more than she expected. When Rox first made it to his house, she was greeted with a rose, kiss on the cheek, and a soda. She figured it was kind of odd, but she just didn't care. Her and Terrance sat down at the table and started studying English and comprehension, because these were the classes he was having the most complications with.

Well as Rox was talking, Terrance told her to hold up a minute while he excused himself to go to the bathroom. Rox got up to be nosy. She noticed on the coffee table across from her, that there was a big thick book on the table. She picked it up because a school picture of her was lying on top of it. She knew Terrance had a picture of her because he went to grammar school with her. Even being two years older than her, he still ended up at Maxfield Elementary School with her.

When she picked up the book it was a 'Sexual Position book.' She opened it up and couldn't believe all the different positions there was for sex. It had animals, insects and every creature of the world in that book. Rox's pussy started getting wet, as she imagined and fantasized about all the positions that were in this book. As she looked at the book, Rox didn't realize that Terrance was standing behind her butt-ass naked. Terrance knew that the book was the bait for her. Even though she had a man, he didn't care. Terrance was 6'2, had long arms, big hands, caramel skin and charcoal black curly hair. He was fine as hell, "fire" as all the girl's around the way would say. All he had to do was look her in the eyes and he got her. His eyes were his best asset, and that usually won any girl over.

As Rox turned around and felt the heat on the back of her neck, she couldn't believe her eyes.

"Damn boy! What the hell is wrong with you, put some clothes on crazy!"

"Don't fight it Rox. You know you want it and so do I." Rox thought like damn, this boy is packin like a plumber, his body is cut the hell up, that damn weight lifting has paid off. She thought damn this boy is a fool brick hard and ready to give my pussy a black eye. If I say no, he might rape me.

"What make you think such a thing? You need to put your clothes on please!" Rox loved looking at his body. It made her pussy drip like a faucet as her body broke out into a sweat. Terrance didn't take his eyes off of Rox, as he watched her view his body while she stepped back to cover her mouth with her hands.

Terrance started to walk towards Rox and grabbed her around her shoulders and gave her a hug. Even though Rox was a little scared of his boldness, she didn't resist. Terrance took that to his advantage and grabbed her by the hand and lead her to the bedroom.

Rox walked slowly, while she wondered what he was about to do to her.

"Terrance, what about your test? Huh...T? T, answer me...." Terrance didn't say anything, he just turned around to kiss her. Rox couldn't resist once again. Terrance' kiss was almost as good as Carl's. Terrance bent down on his knees and continued to kiss Rox and at the same time, pulling her skirt down, He pulled her panties down and softly kissed her stomach and softly licking around her belly. He kissed her down to her feet, as he felt her legs shake, He then lifted one foot at a time, to release her skirt and panties to the floor.

Rox kept trying to talk, so as Terrance made his way back up to her titties to unsnap her bra, he slid his index finger into her mouth. Rox didn't want him to think that she was no punk, so she sucked his finger and grabbed him by the head. Terrance started sucking both of her titties, taking both his hands to cup them. Rox let out a loud moan. This almost made Terrance cum. He was so hard. Ready to release his nut into her mouth, as he had thought about it the whole nine months of tutoring. Terrance quickly pulled Rox's bra and shirt off and threw it down. He stood up and took a good look at Rox's naked wet body. He didn't realize how much she wanted him. Rox was staring at him, "What's wrong?"

"Are you ready to handle all of this?" As Terrance talked and admired Rox' body, her nipples set out at attention, like a soldier to a sergeant. Rox shifted from side to side, like she had to pee.

"Come to me baby. I'm ready." Terrance grabbed Rox, kissed her, sucking her bottom lip and guiding her to the black sheets, that were on the bed. He then laid her on her back, spread her legs open with his, and started grinding. As he rubbed her titties and licked in her ear, she moaned out of control.

"T...please...put it in. Please....baby..please!" Terrance was brick hard and he was about to release his nut. He moved his way down to the top of Rox' hairline and grabbed one leg, with his other hand he took his long dick and stuck the tip of it in. Rox screamed out in pain, asking Terrance to stop. Terrance continued to push his way in her tight pussy as she wiggled. This wiggling was making him weak. Terrance started pumping hard and fast.

"Stop T! Stop! It hurts! Baby stop!"

"Make up your mind. You said I can hit it, now you cryin in shit!"

"I said make it feel good, not hurt me!"

"Oh, well I been waiting too long and I'm 'bout to beat it up."

Oh God, Rox thought in her mind. What the hell does he mean? She soon found out.

Terrance lifted both of her legs up and put his whole 10 1/2 inches in her. Rox wasn't ready for this. While she screamed and put her finger nails in his back, that just turned him on more. Terrance pulled his dick out and turned her on her stomach, and beat it up from the back, while Rox moaned and screamed. Terrance then pulled her off the bed and bent her ass over the chair so he could get a better look at her cherry red ass bent over the chair. Rox tried to make a run for it but couldn't. Terrance was going so deep, he couldn't bust a nut but he really didn't want to until he left his mark. He played with Rox' titties with one hand, while he played with her clit with the other. He then pulled out to sit her on his dresser and let her rest while he positioned her ass on the corner, so he could hit that spot. Yeah he thought, I better hit that g-spot so this pussy will be all mine. Rox thought he was finished when he put her legs on his shoulders and cupped her ass. He went in deep at this point.

Rox was feeling good. She took one hand and held the dresser, and held the back of his head with the other. She started rolling her hips around in a circle and at the same time, she was gripping her pussy muscles around his dick. This was about to make Terrance cum.

"Oh girl, oh girl...yeah! Fuck big daddy! Yeah..I told you...I'm the shit! Yeah" Right at the time they bust a nut, hell broke loose. Aunt Donna bust right in the room.

"What In God's name boy! Terrence yelled "Oh shit." They both jumped down trying to cover themselves up.

 Terrance! What are you doing courtin this little girl ...in my house?"

"I'm sorry Auntie..." Donna cut him off.

"You get your stuff and get out now! You know you have to be married to be having sex with anyone. God will get you for this! You hear me? Get dressed!" Rox laughed as she and Terrance got dressed.

Rox looked at the note and it said: "May 1 Me and Terrance". Rox was shaken out of her thought by the bell ringing. School was out and she had to meet Monique out front. She folded the paper up and put it in her pocket for later.

Chapter 2

Messy

The Elks was a grown folks lounge, that was on the corner of Selby and Grotto. They were a bunch of older people that wanted to get involved with the youth, so they sponsored the Martin Luther King Center, to create a drill team. It was something like cheerleading, but with a twist of street dancing and marching, practice started every year from March until July. This was a black tradition that had been around as long as anyone could remember. Rox asked her mother did they have drill teams when she was younger. She says yeah, but she couldn't give her an exact date of when it started.

Rox was going to Maxfield with Angie, Darlene and Mo, to try out because a couple of girl's quit and everyone heard that they had open tryouts and the deadline was June 7th. They were preparing for the "Rodeo Day Parade." They had to compete against Minneapolis, Kansas City, Chicago, Nebraska, Milwaukee and Iowa. For some reason, the only people that came to Minnesota was people in the midwest, because other states really didn't have the income to travel that far.

Mo, Darlene, Angie and Rox were called Perfection. They made up dance steps and use to practice on weekends and after school someday's. They use to do it for money whenever a local talent show was having a contest, but that rarely happened. The only time anyone wanted to compete against them was when Rox wasn't around, because she did the splits and could put her legs behind her head at the end of their routine. This always made the crowd go crazy.

"What's up Mo? How long you been waiting on me?"

"Hey girl, where has your butt been all day? I've been waiting to catch you between classes, but I never could. I know ya ass ain't been at Carl's house. You know you've missed enough school and grades come out next month."

"Nah girl, I ain't went to C's house shit, but I've had a bad day."

"What? What is it? Do you need to make up any classes or do you got to go to summer school?"

"Mo! No! You know damn well I got too much sense to ever have to go to summer school. My ass is covered okay? I know the last day is June 6th."

"Why the hell you trippin? I'm yo sister. I told you, shit!"

"I'm not! I'm sorry! I'm just having a bad day okay?'
"Well let's meet Angie and Darlene at the car okay?"
"Cool."

Mo knew something was wrong with Rox. She had been hangin with her for a while. Mo was just a year older. Angie was two years older, and Darlene was three years older. That's probably why she was jealous of Rox, but would never admit it.

Darlene was 17 and the one with the wheels. This was very convenient for Rox because she was going on 15 this summer and in the summer for some reason everyone is tryin to get somewhere fast, but never on a bus. Vicki didn't like the idea of her daughter hangin with older girl's, but she never complained because she didn't want Rox to later complain about her never letting her make her own decisions in life.

Darlene was a beautiful girl, with a nice thin frame. She had a big butt, long legs, reddish brown skin, this straight long hair and pretty slit eyes to match, not asian looking, but native looking. Everyone knew how much Darlene despised Rox, and for what? She was just as pretty as Rox, and had more than Rox. I guess when the old people say "It's what's inside that counts, they mean if you don't have inner peace, respect or love, then you ain't got nothing, no matter how much money you have."

As Mo, Rox and Angie walked towards Darlene's Volvo, they saw Darlene watching them walk towards her. They could hear her yelling out something.

"What is she saying?" Rox asked the crew as they headed towards the car. Mo and Angie couldn't make out what she was saying, until they got right up on her. As Rox reached for the passenger's door,

"Didn't you hoe's hear what I said?" She asked them, as they all stood outside the car looking at each other like, who in the hell is she talking to? Rox spoke up.

"Who you talkin to, calling us hoes?"
"You, dumb ass. You heard me!"
"What's yo trip now Darlene? Yo man didn't break you off last night or what?"

Darlene started to run around the car to catch Rox as Rox laughed and ran to make Darlene even more mad.

"I'm so tired of you hoe. I'm going to fix that face of yours. I'm gonna make that everyday smile to a frown, young dumb broke bitch!" Rox just laughed and kept taunting her. Rox really didn't feel like fighting today. Darlene was her friend in some ways, but she knew Darlene was quick to pull a knife.

I guess she got that from her roots. Indian people knew how to use knives, and will use them if they are provoked. This wasn't the case for Darlene. She was just having a bad day because her man that lived across the water in North Minneapolis, played her once again, as Rox teased her about.

Angie and Mo grabbed Darlene, so she wouldn't hit Rox.

"Okay Darlene quit trippin so we can make the cut for the drill team! Come on, we gonna be late!" Darlene was trying to wiggle her way out of Angie and Mo's hands, but she couldn't, so she had to let it go, for now.

"You better be lucky I just remembered what we have to do hoe, otherwise I would whoop yo ass for even thinking you can disrespect me little girl!"

"Whatever. I can walk, I don't need yo ass!"

"Well get to walkin hoe!" Mo interrupted.

"We are girl's. Y'all please stop okay? We ain't gonna be able to do shit together, cause y'all always argue over dumb shit, and Darlene you are older than all of us!" Darlene yanked her arms away from Angie and Mo's grip.

"So you taking up for this hoe? You know she got a smart mouth!"

"Yeah, but you started this time Darlene, so let it go okay?" Darlene felt like shit, because everyone seen she was trippin for nothing just because she didn't have her own shit together. She couldn't let anyone know that she knew she was wrong, so she just rolled her eyes and said "Yeah, whatever. Rox you get your smart mouth ass in the back, so I ain't got to look at you."

Rox just kept smiling and sniggling inside cause she knew Darlene wanted to beat the brakes off her, but she had a reputation to hold down. Miss Darlene couldn't let people know that she was jealous of little ole Rox.

They all got in the car and headed towards the Ave.

Selby Avenue! Where all the older boy's, drug boys, dope fiends, prostitutes and wannabe's hung out. As they rolled down the Ave., admiring the people that were out there handling business as usual.

They all jumped out their seat, when they heard a loud crash. Rox' head hit the back seat. Darlene's face hit the steering wheel, Angie jerked forward and Mo started screaming for no damn reason at all. When everyone made out what was going on, after the smoke cleared, Darlene jumped out the car snapping and japed out on this fool that fucked her car up.

"Who the fuck hit my car! What the fuck are you doing! Can you pay for this!" Darlene was upset that a bunch of kid's was in a beat up pick up truck, and had lost control of the stolen car and crashed right into us. Darlene couldn't do much but complain, because it was about seven kid's and all of them except for one, jumped out and ran. The one that couldn't run was the one person that was stuck in the passenger's seat. The seat belt broke on her and she was stuck. Why she had on a seat belt in a stolen car, I still don't understand what was her dumb ass thinking that the seat belt wasn't a part of the stolen car.

How much more can go wrong in one day? Rox was so pissed off that they couldn't get anything right all that day. Oh God, please help us in our time of need. Please make this better and please make Darlene have a soft heart for this young woman standing in front of us, Lord. Amen.

Darlene broke in, "You need to tell God to get my car fixed now!"

"D, you have to ask God what you want yourself, in your own way. I can't do it for you, and you have to believe in him or it's not going to happen."

"I don't know nothing about that! So, right now, you need to shut up, cause he can't help us!" Rox didn't say a word. She never understood Darlene and her mood swings and anger. Why would someone not believe in Jesus Christ or a higher power for that matter? Rox thought of how her mother and grandmother taught her how great Jesus and God are and what they have done and will do for you. Angie and Mo just patted Rox on her back, as she held her head and talked to God.

The police came and wrote a report. Darlene's car had a big dent on the back bumper, it wasn't bad at all, you could barely see anything, except the paint from the red truck was left on the middle of her bumper. We were embarrassed because everyone stood there looking and laughing, and the police took the young girl away. It turns out, that she was a 12 year old runaway and her parents had been looking for her for months.

Everyone got in the car and headed towards Maxfield. Darlene was quiet and upset. Rox seen how mad she was, so she offered to treat everyone to some good soul food. As Rox asked everyone in the car if they were hungry and she would treat after tryouts, that put a smile on D's face. Rox felt at ease, when she seen Darlene smile.

When everyone got out the car to meet the leader of the drill team, all the girls just stared on as they walked past. Everyone was whispering pointing and frowning like "Look at them stuck up hoes...they think they cute." Then some were like "Oooh, I hope they make the cut because they are good."

Rox, Mo, Angie and Darlene didn't say anything back to the player haters at all, they just lined up against the wall as they were told. Everyone stood there as each one took turns to try out for the team. The whole crowd was chanting for Rox after she did the stomp routine, a circle, the splits, then a one hand stand. The drill team coach was a 21 year old gymnast. Her name was Terry and she enjoyed new talent. Terry was strong and didn't stand for any arguing and bickering. If she seen any new talent she jumped right on it.

Terry knew as soon as she seen Rox do her routine, that they would win the competition. Mo, Angie and Darlene all smiled and clapped with the crowd, because they knew their girl had done her thang.

"I just wanna congratulate you and your friends for tryin out today, and ya'll are accepted."

"Thank you....but I'm not finished..."

"Oh, I've seen enough. You will lead the other group members and we will have practice everyday after school at 4 pm, and when school lets out in two weeks, we will have it Monday, Wednesday, and Friday at 1 pm, and Saturday at 11 am."

"Ah...okay."

"What's wrong? You can't come on one of these days?"

"Oh if anything changes, I'll let you know."

"Okay, well I'll see you Friday then."

"Okay, thank you!"

Mo, Angie, Darlene and Rox all got into the car to go to Mrs. Ann's to eat, as Rox told them she would. Mrs. Ann greeted the ladies with drinks at the table, while they all looked over the chalk board, to see what they wanted.

"How are you young ladies doing, and why do ya'll look so worn down?" They all started to answer at once. "Hold on ladies! You can all sing together, but not talk together. You always respect people when they are talking. Never speak out of turn and only speak when spoken to, and always speak to everyone when you walk into a room."

All of them looked at each other and sniggled. Mrs. Ann looked confused of why they were laughing and that made her furious, so she snapped.

"You girl's hurry and order your food, so you can get your too-cute tails out of here! Humph! Disrespecting your elders when they tryin to teach you some wisdom!" They all continued to laugh.

"Oh ma'am, we don't want any problems, and we would never disrespect you."

Darlene continued to laugh and look at everyone in the restaurant like they were crazy. They just turned their heads. Angie and Mo apologized right along with Rox. Rox had a cheeseburger, fries and a Pepsi, Angie had a dinner that consisted of fried chicken breast, mac & cheese, greens and a cornbread muffin with a Tahitian Treat soda. Mo had 5 fried chicken wings, french fries and a orange soda. Darlene had a dinner as well, smothered steak, yams and corn with a cornbread muffin and a grape soda.

When they were all full and ready to pay for their food, Darlene bust out "I'm still hungry. I want some dessert."

Rox just rolled her eyes and smiled. "I said my treat but you're going overboard."

Darlene laughed and stood there waiting.

"Mrs. Ann, can you get me a peach cobbler to go ma'am?"

"Yes lovely lady, I sure can...with your respectful self."

Everybody ran to get into the car, while Rox paid for the food. As Rox stood there to pay and get the peach cobbler that Darlene ordered, Mrs. Ann had to continue with her words of wisdom.

"You know I need to tell you something and you better take heed young one."

"Yes ma'am."

"That little girl you're with is dangerous and she means you no good! You hear me?"

"What makes you say such a thing Mrs. Ann?"

"Listen to the gray when the gray speaks...respect that." This hair ain't gray for being a dumb old lady you hear me baby!

Rox paid for the meal and said goodbye to all of the old veterans that hung in the VFW lounge. They said goodbye as well, as they watched her leave. Rox thought heavily of what Mrs. Ann said and walked to the car to get in. Everyone was nodding their head to Prince' Purple Rain tape, and singing along to the song. As Rox got in the car, Darlene snatched the bag out of Rox' hand, and turned the music down. Rox snatched the bag back and said "What's up with you girl, damn!"

"Ha, I'm just making sure you still got it."

"Got what girl?"

"Heart! Dummy! Cause you can't roll little girl, if you ain't got it."

"I got more than you. I just don't throw my weight around and let everyone know it."

"....what you say that for stupid?"

"Women are to be seen and never heard, meaning, never talk about what you're gonna do, unless you're gonna do it."

Darlene just got quiet, rolled her eyes and started the car.

Everyone sang along, as Rox watched out the window and thought to herself. What is a young girl to do if she is pregnant? I'm going to make my mom real upset. Oh God, please help me in this situation. I want this over, can you please make my period come and if worse comes to worse, could you forgive me for what I'm going to do? Rox' thoughts were broke when the car stopped.

"What are we stopping here for?"

No one answered, they just looked on and continued to nod their heads to Vanity's Nasty Girl. When Rox looked around, they stopped on the Ave, at the "Pop Shop." This was the hang out spot for all the local and non-local dope boy's, as people called them. Darlene was on a mission to find her man "Tobby."

As everyone except Rox jumped out to walk around and flirt with the locals, Rox decided to stay in the car, to think out her plan.

I don't know where I'm gonna go, but I'm not moving to that gang bangin ass South Minneapolis. My mom is going to kill me and be disappointed with the outcome of this test. Damn, Damn! I'm gonna say it....I slipped! I know I did it!

Rox continued to get caught up in her thoughts, and wasn't even paying attention to what was going on right outside the car. Mo and Angie were standing there talking to some dope boy's and getting all their tomorrow's lunch money taken, by the 3 card marly. As I watched, Mo and Angie was so busy shakin their butts and dancing, they never saw the dude put a card behind his back and right after, telling them they lost the ten dollars they both put up. I never said a word. I mean...I could of easily yelled out "Quit jackin my friends!" But, I didn't. My mind was on all of the events of the day. This day was the worst day of my 14 1/2 years of living, and I'm gonna make it better, "Sho Nuff."

Mo and Angie headed towards the car and Darlene was down the block. It was late and I was getting sleepy, plus it was 9:55 pm, and I had to meet my mom's 10:30 curfew. I always felt 10:30 was too early, but my mom would always say "What does a 14 year old have to do after dark, except something she can get in but have a hard time to get out of? Trouble! Trouble! Trouble!" She was right, because every time I sneak out after dark, I get my butt in trouble.

Darlene finally made it to the car, with an attitude, of course. "What's up ya'll? Why ya'll didn't help me?" Everybody looked at each other like they was crazy.

"What you looking at me for? You heard me! Why ya'll always missing when I get in a fight?" Mo and Angie started explaining what they were doing and why they didn't help.

"What's up with you little girl? Why you ain't help, huh?" "Help what..and when?" Rox said with an attitude.

"I was fighting Tobby dumb hoe, and you ain't do shit!"

Rox was pissed with an attitude and she was ready to let D have it.

"What's up Darlene? You wanna go toe to toe?" Darlene wasn't ready for a challenge from Rox, so she just started the car up and began to pull off. While they were pulling away from the "Pop Shop", they saw Tobby running towards the car. He made eye contact with Rox as Rox continued to argue, her words slipped out of her mouth as her eyes met with Tobby's. His thought was the same as hers.

"Damn! That boy is fine! Who is that?" Everyone except Darlene turned to see who it was, Mo and Angie already knew who it was — Tobby, the biggest dope boy on the North and South side of Minneapolis. He supplied every top notch, curb server, and dope fiend with heroin. They called him "The Smack Man", but if he never knew you, then he wouldn't answer you by that name. Tobby blew a kiss at Rox, as Darlene spit out the window at him and passed him by. She just knew that he was blowing a kiss at her, but he wasn't. Mo and Angie nudged Rox, as she sat in the front seat. She didn't know if they were telling her to be quiet and stop arguing with Darlene or she better not let D catch her looking at her so-called man.

Rox turned to D "What's up? You wanna get your scrap on with me or what hoe?"

"Oh young one, you tryin to challenge the native one huh?"

"If that's what you call yo self trick!"

Darlene was making a turn down Ashland Avenue where Rox lived. Rox knew when she pulled up to the house, it was on and she was prepared.

Darlene made it right in front of the apartment that Rox shared with her mother. Rox seen that her mom had not made it home yet. She figured she was probably out with her soon-to-be step daddy, Mr. Davis. Rox reached over and sucker punched Darlene. Plow! Plow! A left caught her in the lip and her head hit the window. Mo and Angie kept trying to stop Rox, but not really, cause they were tired of Darlene's attitude but they didn't have the guts that Rox had. Darlene started crying and screaming like a punk. Plow! Plow!

"Bitch, you talk all that shit and you cryin hoe!" Rox yelled out, with a kick right in between Darlene's legs. Darlene, Mo and Angie all tried to make Rox stop, but she just continued to well on top of Darlene like a mad woman.

"Please stop! Okay! I'm sorry! I'm sorry little girl....I mean Roxanne!"

Rox started to stop and asked "You going to keep my name out yo mouth, you old bitch ain't you?"

"Yes! I will! Now let go of my hair!" Rox slapped Darlene around a little more, before she released D's long hair.

"Why you got to pull my hair hoe?"

Rox didn't say a word, she just grabbed her purse and bag and jumped out the car. Mo and Angie jumped out behind her.

"What y'all want? I'm fine," she said, as she proceeded toward her apartment door. Mo and Angie tried to help Rox, but she wasn't having it. She was upset that Angie and Mo tried to stop her from fighting.

Darlene fixed her clothes and was combing her hair as she yelled out the window "Yeah hoe, I only let yo young ass get one on me cause you're pregnant, but I'm gonna get you!"

Mo, Angie and Rox busted out laughing, because they knew Darlene was embarrassed about getting her butt kicked. Rox' mind was still on the comment that D had made. Pregnant...pregnant, ran threw her mind, as she turned to speak, Darlene pulled off and left Angie and Mo at Rox' house, without a way home.

"Oh, y'all girl left y'all. Where y'all gonna go now?" Mo spoke first.

"You know we love you Rox. Why you acting like this, huh?"

Here they go again, treating me like the bad one, everything my fault.

Angie broke in "Yeah Rox, you've been real upset and I think it's time for you to take the test."

"Whatever. Y'all just better get in here and call a cab or something, cause it's almost 11:00 pm, and we got school tomorrow."

They all made it in the apartment. Rox headed straight for the room, so she could take a bath. Mo yelled to tell Rox that her mother had left a note by the phone, that said she would be in late and if she didn't make it in, then she would be in at 6:00 am, to get her up and ready for school. Rox was happy. She had a long day and was ready to get this day over. Angie made a call to her cousin, for him to come and get her and Mo, but he said it would be about an hour or two.

Rox made it out the bathroom and looked at herself in the hallway mirror. She could see some thickness around her stomach. Her stomach was flat, but she knew her body. Rox felt better and sat down on the couch next to Angie and Mo. Rox knew that the rules in both their parents house was if they didn't get in by 11:00 pm on a school night and 12:00 am with exception sometimes, then they better not come in at all. Rox broke the silence.

"What's up? Y'all can't get no ride?"

"Angie cousin said he would try and make it in an hour, so I'll call him at about 12:15 okay!" Angie spoke in a soft tone.

"I'm pissed off at that damn Darlene. I'm gonna get her ass, you watch."

Rox just laughed and said "She won't be messing with me no time soon."

"She sho won't. You put a whoopin on her butt."

They all laughed and talked, until the clock read 12:30.

Mo picked up the phone and asked Angie for her cousins number. Rox looked at the time and seen it was late. She told Mo to take the couch, Angie to take her bed, and Rox took her mother's bed.

Angie was very grateful that Rox was getting her rest. Angie had a trick up her sleeve that she knew Rox would be mad about at first, but would thank her later.

The next morning, everyone was waken up by Ms. Adams loud voice. She had arrived at the house at 6:15 am, to wake Rox up for school, but was a little mad that Rox had company on a school night.

"Get up ladies, it's time for school. I know y'all must of had a long night, but you got to get to school in one hour." Mo turned around and rubbed her eyes.

"Hello Ms. Adams, I hope we didn't make you upset for sleeping over."

"Yes ma'am, my cousin was supposed to pick us up, but he never made it" Angie said as she stood up.

"No! I would never want you ladies to be stuck out in the streets and plus I didn't want my baby here all by herself."

Rox was groggy as she always is in the morning. Rox made her way into the bathroom. She had clothes in her hand, that Mo and Angie had left over from other times that they slept over. They were both happy to know that they had a change of clothes, and didn't have to go home to get a change of clothes. Mo didn't want to hear her mother's mouth about sleeping over Rox' without asking. Angie didn't feel like the long lecture that her dad would give about her being out all night, so she didn't call him. Angie felt because her dad was white, she could do whatever or say whatever to him.

Mrs. Adams asked Mo and Angie did they call their parents and inform them that they had slept over, but knew that they were lying. Ms. Adams could see in the girl's attitude, that they were a little nervous about her question, so she didn't bother.

When Rox, Mo and Angie finished in the bathroom, Ms. Adams told Mo and Angie to go to the car and asked Rox to stay right there, so she could talk a little bit about the events that would happen in their life in the next couple of months.

"Rox baby, I'm sorry that I've been gone with Mr. Davis, and haven't talked to you about us moving. I shouldn't drop that on you without having Mr. Davis present."

"Yeah, I was a little upset, but it's whatever makes you happy Mommy."

"Oh baby, I thank you for being so understanding." Vickie proceeded to hug Rox, and Rox started to panic.

"What's wrong? Why are you hesitant baby? You don't want me to touch you?" Vickie put her head down and started getting sad, as tears welled up in her eyes. Rox wanted to hug her mother, but she was afraid she would feel the bulge in her stomach. Rox had to think fast.

"Stop Mom! We got to get to school, and Mo and Angie are in the car waiting, or did you forget!"

"I forgot all about the girl's sitting in the car!" She just did as Rox told her to do and headed for the car. As she locked the door to the apartment, she kissed Rox on her forehead and told her she loved her.

"I love you too Mom, now let's go!"

Chapter 3

Get It!

The girl's made it to school. Rox wasn't prepared for what was going to happen today. Rox made her way to her class. She hadn't seen Carl, and that was pretty unusual. Rox went looking for Carl in between classes. She asked everybody had they seen him, but no one had seen him. Rox decided to wait until lunch time, so she would have 40 minutes to at least talk to Carl, because she hadn't seen him since the day before.

All kinds of thoughts ran through her mind. Was he with that hoe Denise or had he found out about her and T having a day of mistaken sex? It was only one time. She just knew he didn't find out, cause T don't like Carl at all. I mean, I could understand why Terrance was a struggling student, that hustled for his uncle and had so many cousins and uncles that he didn't need any friends.

Carl was a football star, fine as hell and didn't have to have a tutor to help him pass or graduate. Carl hustled for his self. He never wanted his love, Rox, to be involved, so he never let her in on what he actually did.

Rox made her way to the lunch room to scope out the few people, that were in there. On the way in, she bumped into Angie and Mo.

"What's up y'all seen Carl at all this morning?"

"Yeah, I seen him", Angie said.

Mo nudged her in her side to signal her not to speak. Rox seen her do this, and instantly she got angry.

"What you hit her for? What y'all hiding?"

"You know we wouldn't hide shit from you."

"Then why you stop Angie from talking?"

"Come on Rox, let's not do this here okay?"

"Yeah, not here. We're going to tell you after school okay?"

"Nah, I said where is Carl? If you seen him, then tell me where he's at, cause y'all acting shady." Angie got an attitude, and smacked her lips. She waved her hand in the air as to say forget Rox. Rox was ready for a fight.

"What you smackin yo lips an shit for? I'm the one who should have an attitude girl!"

"I know, I can do what I want....shit I'm older than your butt and plus I got your back."

"Okay. Well spill it out! Stop playing the guessing game shit!"

"We will tell you after school, and drink a lot of water at 6th hour", Mo said.

"Drink water? For what?" Rox yelled at the top of her lungs and everyone in the lunch room turned to look. She was so embarrassed, that she covered her mouth and laughed.

"Oops! I'm sorry, but will y'all please tell me what's up?" Angie and Mo leaned in close to Rox, to get right in her face. Angie put her arm around Rox' shoulder and spoke "I have a pregnancy doctor, that will test you without your mother knowing. I'm 16, so I can take you and say you're my sister okay?" Then Mo added "Yeah, and if you're pregnant, I can take you to get an abortion."

"What! Oh God! What makes y'all think I'm gonna kill my...." Rox stopped speaking, as she felt a tap on her shoulder. It was Carl standing there with the tape recorder in his hand. Rox didn't have a clue what he was smiling for, but she knew something wasn't right.

"Hey my love, where have you been? I heard you was looking for me."

"Oh yeah, I was. Where was you? I went to all your classes and I hadn't seen you at all."

"If you would of checked, I left a message on the door of your home girl's car, when you was at try outs."

"Um..I never got it."

"When was you there, we didn't see you", Mo said.

"Yeah, why you ain't say shit? Your girl turned that shit out!"

"Yeah, that ain't the only thing her ass done turned out."

Rox, Mo and Angie looked at each other confused, as they started to laugh. Carl was pissed off, so he started to walk away and deal with Rox later.

"Where you going baby? I just seen you for the day. You ain't gonna give me no hug or nothing?" Carl turned around and grabbed Rox by the waist and kissed her slow and long. He then slid his hand down to her butt, gripped it and grinded on her, then let go.

"You better not let me find out you gave this pussy to somebody else, or somebody is gonna die." Rox stood there and looked at him like he was crazy, because she knew he must of known something. Rox knew she had to say something to convince him otherwise. Mo and Angie started speaking for her.

"Oh Carl you trippin boy! You know young one ain't cheatin on you boy!" Mo said. Then Angie said "Yeah, she don't talk about nobody but you nigga...stop trippin."

"Ah, you need to watch yo mouth calling me nigga, and you Monique, you're gonna say anything to cover up for her."

"Hold up. Don't start trippin on my crew boy, and they right, I ain't did shit!"

"Whatever. You better cover that shit up or else somebody gonna die, like I said."

Carl just walked away from us standing there speechless. We were so scared of what we had seen in his eyes. We saw that he meant business.

Mo broke the silence "Rox, go to class and meet us out front and drink the water, like Angie said."

"Okay, but how we gonna get there, cause I ain't going in D's car, fuck her."

"Oh yeah, we ain't seen her all day, but my cousin dropped me the keys off to his Monte Carlo, because he felt bad about not coming to get us last night."

Rox was so nervous she couldn't function in the next three hours of classes she had left. She felt that she would sit in the back of each class, so the teachers wouldn't ask her any questions. Rox made it out of class with a leveled head. She had to meet Mo and Angie in front of the school. I'm so mad at myself. Damn! Oh God, I can't get no abortion. You or my mother doesn't believe in that. Will I be wrong if I try to fix it myself? I could do what all the girl's around school talk about. I could drink some castor oil. Um yeah, I could do that.

Rox thought that through in her mind for the rest of the day. She didn't even realize that drinking that castor oil was dangerous. It would send her into early labor. It would also be very painful. She didn't know that her mother would find out anyway.

"What's up y'all?"

Mo and Angie didn't see who was speaking to them. When they turned around, it was Darlene and Denise. Mo knew that it was about to be trouble, and so did Angie. Angie spoke up "What's up? What's up with you hangin with that hoe..." Before Angie could finish her sentence, Mo broke in "You are a fake silly trick! You know if Rox seen y'all, she would flip the hell out!"

Darlene started rolling her neck to say "Rox young buck ass don't tell me who to run with. Fuck her!" Angie busted out laughing.

"Oh, you mad that young buck dropped them b's on ya! Ha Ha."

Denise was uncomfortable, because she knew Angie and Mo knew she was up to something, and dumb Darlene was in on it. Mo grabbed Angie by the arm and looked back at Darlene.

"It's a damn shame D, that you had to go pick up strays to hang with." Denise rolled her head and turned around, "You hoes are gonna see who's a stray, when Carl has me on his arm."

Mo and Angie walked away from Darlene and Denise huffin and puffin.

"How dare that trick dis Rox like that! I knew D had low self esteem, but damn! She would go that low?" Monique said to Angie, as they were approaching Roxane. Monique didn't want a problem, so she told Angie to keep that incident to themselves.

Monique didn't want Rox to get side tracked. Monique knew the doctor that they were taking Rox to. First Angie had to find out how far along Rox was, before she could set up an appointment. Angie called the doctor "Mrs. Snatch Out", this was her name, for the obvious reason. Angie didn't let her friends know that she also had an abortion at 13. Her mother never knew, because her boyfriend's sister took her to get it. If Angie's dad knew that a grown woman took his underage child to do such a thing, he would be furious. Mr. Mackman was a Corporate Investor. He made a seven figure salary, and he felt he was unstoppable. Angie knew her dad was rich and too busy to pay attention to what was going on with her. She knew what she could get away with.

Mr. Mackman was a tall white man, with a long ponytail. He thought it was cool for him to have a ponytail, even though the rest of his corporate friends and uppity family members were worried about stereotypes, he never paid it any attention. He had his beautiful black wife and baby girl, so they could kiss his ass. They had to answer to him, so it didn't matter.

Angie, Mo and Roxane left the school to go downtown to the doctor's office. Roxane was so nervous that she started saying her thoughts out loud. "Yeah, if I wouldn't of did what he wanted...damn...shit! I should just killed him...damn! What was I thinking...oh God, forgive me for thinking of killing anyone...but, cousin Kane told me the rules of the streets is never trust your friend, keep your enemies close and family and friends closer, cause they're waiting on me to slip up."

Monique and Angie thought she was on dope. They didn't understand why she was saying that. They didn't realize she was speaking her thoughts out loud. Monique kept pinching Angie and making eye signals to tell her not to say nothing until Rox opened her eyes.

Rox kept going with her thoughts out loud. "Only the good dies young and I'm gonna make it in this hood....yeah...won't no hoes make no fool out of me." Monique turned around to stop Rox "What's up young one, you trippin."

"Ahh, oh man I was just thinking of something...um um how long have you been listening to me?" Rox said, as she looked Monique dead in the eye. Rox was good at reading people. Cousin Kane told her that as well. You can read a person by watching their eyes and hands. Rox was unsure of what she said. She didn't want Monique knowing nothing about her family. That was personal. Especially when it came to her cousin Kane. He was everything to her. She had his back and he definitely had her's.

Monique knew that she couldn't lie, so she decided to tell her. Angie started laughing and called Rox crazy. Rox never took her eyes off Monique.

"Um....you said only the good die young and you don't trust nobody, especially your friend, and you said something about you should of killed him."

"That's it? You sure that's all I said?" Rox said, still never taking her eyes off Mo.

"Oh...you said your cousin Kane taught you that."

"That's it? You sure?" Rox said, still not moving her eyes off Mo. "Yes, yes, young one! I told you, I'm loyal and you have no reason to worry. I'm yo sister."

Rox looked Mo straight in the eye and busted out laughing and pointing at her. She had to play it off, so she wouldn't think Rox was losing it. She laughed so much, that Mo was kind of scared of what was going on with her. So Mo just turned around and looked at Angie. Angie shrugged her shoulders and laughed with Rox. Rox stopped laughing, and patted them both on the shoulder, at the same time.

"I'm not crazy y'all. I just black out sometimes. That's why the good Lord is so important to me. Y'all need to try him out sometimes."

Monique turned and gave her a hug. Angie told her "Do whatever you want, I'll always have your back, just be careful how you say things and who you say it in front of." Monique busted in "Yeah, cause girl with the stuff you said, you sound like you was confessing for not killing someone."

Rox sat back in her seat and thought about what she had just done. Damn, I better be careful. Shit, I promised Kane I would never tell...., I won't...I won't, as she continues to think and look out the window. Her thoughts were distracted by Angie's voice.

"Come on Rox, we're here and I hope you been drinking that water."

Rox looked up to see that they were in front of the St. Paul Board of Health. This was the big building where all the young boy's talk about going, when they get burnt (disease). Rox hear's all the kid's in school talking about their going to the free clinic to get some penicillin for that green stuff that been coming out of their dick. Rox knew that this had to be the place everyone in school was talking about.

Rox was scared. She didn't want anyone to know that she had been there. She didn't want anyone' thinking Carl burnt her shit, or Terrance. Rox quickly ran and caught up to Mo and Angie.

"Y'all...I ..... I ain't burning. Why are we going in this building?" Angie and Mo laughing, Mo spoke "It's okay Rox. This is the Board of Health girl, this is for free so anyone can come without insurance okay? You're cool."

Rox put her head down with embarrassment and relief. Angie grabbed her hand "You'll be okay. You're just getting a pregnancy test. That's it. No pain at all. We need to get this to see how far along you are."

Rox just did what they told her. She walked in the clinic and looked at all the people in there. Rox prayed that no one seen her. She didn't know how she would explain herself. Rox was moving from side to side in her seat. All that water she had drunk was really taking a toll on her bladder, plus she was pregnant and didn't understand the first about pregnancy, so she didn't understand why she had to pee so bad.

The nurse called Rox in for her appointment. She went over the chart with Rox and asked her everything pertaining to her health. When the nurse asked her how many sexual partners have she had, Rox coped an attitude.

"What you mean how many partner's have I had? You don't know me!" Rox said, waving her hands in the nurse's face and rolling her head. Thank God the nurse was understanding and didn't take offense to Rox. She had seen this time and time again, when young girl's try to out slick their parents by coming to the free clinic to get tested for pregnancy or std's. The nurse just smiled at Rox and politely broke it down to Rox, why she has to ask these questions and it's her job to do this. Rox felt so bad about snapping at the nurse, she apologized to her.

The nurse stepped out of the room for 10 minutes, to only return to Rox' worse nightmare.

"Yes, you are pregnant young lady." Rox put her head down and started crying. The nurse just gave her a hug.

"It's going to be okay young lady, just pray and the Lord will help you okay?" Rox continued to cry out to the nurse

"This is a curse for disrespecting my mommy. She's gonna be so upset at me!" Rox said, as she wiped the snot and boogers from her nose. The nurse was heading out the door so Rox could change her clothes. Before leaving, she turned to speak to Rox.

"Young lady, here is a pamphlet to 'Planned Parenthood', these people should help you figure something out, okay?" Rox lifted her head up and smiled. It was comfort in that woman's voice, that made Rox relax.

"Thank you for being so understanding ma'am."

The nurse walked out and shut the door behind her. Rox sat on the exam table and cried harder. Man! I'm going to disappoint my mom. So she did as she always does, she began to pray.

"Oh God, I ask that you be with me in time of trouble. Please God.

I know I did wrong, but help me. Please make it so my mother isn't mad at me, please. Amen."

Rox put on her clothes and looked at herself in the mirror and said

"You're a beautiful queen, you are not a disappointment. You love yourself, you love yourself, that's right, you love yourself."

Rox walked out of the nurse's office, past all the poor people that were waiting to be seen in the clinic. Rox' head was held so high, that she didn't even see the people that noticed her. Later, she will soon find out. Rox walked out to the car because she didn't see Mo or Angie anywhere in the clinic. While she was approaching the car, a thought went through her mind,

"Um...I know what I'm going to do. I'm going to drink that labor potion, that stuff the girl's say will make you have an abortion." Rox continued to speak out loud and not being careful about what she's saying or who she's saying it in front of. Mo and Angie were in the car sleep, but was soon awaken by Rox' loud voice. They heard Rox babbling about what they didn't know. When they raised up out the car, Rox jumped back.

"What the hell are y'all doing in the car?" Rox said while opening the door.

"We fell asleep, because it was so crowded in there." Mo said, while getting out to help Rox in the car.

"You woke us up with that babbling again." Angie said, while she was starting the car.

Rox was so into what she was thinking, that she didn't pay attention to what Mo and Angie was telling her. Rox was always embarrassed about her black out's, that she didn't want to address them at this time.

"What is that girl's name that took that castor oil to make herself go into labor?" Rox said to them, while they were driving. No one said a word at first, because they didn't want to make Rox mad, so Angie decided to speak.

"Why? Do you want to go that route? Because if you do, then you can just get an abortion like I said Rox."

"No!" Rox yelled, rolling her eyes and looking out the window.
Monique seen the tension start to flare, so she busted in the conversation.

"Hold up young one, we are here to help you, not hurt you, so you need to chill, okay?"

Rox just kept looking out the window thinking damn, I have to calm down, because they really do care about me. Rox turned to Angie and said

"No, I'm not going to take the stuff. I was just asking okay?"

Angie looked at Rox through the mirror and smiled at her. Angie understood what her friend was going through, so she didn't say much to her on the way home. Angie knew that Rox was gonna have to re-think her future.

Monique didn't want to bother Rox about the pregnancy, so before approaching Rox' apartment, she decided to spark up another conversation. Monique was always so worried about Rox, because she was young, wild and out of control at times.

"What are you gonna do to your hair for practice Friday?" Monique said to Rox while turning around towards her in the back.

"I'm gonna wear a ponytail to the side with flip bangs, a blow pop (purple), and purple and black ribbons." Rox said while turning from the window. "Why you ask?" Rox said.

"Oh, I was gonna do me and Angie's hair similar, so we can all look alike, since it's gonna be Friday I figured we could go to the Hip-Hop Shop."

Rox began to smile at Monique's thought and wanted to dress them the same as her.

"Okay, I'm gonna make us some shirts with flowers on it and I'm gonna put flowers on our jeans and y'all can wear your dope man Nikes okay?" Rox said, while looking back and forth from Angie and Mo, in the front seat. Angie was excited about the thought and had to put her thoughts in, "Yeah, and you can make those pretty paper flowers you make, and put them in our hair." Rox' eyes lit up.

"Yeah Angie, that's a good one cause you know I love flowers girl."

"I'm gonna pick you up for school tomorrow, so tell Ms. Vicki that she don't have to bring you to school."

"Okay. I'll check y'all out tomorrow morning!" Rox said while getting out the car. Mo watched Rox run up the stairs and let herself in the apartment. Once Rox yelled that she was straight, Mo and Angie pulled off.

While Rox was in the house, she kicked around and relaxed. Ms. Vickie wasn't home, so she knew that her place was to sit in front of the TV, with her t-shirt and panties on. After Rox sat on the couch and channel surfed, she got up and went to the table to create the outfits that her and her crew would wear to practice Friday and to the spot tomorrow night.

Rox took pictures of flowers out of magazines and her scrapbooks. Rox would take tissue paper and fabric to create her designs. As she designed her pants and shirts, her mind began to race.

"I'm going to be the first black woman to own a Floral Shop. I'm pissed at myself for getting pregnant. Damn, my mom is going to be disappointed at me, but I'm gonna fix this."

Rox picked up the yellow phone book and decided to call different drug stores and ask for the castor oil medicine. Rox became frustrated, because every drug store she called, they told her that the only thing that castor oil would do, is make her have heavy bowel movements. She continued to call different drug stores, over and over and got the same outcome.

Rox began to cry continuously; she knew sooner or later she was going to have to tell her mom. Rox began to have a tantrum and destroy all of her things that she had just made to wear out Friday night.

"What's going on in here....who's in my house?" Ms. Adams said, while walking through the house with Mr. Davis.

"Roxane, where are you at?"

Ms. Adams began to walk through the house, because she could hear Rox crying, but she couldn't see her. Rox said nothing. She just cried on the toilet, bent over.

Rox had found some castor oil in the cabinet, and began to take it, when her mother walked through the door. Ms. Adams seen Rox bent over on the toilet, and felt an instant pain in her side. What she thought of her daughter all along was true. She knew Rox was pregnant. Rox seen her mom walk through the bathroom door and stopped crying.

"Hey Mom", Rox said while wiping her eyes and trying to clean herself up.

"Don't hey mom me! You didn't hear me calling you?"

"No Mom, I didn't, cause I got a stomach ache."

"You think you're slick don't you?" Ms. Adams said while looking at Rox and standing in the doorway.

"No Mom, I don't. What do you mean?" Rox said, while wiping herself.

"Yeah, you are pregnant and I know you are! Um hum..didn't I tell you that you can't out slick the slicker?"

"Mom, I'm not pregnant, see!" Rox showed her mother the tissue she wiped herself with, that had blood on it.

Ms. Adams was so disgusted with Rox, that she just slammed the door. When Rox seen her mother leave the bathroom, she looked at herself. When looking in the toilet, she seen lots of blood and flushed it away.

"Oh God! It worked...it worked!" She began to say out loud, not knowing that her mom was right outside the door listening. Rox put on a pad and opened the door and walked right into her mother.

"Oh shoot! I'm...oh..oh...Mom, what you doing?" Rox said while pulling her t-shirt down to her knees.

"I'm checking on you like I'm supposed to", Ms. Adams said.

"For what? I'm cool. I told you okay?" Rox said, looking her mother straight in the eye.

"Well put some clothes on and clean up this mess, Mr. Davis is in the front room, and he wants to talk to you now."

Rox skipped past her mother to make it in her room to put some presentable clothes on, she didn't want her soon-to-be stepfather to have a bad impression of her. Rox walked down the hallway, to see her mom and Mr. Davis sitting on the couch. To break the ice, Rox decided she'd be on her best behavior and speak first.

"Hello Mr. Davis. It's so nice to finally see you sir." Rox said while looking back and forth from Mr. Davis to her mother.

"Hello yourself young lady. You're pretty nice and presentable for the occasion." Mr. Davis said, while looking Rox up and down and smiling.

The conversation between the new Davis family went on for about an hour and a half. Rox started off being happy that her mother was happy. When it finally was about to end, Rox was a little irritated that Mr. Davis informed her that she was going to be a big sister to his daughter, that was four years younger than Rox. Rox was a little jealous, because she was use to all of the focus being on her.

Rox was beginning to feel a little better about moving, she wanted to start her new life over. Starting out at a new high school, with people that didn't know her past, wouldn't be a bad idea.

After Rox got her lecture about curfew, chores and obligations, she decided to press her luck.

"Mr. Davis, so do I have to baby sit this girl, cause I got thangs I got to do." Rox said while looking him straight in the eye. Ms. Adams raised an eyebrow, because she knew her daughter was going to make her mad.

"Ah....yes." Ms. Adams tried to butt in and answer his question with an attitude.

"I can answer that honey. Roxane, I would never put my daughter off on you. First of all, I'm a grown man that happens to be in love with your mother, I have a daughter and that's my obligation to take care of her. Anyone that I'm with, has to accept her, just as well as if anyone is with your mother, they have to accept you okay?"

Rox was so shocked at her soon-to-be dad's intelligence. Rox had never heard a man speak so well, except her teachers at school. Being as though Rox was from the wild inner city of St. Paul that language wasn't too common from men that had children.

Most of the dads in her hood that had kids didn't take care of them or did a half ass job and wanted credit for anything they did do. Mr. Mackman was the only man that took care of his family and that was because he was so happy to be with a black woman.

"Okay Mr. D! I'm gonna call you that for short, cause people don't have to know your whole government name, okay?" Rox said with one hand on her hip and waving her hand.

"Why thank you Roxane. I guess that's cool if you like."

"Well good, we are gonna get along good, and don't worry, I'll look out for my little sis okay!" Rox looked in Mr. D's eyes for approval.

"Fine with me Rox, as I see you would prefer to be called. Anything for you."

Ms. Adams was so relieved that the conversation went well. Ms. Vicki was ready to move as soon as her lease was up. That would be right before Rox and her soon-to-be step sister Latasha, would start school.

Mr. D and Ms. Adams continued to talk, while Rox went in her room, to finish making the outfits for practice on Friday. Rox came up with more ideas and wrote down everything to prepare herself for when she became a florist.

It was getting pretty late, so after Rox cleaned up her mess, she set the three outfits out and was pleased with her designs.

"Thank you God for my designs and for saving me from my mother today. Thanks for my period. Amen." Rox said out loud, before turning her light out to go to sleep.

As she drifted off to sleep her thoughts keep going. "Damn Hood makes fresh water — in my hood pussy is what makes the world go around and niggas love when your water falls."

Wow, what was I thinking? Da Hood makes fresh water...huh...I'm trippin'... what is that?

Huh... I guess I'll tell every dude I'm freaking that my pussy is as good as life is to water. Nobody's hearing me!

Go to sleep girl.

Damn, I can't sleep.

Rox was in for a rude awakening tomorrow and she wouldn't be able to handle it.

Chapter 4

It's A Problem

    The next morning, I got up for school. I put on my Addidas sweat suit and shell toe Addidas. I had to have a all white bra and panties to match. My hair is in a ponytail to the back. I put my matching Addidas hat to match and my lip balm on my lips. I looked in the mirror and told myself "Damn! I'm sharper than Dick was when Hatti died!" Ha, Ha, Ha, I have to laugh at myself sometimes. I use to hear this old lady say this to her husband, when she was leaving the house clean as a whistle, after he cheated on her. It's funny how old people have a major influence on your mind when you least expect it.
    Damn, I look good. Today, Carl is gonna love looking at me today. My booty is bangin and I can unzip my jacket a little to let my tits stick out and have his head spinning.
    Monique and Angie pulled up in front of the house and blew the horn for Rox to come out. It was one more week left from school and Rox was very happy. Damn, I got to pee so bad.
    "Let me use the bathroom and I'll be right out okay?" I yelled from the window in the living room.
    "Oh shit!" I looked down in the toilet and it's blood mixed in my pee. "Okay God, help me here. Ooh, my stomach…it's hurting bad. Help! Help!" What am I going to do? If I tell Angie and Mo, they gonna take me to the doctor. I'm not going back downtown to the green door, red door or what ever they call that place. I can't be havin no chicks from school peepin me in nobody's clinic. I'm just gonna take some more castor oil and I should be cool in about a week. Yeah, that's what I'm gonna do. Rox made her way down to the car. Monique looked Rox up and down.
    "What the hell took you so long?"
    "Oh, I had to pee and straighten my room up."
    Angie looked in the rearview mirror, to see if Rox was lying.
    "You sure you straight? I don't want no accidents in school. You know Carl is gonna be on you today."
    "I'm cool Angie, and I'm expecting to see my man today. I miss him and I

ain't talked to him in two days." Monique broke in.

"You gonna go see Dr. Snatch Out today, just for a little bit, to get checked out okay?"

I just looked up at my two friends and shook my head. Damn, they are really buggin out about this abortion, so let me do the over lay for da under play.

"Cool, she can let me know how much it cost and I can get the loot from Carl, without my mom knowing, cause I ain't tryin to upset her at this time. She's happy with Mr. D, and I won't let my mistake get her distracted."

"Bet dat up young one." Angie said, while pulling into the school parking lot.

Today was about to be long. I have final exams all week, because next week is only for 3 days. The last day of school is on Wednesday, and our first drill team competition is that Friday, with the South Side Minneapolis Show Stoppers.

I guess this would be the perfect time to get to know people, since I'm gonna be living over there. I could at least meet some of these chicks to learn my way around over there. See by me being a St. Paul girl, they might not like me! What they don't know, is that I'm my own leader, gang, big dogz, head honcho, boss chick... well you understand. I don't let nobody run me. Never have, never will.

Ever since I was in grade school, my mom always knew I was gonna make it on my own. She said everyday when she came to get me, I was always making my own way to play by myself. When the teacher told us to make anything out of the building blocks, I was the first to finish, without help. Kid's always wanted me to be in their click, or to come to their house to spend the night, but I never would, until I was older. I'm sure it was because I had an older sister, that use to treat me like shit.

That damn Lili use to make me go to the refrigerator and get her popsicles in the middle of the night. My mom caught me one night, and whopped my butt, because she said that drinking and eating before I go to bed would make me pee in the bed. Lili's evil ass would just laugh every time I got whopped. I don't know why I was so loyal to her ass, cause she never was to me.

Loyalty is a major deal to me. I don't know what I'm gonna do if Carl finds out I was messing with T, and if he finds out that I really got my virginity broken by Monique's cousin, then hell, he will really beat the brakes off me.

I mean, Mo's cousin only got it in for about 2 seconds, before I kicked and screamed. He was so upset at my ass, that he jumped up, put his clothes on and cursed me out. He called me all kinds of young dumb full of cum hoes, that he made me think that that's how all dudes felt. Then shortly after and even to this day, I can't get rid of his ass. Always calling Mo and asking when yo girl gonna let me open that shit all the way up. I told his ass that he had his chance, and it won't be no one but Carl jumpin in and out of me. Bless Mo's heart, she always wanted me to make more out of the relationship because she would figure that we would get married, have a baby, and I would be her cousin.

I said "Please Mo, I'm barely a teenager and you talking grown folks shit already."

"Yo, yo baby." A loud voice said, startling the heck out of Rox. Rox continued up the stairs and headed for her first period class.

"Yo, yo sneaky." The voice continued, as I made it to the door of class.

"What dummy?" I said, before I stepped into class. "Show your face faggot." As soon as I was about to close the door behind me, the face appears. "Oooh, damn, you scared me!"

"Where the hell have you been all week? What you ain't my girl no more? You been being sneaky and shit."

I had to ask my teacher to let me step out the class for a little bit.

"Carl, I've been chillin with my girl's, you know that, plus yo ass ain't been at home and I know football practice don't start for 2 1/2 months."

"Yeah, but that ain't no excuse for you not to come by and see about me. You act like you don't care no more."

"I love you baby and I have some things I need to tell you, but I have to get in class for the finals."

"Yeah, whatever, you been sneaky and when I find out, I'm gonna beat your ass." Carl said, while letting go of her arm.

"Yo whatever, but like I said, I have some things that I need to talk to you about."

"Cool, give me a kiss."

Rox turned around to give Carl a kiss. He had to make a scene so everybody in the class could see him grabbing her butt and cupping it. Carl was kissing Rox so long and hard, that she had to pull back just to get some air.

"Okay Carl, that's enough. I got to go. I have finals I told you." Carl let go of Rox.

"Okay, I'll see you later."

"Bye."

Rox turned and shut the door behind her. Damn, I can't even function now. I'm horny as hell, but I'm in enough trouble with this shit. I've got to get it together.

I wonder why the hell he was calling me sneaky? Shit, I've been doing a lot of sneaky shit lately, so I know he could be talking about a lot of things. I know that I'm gonna have to fight Carl. I don't want to, but I'm gonna have to. He's not gonna take me moving to Minneapolis lightly, shit now on top of that, I'm pregnant and yes, I'm gonna take care of it, whether it's with this castor oil or with Dr. Snatch Out. I'm doing it. I ain't having no baby at my age, and be like all the rest of these hoes dropping with babies, and the daddy just gone. No, not me!

Rox was interrupted by her thoughts from the sound of the bell ringing. I've got to make it through these damn finals, so I can get out of school early. "Duch...ooh...ooh!" What the hell is that? Rox was interrupted throughout the whole day by pain, but there was no blood at all. I keep checking in between classes, and there ain't shit but clear shit coming out of me. "Oh God, please deliver this pain out of my body, please. Amen."

"Roxane Adams." A loud voice said over the loud speaker. "Roxane Adams to the counselor's office."

I wonder what the hell they want with me? I've already told them I won't be back next year and my GPA is up. I haven't missed any classes or tests, so what the hell! Rox continued to think, as she walked through the door.

"Yes, I'm here to see the counselor." The secretary buzzed for the counselor to come out. Rox took a seat and waited.

"Hello Miss Adams, can you step into the office please. I have good news for you."

Rox was confused by this, she never liked being bothered by teachers, police, or doctors. That just wasn't her thang, she figured that they would bring bad news.

"Yes sir, what is it that you have?"

"Well you have completed all of your classes with straight A's, so we have decided that since the school can't afford to send you all out on a field trip this year, we're letting you take your finals today and tomorrow, and you won't have to come back next week."

"Oh thank you sir! That's music to my ears."

Rox walked out the office feeling happy as ever. All these things in her life happening at once, was beginning to wear on her brain. All the people in school was looking at her upside her head. People were saying "Why you so damn happy?" Another dude looked on. "Did that nigga C finally put a ring on yo finger or some in?"

Rox just continued to move through the crowd, ignoring all the comments of the jealous people, that watched her move on. Rox never understood jealousy, because her mother always made sure she showered her with love. Rox felt that people with low self esteem came from somebody not showing them love when they was younger. Rox' esteem was even higher now that she had all these older men after her.

Once she was walking to her cousin's house in the hood, right off of Selby and Grotto, and some old head told her she was so fine, she looked like a fresh glass of water that he ain't tasted in years.

"Yo old head, what in the hell does that mean?" Rox said, while walking and laughing.

"It means you have a glow. Your body language is sayin something ya dig? It's sayin that you have a look of strength in you and you're beautiful to top it off."

"So yo, if I was ugly, I wouldn't be fresh water?" Rox said with a smile, as the old man stopped her in her tracks.

"Nah baby girl, you would be tainted water and it would show. Now move around 'fore some of these tainted hoes around here start trippin."

Rox continued on, and remembered the old man's words and kept them near to her heart.

"What's up Mo and Angie? I've been waiting on you."

"Yeah, we been tryin to get out of here. Shit, all these damn people been tryin to move out at the same time, ain't gonna work."

"I know they're happy cause tomorrow is the last day for most, and the dummy's have to come back and finish next week." Angie and Mo looked at Rox and busted out in laughter, as Darlene gave Rox a screw face.

"What did your dumb ass just say hoe?" Rox didn't even see Darlene behind her.

"You heard me, shit, what you mad for Miss High and Mighty? You ain't slippin in yo pimp on the grades are you?"

Darlene was so embarrassed, that she couldn't even respond to what Rox just said to her. She knew that Rox had a point. She knew that Rox was a young girl who was smart and swift as a whip, and had her game on lock. Darlene decided that for now, since she couldn't beat Rox verbally or physically, then she would join her.

"Yo, young one, you can quit all that smart shit, I have to come back for one test, because I skipped a couple of times for my man Tobby, ya dig?"

Rox just laughed at her response and said "My fault, I wasn't considering you dumb."

"Thank you, now can we just get to practice since we just made up."

"Who said we made up? You need to apologize for dissin me in front of that hoe Denise."

"Yo, she was tryin to make me tell her shit about you."

"And you was wit it, wit yo fake ass. I should whoop you again."

Mo and Angie stepped in between Darlene and Rox, because it would of been so stupid for them to fight on the last week of school and get their final grades taken away. Mo screamed out "Stop this shit now! Either y'all gonna get along, or you're not." Rox turned and started with the finger pointing.

"What the fuck you mean? You on this snakes side or what?"

"No, I told you you're my lil sis, my ace, my road dog, all that shit."

"Then why you always tryin to make peace with this hoe?"

Darlene looked on with disgust, because she knew that she was jealous of Rox and everyone could see it. Angie was so tired of all the bitchin between Rox and Darlene, that she stayed quiet.

"Yo, I said I was sorry and if that makes you feel better, then I said it." Darlene held her arms folded and stared directly at Rox.

"Yeah, whatever for now. We'll see how you gonna act later, or when I ain't around."

On the ride to practice, Rox just sat quietly in the back seat. Everyone offered her the front seat, but she refused. This summer was gonna be a long summer, but all Rox could think about was her moving away from her friends that she had grown to love so dearly, especially Mo. She knew that Mo had her back on whatever.

Angie was her friend as well, but she held some things in, Angie always felt that because she was mixed, she didn't really fit in as well. Rox and Mo always told her that she was their sis, and color didn't matter. Angie believed them to a certain extent.

See, when Angie was twelve, she got pregnant by an older, black drug dealer. He would shower her with gifts and spend time with her. She was spending so much time with him, that her dad started questioning her about missing school and creeping in the house at all hours of the night. Angie got so out of hand, that she started disrespecting her parents.

One day when Angie went to meet him at his apartment, she overheard him telling one of his homeboys "Man, I don't want that young ass half-breed bitch. Shit, her daddy's white ass has all that money and I'm just baiting her in, until I can have her taking everything out his account. Shit, she's so slow, she lets me call her H-B. I told her it means Honey Bunny, but you know it means Half Breed."

Angie just listened on. She cried as she heard somebody that she thought loved her, really felt different about her, and was using her. Angie got five bricks, tied them up in her sweat shirt that she had wrapped around her waist, and busted all the windows out of his apartment, like a mad woman. He was so scared, because he knew she must of heard what he said, so he just sat quietly, until she was done with her rampage.

Angie went home, cried for about a week, and got herself together. That's when she met Dr. Snatch Out, and got rid of her first child. After her boyfriend felt she had cooled off, he tried to send his sister over to talk to her. Angie refused, and told him to give her the money for her abortion, or her parents would send his ass to jail for statutory rape, because he was 21. He quickly agreed and sent his sister with her, to make sure that the job was done.

"Rox, what's on your mind girl?" Rox was so into a daze, that she didn't notice that Mo was looking dead in her face, with the door opened.

"Oh shit girl, I was thinking about where I'm gonna get a job at this summer."

"Yeah girl, I heard that they were hiring at that new Hardees on St. Anthony and Hamline."

"Good, then tomorrow after I take my last final, let's go apply okay?"

Rox stepped out the car, with dancing on her mind. Shit, when it came to money or dancing, it made her get hyped up. Practice went as they all knew it would. Shit, nobody wanted to compete against Rox and her girls. So the team leader told them that since they knew the routine and school was about to be out they only had to come to practice on Saturday mornings, until competition week. They wouldn't have to practice all week, until the day of the competition, and that was a month and a half away.

"Take me to get something to eat Darlene, before you drop me off. Your treat." Rox said, looking at the back of Darlene's head, while she drove. Rox was testing her ass, and Mo and Angie knew it. Angie nudged Rox, while sitting next to her. Mo just snickered and kept quiet.

"What you say?" Darlene said to Rox, while looking in the rearview mirror.

"Take me up to the Wing Shop, so I can get something to eat and peep some tricks."

"Oh, bet that up!"

Angie pinched Rox on the leg, cause she knew what she was up to, and Darlene had no clue. They made it up to the hood and as usual, it was a gang of dope boy's hanging in front of the Pop Shop, shootin dice, talking shit and curb servin (means petty drug hustling).

Rox jumped out ahead of everybody else. She thought she seen Carl bent over in a car, talking to some girl's, but when she made it that way, the car was gone. She knew her mind wasn't playin tricks on her, so she went in the wing spot, and made her order.

Darlene, Angie, and Mo walked in with three dudes right on their heels. Darlene approached the table, after making her order.

"Why you leave us? Walking all fast and shit. Girl, you act like you seen a ghost." Rox just looked up in the face of the three dudes that were standing there, to make their order.

"Yeah, I'm hungry. I told you. You treatin ain't you?" Darlene tried to pat her pockets as if she was tapped (meaning broke). Rox rolled her eyes, and was about to snap, but Angie interrupted.

"Yo, I got it. My cousin hooked me up."

Rox saw Angie not wanting to make a scene in front of the ballers that were looking here up and down. Rox seen the fine men paying close attention to her, so she decided to chill, because the one with the black ball cap on looked real good to her. He kept making eye contact with her.

"Okay, but next time it's Darlene's turn to pay, cause I treated last time."

Darlene just smiled and tilted her head towards the direction of the three dudes that just made their order. Rox seen what Darlene was talking about, so she spoke up since everybody was scared.

"What's up?" Rox said, looking at the guy with the black ball cap. Shit, she took a good look at that fat bank roll that he had in his hand when he peeled off that hundred dollar bill to pay for his food, and told the woman to keep the change. The dude was so hungry, he didn't really hear her.

"What's up, you can't hear nigga?" Everybody in the place busted out laughing. His boy's was slapping each other five and pointing at their boy.

"I heard yo smart ass, and I ain't yo nigga." He was shocked at her boldness, and knew right off the back that she was a mess.

"Cool, then answer me and stop looking at me like you gonna eat me or something."

This made him laugh real hard. Shit, he was eyein her fine ass in that Nike suit huggin her ass.

"Okay Miss...Lady, what's your name?"

"Oh, you think it's that easy huh?"

"Damn girl you trippin! Just tell me yo name shit!"

Rox stood up to walk to the counter to get her food. Angie, Mo and Darlene stood to head for the door. Rox reached to grab her order.

"Stop, quit playin with my food. I don't know you." He pulled the knot out his pocket and handed Angie a hundred dollar bill and said

"Nah, it's mines and yo smart ass is bout to be starvin like a hostage in Saudi Arabia."

Rox got pissed off, while everybody laughed.

"Give me my food boy!" As Rox followed the baller out the door, running up behind him, she could smell his fresh scent in the wind, and it turned her on. Rox reached out to grab him. He started walking a little quicker, so she kept tryin to keep up with him, but couldn't.

"Stop boy! Please give me my food. I'm hungry okay!" He turned around and waited for Rox to get a little closer.

"Why you playin? I'm out here on this dusty ass block, following some ni...I mean, boy, I don't know."

Rox stood there and was going off, until her girl's caught up. When he seen them approaching, he handed Rox her bag.

"Have a nice grub. If you ever want something better in your life, get at me." He handed Rox a card with his name and number on it, then kissed her on her lips real quick, and ran away.

"What the hell! Hey boy! Where you going?"

Rox, Mo, Angie and Darlene watched in shock, while all of them watched the dudes run and jump into a blue Cadillac coupe. Rox was happy that they came up on a hundred dollars, and she knew that the heart Angie had, she would split the money with her.

They all walked back to the car laughing about what just took place. Rox slid the card in her pocket, with intentions on calling him when she got home.

"What's up Angie? I know you gonna break me off something from that c-note. Give a chick a dub (dub meaning $20) or something."

"You know I got a 40 spot for you, don't trip shit, our food only came up to $20 bucks."

"Cool, I'm bout to go in the crib and get some sleep, shit I got my last final tomorrow, and after practice Saturday, we're going to find a job." Angie looked at Mo and Darlene and started laughing.

"When did you wanna get a job? I never heard you say that before."

Darlene joined in, "Yeah, where did that bright idea come from?"

"Oh, you always gotta say some slick shit." Monique jumped in.

"Well, I know y'all ain't said shit to me about getting no job!"

Rox shut the door to walk towards the house. "Yo Darlene, you just be around to do what I said. We going to get a job Saturday, you dig?" Darlene stood up out the car and yelled out, "I ain't yo fuckin "do-girl".

Rox busted out laughin and opened her door to the apartment, before they pulled off, Rox yelled "You'll do for now until I'm done wit cha trick!" Darlene sat back in her car and pulled off. Angie and Mo just laughed and shook their heads.

While inside her apartment, Rox noticed her mother in her room, with the door shut. It was only 10:30, and that was weird for her to be home so early.

"What are you doing home so early Mom?" Rox walked in her mother's room and sat on the end of her bed.

"I'm home because I'm concerned about my daughter."

"What you mean, you worried about me? I'm okay Mama," Rox said, while huggin her mom with tears in her eyes.

"Carl called, and said that you're pregnant."

Rox just looked with shock. (How the hell he tell my moms I'm pregnant? Shit.)

"I know you're pregnant, and I'm gonna fix it, because you are not gonna be like your sister, you hear me?"

Ms. Adams just hugged her baby, while Rox cried. She knew that something was wrong and she should of paid more attention to her, instead of work and Mr. Davis.

"It's okay Mom, I told you I ain't gonna disappoint you. I promised you that."

"You'll never disappoint me baby, and anytime you have an emergency, you better tell me. You hear me girl?" Ms. Vickie said, while shaking and looking Rox directly in the eye.

"Yes Mommy. I'm sorry I won't do it no more." Wiping her face and her mother's nose, Rox had to tell her mother, "Mom, I've been taking castor oil, to give myself an abortion, but it didn't work, and I be bleeding off and on."

Ms. Vicky was irritated by the sounds of it. She knew girls did things like this.

"Okay baby, don't panic. Are you bleeding now?"

"No Mom, but I'm scared."

"Yo butt should of told me when you first missed your period, with your hot tail." Rox just looked at her mother with disappointment.

"Go get in the bed and we're gonna get you taken care of tomorrow."

Rox just walked out the room and went straight to get ready for bed. Before she pulled all her clothes off, she thought of calling Carl to curse his ass out, then all of a sudden, the baller that paid for her meal went through her mind. Rox ran to her pocket and there goes the card. It read "Brian's Barber -n- Beauty", it had a south side number, with a pair of handcuffs on the bottom of the page. Rox put the card in her address book. She planned on calling him after she got out the shower.

While in the shower, Rox replayed the events of the day and asked God to forgive her and also thanking him for letting her mother be so understanding.

"Rox!" Her mother called out.

"Yes Mama, I'm fine!"

Rox put on her Pj's and laid down. She had to get ready for tomorrow, cause it sure was gonna be a problem.

Chapter 5

I'm Sorry

Damn, 5:30 and I still haven't slept yet. I wonder what Mom means, that we're gonna take care of it. Shit, I know damn well that she means "Abortion." When I was a little girl she always told Lili that it was wrong, murder, the devil's way to get rid of God's blessing. "Um", I guess her mind changed. She probably don't want Mr. Davis to know she got a hot ass daughter. I'm glad as hell she was so understanding, shit, I got thangs to do. I can't have no damn baby! My dreams will be over.

"Louise Lovely Floral Designs." It just hit me. "That's it! It's it!" That's what I'm naming my floral shop.

Boom! Boom!

"Who is that?"

"Me, open the door!"

What the hell is he doing here?

"I know that ain't Carl." Rox jumped out the bed to slip some clothes on. The male voice that was on the other side of the door...damn it sho don't sound like Carl. Rox reached the door to open it, before she could open it, "Damn! What you....oh...what the....you...."

"I've been tryin to call you and you ain't been here, so I came over."

"How the hell you get in here?"

"Through the front door. Did you forget that I know where the hiding spot is, to let myself in?"

Rox looked at Terrence like he was crazy. She knew that he was bold, but not this bold.

"Did my mom hear you come in? You was loud as hell." Rox said while looking T's sexy ass up and down.

"Nah, I thought she was at work, but I seen her and some man on the couch sleep, so I crept past them."

Oh shit, Mr. Davis is going with us. My mom didn't tell this damn man my business, I know. Rox crept out the room, to go look and see if her mom and Mr. Davis was still sleep. She took a peek and then looked at the clock in the kitchen. It was 5:45. Mo and the girl's would be over to pick her up soon, and her mom's alarm would be going off at 6:15.

Rox made it back to her room. Stepping back in, she seen Terrance sitting on her bed.

"What did you come over here for, boy? You need to call before you come... shit....I do got a man, as if you don't know." Rox was pissed with her hands on her hips. Terrance was lost for words. He really liked Rox, but she was too young to understand him.

"Oh, I need you to help me with my English, you said you would, and you forgot I have finals."

Rox knew that Terrance needed help, but she was so into her own thang, that she totally forgot her obligations she made to Terrance.

"I'm so sorry," Rox said while putting her hands over her mouth, then reaching out to hug Terrance. He reached to embrace her with a hug a little too much, and started feeling on her ass.

"Stop Terrance!" Rox said, stepping back and poppin him slightly on his shoulder.

"Oh, I'm sorry girl, it just felt so good to have you in my arms again, that I just..."

"Yeah, you wanna take over my kindness again, huh," Rox said, cutting Terrance off.

"Nah, I just wanted to savor the moment for a beautiful queen like you."
Rox knew Terrance didn't want to leave, but she had to get him out, before her mother woke up.

"Thank you Terrance, but I got to get you out, before Ma Dukes get's up, you dig?"

"Okay, Okay, but when can you help me, because I have to go back next week, to finish my finals." Terrance got right up on Rox, making her feel uncomfortable.

"I'll be over Sunday okay? Now let's go okay? Shit, we already been caught doing shit. I ain't wit dat no more."

Rox grabbed Terrance by the hand and lead him to the door, without him having a chance to respond. Rox and Terrance crept past her mom and Mr. Davis, sound asleep on the couch.

"I'll see you in school today, okay? If not, then I will see you Sunday, after church."

"I need you Rox, please don't dis me." Terrance said, after kissing Rox on the forehead. Rox never answered him, she just nodded her head and jumped back in the door, then locked it.

"Rox, baby what are you doing locking the door?" Rox jumped up against the wall, startling Mr. Davis.

"Hello Roxane," Mr. Davis said, with a smile, while rubbing his eyes.

"Oh...ummm, Hi guy's, I was locking the door behind T."

"What was T doing over here this early for baby? Is something wrong?"

Ms. Vicki looked with a confused look on her face.

"Nah Mama, he was tryin to catch me before I go to school, cause you know finals is this week."

"Yeah, and how have you been coming along?"

"I'm cool, as a matter of fact, I get out today because my grades are an A-."

"Oh is that right? How is Terrance coming along?" Ms. Vicki asked, while looking Rox in the eye.

"He's cool, he just scared of the English test, that's all. He'll be fine Ma!" Rox knew her mother could sense something, so she had to change the subject.

"Ma, don't we got something to do today?"

"Oh...yeah...ah..later." Rox seen her mom moving her head towards the direction of the room. Rox seen her mother, so she shut up and headed towards her room.

"See you later Mr. Davis." Mr. Davis was returning from the bathroom and headed for the door.

"Bye, young lady, and be ready for tonight okay?"

"For what Mr. Davis?"

"You're gonna meet Latasha, if that's okay with you." Vicki stood at the door grinning from ear to ear.

"That's cool Mr. D, I'll be ready okay?"

"Sho Nuff." Mr. D said.

Mr. D and mom stood at the door and talked a little, before he kissed her and said goodbye. When Rox heard him leave, she immediately ran out the room, to talk to her mom.

"Mama, what are we gonna do today?"

"You know you are going to get an abortion today, and don't try and get out of it, cause I know you're pregnant. I won't wait until it's too late." Ms. Vicki stood in the middle of the living room floor, pointing her finger.

"Okay Mama, cool. I'm ready but..."

"What you mean you're cool but? But what? It's a done deal. No babies I told you girl!" Ms. Vicki was so upset that she was ready to slap the piss out of Rox, if she got flip at anytime. Rox seeing that her mother meant business, she knew that she shouldn't say anything smart at all.

"Mom, I'm ready for whatever, shit..um..um, I mean, I don't want no kids." Rox said, stepping back, because she knew she just slipped and cursed.

"Alright, that's what I'm talking about. Now get in there and get ready for the doctor."

"Mom, you got to take me to school first."

"Girl, I said you are getting it done today!" Ms. Vicki got angry, and was headed towards Rox.

"Mama no, I got to take my last final remember?" Rox said, looking at her mother with a surrendering face.

"What time?"

"At 7:30, so we got to go, it's almost 6:30 and I haven't showered yet."

"Okay Rox whatever! I'll wait in the car while you take it, because your appointment is at 9:00 and we have to be there for at least 4 hours."

Rox went back to her room to get ready for school. While pulling out her purple Guess jean shorts and matching shirt with jelly bean sandals, she picked up the card that was laying on the floor. Damn, I must of dropped it when I was looking at the number last night. Rox was saying to herself out loud. Looking at the number, Rox couldn't understand why the card had handcuffs on it. Damn, she thought, does he work for the police or something? Did he do time or is it just a baller thang?

"Uhmm...I'm bout to call this nigga." Oh I better stop that. He told me about calling him that.

Rox made it in the shower and got dressed, then headed for the door. Ms. Vicki was already in the car honking the horn.

"I'm coming Ma! I'm calling Mo and dem to tell them not to come!" "Hurry up girl!" Ms. Vicki said, before rolling the window up.

Damn, she sure is bitchy today. I'll be glad when this shit's over.

Ring! Ring! Ring! The phone rang 3 times, before Mo answered. "Hello," she answered, huffing and puffing.

"Mo, don't come get me. I'm gonna get up with ya'll later 'kay?"

"What! Girl, I'm rushing out this house to come get yo ass on time, and you changed yo mind?"

"I know. Mom is taking me to the doctor, so I'm bout to go take my final and then..."

"Well you should of called last night and told us girl. Damn, be considerate!" Rox didn't have time for Mo and her fussing, so she just chilled. "Okay, I'm sorry, but got to go. Moms honking the horn."

"Okay, call me when you get back. You know we going out. Did you get the outfits ready?" Damn. Rox forgot all about the outfits to wear to the Hip Hop Club tonight.

"Oh shit, girl I forgot, but don't trip, it's done. They're cute too."

"Good, I'll see you later then."

"Bye."

Rox knew she was pushing it. It was 7:10 now, and it takes 10 minutes to get to school, so she had 10 minutes to kill or at least 5.

Ring! Ring!

"Hello, Brian's B."

"Ah..ah is this a business," Rox said to a older man answering the phone with a sexy voice.

"Yes it is a detail shop. Can I help you?" Rox could hear LL Cool J's "Big Ole Butt" bumpin in the background.

"Yes, I got this card from this tall medium built dude with a fitted ball cap."

"Oh yeah, it wasn't me, but I think I know who you want. Hold please." Rox held on.

"Mom, I'm washing my hands okay?" Ms. Vicki looked up at the window with a frown on her face, and pointed at her watch, meaning it was time to go. Rox shook her head and mouthed "I'm coming."

"Hello, who dis?" The voice said, on the other end.

"It's me. You don't know who you gave your number to?" Rox said, in a sexy tone.

"Oh yeah, I gave it to a lot of people, shit this is a business you know."

"Oh well you had plenty of business with me that you put your nose in."

Brian was a little confused. He really didn't recognize the voice, but he remembered the incident that occurred yesterday. It was so loud, so he moved into the office.

"Oh yeah, umm, I know who this is."

"Who? Who am I Mr. Running Man," Rox said, with a chuckle.

"Yeah, um humm...I knew you would be calling."

"Don't beat around the bush nigga, ooh....I mean ummm boy."

"Hum, I see you ain't changed that shit over night huh?"

"What!" Rox knew damn well that Brian wasn't no push over, shit, she really didn't know what she ran into, but soon she would find out.

"Yeah, you better act like you know. Don't call me that!"

"What?"

"Nigga. I ain't no nigga, you heard!" Brian said, screaming into the phone.

"Okay cool, I heard you."

"Yeah, act like you know den."

"Shut up boy! What's yo name?" Rox had to make it fast, she had 2 minutes left.

"Why? You feelin me huh?"

"Say I do? Den what?"

"You'll see...yo what's yo name?"

"Rox, but um...you can call me fresh wa." Rox said, with a smile. She was smiling so hard, that she didn't realize time was flying.

"What kind of name is that?"

"It's me, my name, you know...fresh water." Rox said, with confidence.

"Um yeah, I like dat, fresh water huh?"

"I bet yo dick will like it better when it flows on ya!"

"What girl?"

"Nuthin...um...what's your name?"

"It's B, you know, Brian. Call me what you want, but don't call me nigga."

Rox was smiling from ear to ear. She gave Brian her home number and was glad to know that he was from the south side. She knew that he could show her around.

Rox rushed out the house, and jumped in the car, it was now 7:22 am. "What took you so long girl?" Ms. Vicki was real mad, pulling off while Rox was still closing the door, and almost hitting another car.

"Mom watch out, you almost hit that car."

"Don't tell me how to drive girl, I got dis!" Rox busted out laughing at her mother. Ms. Vicki had to let Rox know that she was hip to the broken english that the kid's use these days.

"Okay, burn rubber speedy." Ms. Vicki just looked at her daughter and laughed.

She remembered Rox being just 10, now she almost 15. Dang, she thought, time is really flying. Rox and her mother rode in silence, until they arrived at her school. Rox was watching out the window and wondering about the summer and how much fun she was about to have. Ms. Vicki wondered about how this abortion that her daughter was soon to be having, would affect both their lives.

Ms. Vicki had been teaching her daughter forever, not to have abortions. Even though she would of recommended her daughter Lili to have a couple, because she was such a destruction, after she had all them damn kid's. She loved her grandkids dearly, since they were here now on earth, but she was embarrassed that she had 5 different dad's.

"Mom, park there....right there, Mama dang!" Rox was now yelling at her mom, while pointing at the 15 minute parking sign in front of the school.

"Mom! Mom! Earth to you woman." Rox said, putting her hand on her shoulder.

"What girl? I hear you okay? Don't talk to me like that! You hear me?" Ms. Vicki said while trying to park and point at Rox.

"I didn't think that you heard me." Rox was laughin so hard at her mother, that she didn't realize that she was 2 minutes late for her final.

"Oh shoot! Mama I got to hurry....I'm late!"

"Get your butt in there and hurry up! We have to be there in 2 hours, just make sure you get an A+," Ms. Vicki said, with a smile.

"I'll be back in about 20 minutes, so park over there."

Rox ran up the stairs and in the school. She wasn't paying attention to the eyes that were on her.

Denise was watching her run to her class. She instantly turned her recorder on and made her way to the bathroom. While inside, there were girl's in there, so she had to wait for them to leave, to set up the plan. Denise took the trash can and bolted up against the door, so no one could get in. She put her bag on top of the counter, pulled out a set of Rox clothing, that she got out of her gym locker, a camera, some red panties, and a bottle of mace. She took a pen and some lotion and rubbed it in the crotch of Rox' panties. She made it look crusty, so her plan would work. She then took pictures that she had of Terrance and her talking, then one of them hugged up in front of her house, and she transferred all of her evidence into a bag that she found in the back of Terrance's car. She then pulled out the tape that she recorded of her and Rox having an argument in the bathroom. Denise put everything in order, and headed out the bathroom.

Looking at her watch, it was 8:10. "Damn!" She said out loud, and now having people looking at her like she was crazy.

"What ya'll looking at? Damn!" Denise made her way down to the administration office. Denise didn't realize that the people looked at her funny, because they seen Rox' shirt with her name on it, draggin on the ground.

When she discovered that her plan might of been ruined, she had to act fast. Denise made it into one of the counselor's office, that was already off for the summer. She looked at the pictures that she had taken of Rox and Terrance butt naked, Rox and Carl freaking in the car, and of Rox pointing at a baller in a fitted hat.

Denise started the copy machine, pressed repeat, then color. She made over 25 copies of each picture. She then set up the tape recorder and pressed play. Denise put all the evidence in Rox' bag, and headed to Carl's locker.

Beep... "See...um,...oh....stop Terrance....oh....stop please." Rox's voice rang out over the loud speaker.

"What's that?" Everyone was laughin and listening, as they could hear Rox begging Terrance to stop fucking her so hard.

Rox didn't discover that it was her, until she walked up to the teacher to hand her test in.

"Roxane, do you hear that?" A girl said from behind her.

"Hear what girl?" Rox said, while looking at the girl and heading for the door.

"Your voice on the loud speaker."

Rox looked at her and stood in the doorway, with silence filling the room.

"Oooh....baby please oh it's so good, don't stop."

Rox looked at everyone in the room and the hallway laughing and pointing at her. Rox knew it was her voice and she was about to lose it.

She slammed the door and took off down the hall, to the Principle's office. On her way, she saw pictures of her having sex with both Terrance and Carl.

"Oh my God! What the fuck!" Rox said, while running around and snatching the pictures of her off the walls and out of people's hands.

"Hey Roxane, why don't you let me hit it," one guy said, while she was running and crying.

"I'm gonna whoop Denise's ass when I catch that hoe!"

Rox was yelling like a mad woman. Everybody was laughing and pointing in the direction of the gym. Rox made it to the counselor's office. The teacher's school monitors and Carl were looking for the office that had the recorder playing. When everyone seen Rox run in and grab the recorder, they fought with her, knocking papers all over the place. Rox ran with the recorder in hand, and pushed past everybody.

"Hold it young lady...hey!" Rox ignored the Principal and all the teacher's that were calling out her name.

"Yo Rox, baby, what's going on baby?" Carl was yelling as he was close behind Rox right on her tail.

"Nothing, I got to find yo bitch Denise, cause I know she's behind this!" Rox was yelling as she ran towards the locker room.

Rox didn't see the crowd that formed behind her. Everyone started running out of class, because they knew it was about to be a good throw down. Rox made it to the men's locker room, where everyone had formed a circle around Denise.

Denise stood there in front of Carl's locker, with all the evidence. When she noticed Rox, she tried to slam it back shut. Rox busted through the crowd, and landed a hay maker right upside her head. Bam! Bam! Plow! Rox was boxing her up. Poor Denise didn't even have a chance. Everyone cheered on. "Whoop her ass Rox!"

Mo and Angie was chanting "Yeah, show that hoe you ain't no joke."

"Denise oh she's whooping yo ass!" Darlene yelled out.

Denise was tryin to get up off the ground, but Rox sat right on her chest and was bangin her head to the ground, with her left hand and punching her in the face with the right.

"Please stop! I'm sorry!" Denise was tryin to say, but Rox lost it.

"What hoe? I'm gonna kill you bitch!"

Somebody ran outside and got Ms. Vicki out the car.

"Roxane Adams, you stop it now!" Rox heard her mother's voice but continued.

Carl stood and watched the woman he loved beat the brakes off the woman he used for ill pleasures. Ms. Vicki seen Carl watching as she pulled Rox off of Denise.

"Why are you just standing there? Huh? You say you love my daughter... you don't love nothing, you punk!"

Everyone stood and laughed, as Ms. Vicki took her attention off Rox, and put it all on Carl. While Ms. Vicki and Carl argued, Rox kicked Denise in the face and snatched up all the evidence she had laying around on the ground. Denise was so scared, that she raised up off the ground, to help Rox get the evidence out of Carl's locker.

Rox rummaged through Carl's locker and watched her mom and Carl argue. "Is this yo bitch?" Rox said, while slapping Denise's head against the locker.

"Yes, I'm sorry..." Denise was watching Rox, so she wouldn't get hit again. She put her hands up, to cover up her face. Mo, Angie and Darlene rolled up and helped Rox get herself together.

"You okay girl..."

"You whooped her ass, damn," Angie said, yelling and doing a dance.

"Yeah Darlene, I thought you were my friend." Denise said, while being jealous because of Rox getting all the attention.

"I ain't yo damn friend, hoe." Darlene said, looking nervously at Rox, who was now pissed off at Denise's comment.

"What you mean yo friend? Huh?" Rox turned all her attention to Darlene, as she tried to look at Mo and Angie for help.

Ms. Vicki and Carl walked up as the crowd went their separate ways, still hyped off of the good fight they just witnessed.

"Roxane, let's go...we are going to be late." Ms. Vicki walked off, to the car.

"What you still standing here for hoe!" Rox yelled at Denise, who was still standing around.

"Yeah, beat it bitch!" Mo yelled out.

"Yeah, go kick rocks hoe, before you catch another ass whooping trick!" Darlene yelled.

"Hoe, Carl don't want you." Angie said, while pushing Denise. Denise got the point, and left like she was told.

"What's all this shit Roxane?" Carl said, while looking his girl in the eye.

"I don't know, I should be asking you."

"Nah, you was fucking that nigga that you kept saying you were tutoring."

"I was helping him, I told you."

"Yeah, in the damn bed like I thought."

"No...no I wasn't."

Rox continued to deny the events that took place that day in Terrance's house. She was so ashamed that she just kept walking and talking. Angie, Mo and Darlene walked right behind them, to make sure that Carl wouldn't flip out and fight her.

"I got to go Carl."

"I know where you got to go, but before you do...you tell me something."

"What boy? I told you I got to go." Rox said, with one hand on her hip and the other one holding a tight grip on her bag.

"Is that my baby?"

Rox looked at Carl like he was out of his mind. Angie, Mo and Darlene stood in silence. Rox knew just what he was talking about, but she had to stand firm and make her answer believable. She was so embarrassed, but she didn't want to show it.

"Yes stupid...what the hell you mean nigga?" Rox was acting mad so Carl would have sympathy for her.

"Okay, I'm gonna let you go for now but as soon as you get home tonight, I'm gonna be there to pick you up."

Rox knew that she had plans with her girl's and he had nothing to do with them. She had been neglecting him and he wasn't taking no for an answer.

"Okay baby, I'll be waiting." Rox was ready, waiting for a hug or a kiss for confirmation that her man wasn't mad at her, but she would be waiting, because Carl had a plan that she would not understand.

Carl walked away frowning up at Angie, Mo and Darlene. "Shit Starters!" He yelled at them, while punching the door as he walked away.

"Damn, he's mad Rox!" Mo said, looking confused.

"Yeah, he just better quit trippin before we jump his ass," Angie said, while slapping hands with Darlene. Rox was worried, but didn't say nothing.

"I got to go ya'll, I got a doctor's appointment." Rox let her friends know, as she stood outside of her mother's car.

"We can meet up later, so I can give ya'll your outfits okay?"

"Rox thank you for hooking us up, cause I know we are gonna turn heads tonight." Mo said, while opening the door for Rox to get in.

"Girl, you ain't even seen them yet."

"I know they are cute though."

"We have to go ladies." Ms. Vicki said, with anger in her voice.

"Okay, we'll call you later Rox," Mo said, while Ms. Vicki pulled off.

Roxane enjoyed the ride on the way to the doctor's office. She knew her mother was very upset, so she didn't bother to question her mother about being so quiet. Rox had to get her story together for Terrance and Carl. It didn't matter what she told Terrance, because he wasn't her man. It was Carl that she had to worry about.

Rox and her mother made it to the doctor. Rox had to give out all of her info, of when she last had her period and how many people she slept with, and when was the last time she had sex. She was embarrassed, because she had to explain her sexual history in front of her mother.

Ms. Vicki sat and listened in anger. Half mad, because her daughter was having sex without being married and being too young. The other half, for not preparing her for protection and games that men play on women. Rox went in the room without her mother. There she laid on the abortion table, looking at the ceiling.

"Ouch! Ouch!" Rox screamed out, with tears running down the side of her face. She tried lifting up off the table. The doctors held her down for 5 minutes, that seemed like 5 hours.

Ms. Vicki stood outside the door and listened to her baby cry out for her mom. Rox thought she was so grown, but when it came to pain like that, she still cried out for her mama.

"Knock knock, can I come in please?" Ms. Vicki said, while opening the door.

"Yes Mama, they're done," Rox said, while leaning up over the table. Ms. Vicki cried and hugged her baby tight.

"I'm a failure. I should of told you."

"No Mom, you are the greatest Mom on earth. I'm sorry."

Rox cried, as the doctors left out and left them alone. Rox had to sit in a room for 2 hours. The doctors had to make sure she wasn't bleeding heavy, before they let her go home.

After the doctors checked her out, Rox and Vicki headed home. It was 5:00 and Rox was tired. She had to get some rest before she dealt with all of the embarrassing things that happened today.

Chapter 6

Feelin' It

After a hot shower, Rox put on her pj's, sat in her room and watched TV After about 10 minutes of channel surfing, her phone rang.

Ring! Ring!

"Hello, hello dummy." Click.

Um, I'll watch the reruns of Good Times. "Ha, ha.."

Rox laid there and laughed, while watching Good Times. She reached over the bed to look in her book bag. She was really excited about being out of school. Um...here goes B's number, let me put it in my address book.

After putting the number in her book, she went into thought. I wonder what he's doing? Should I call him? Nah, I'm gonna play this one my way. Yeah, I'll make him sweat me, shit he got the number. I'm gonna make him mine or maybe I'll play with him. Shit, Carl will be in St. Paul and B will be in Minneapolis.

Ring! Ring!

Damn, who is this that keeps calling? It better not be nobody playin games again.

"What!" Rox said, with a irritated voice.

"What? Is that how you answer a phone?"

"Who is dis?"

"It's me."

"Okay, I ain't got time for no damn games nigga." Click.

Before Rox could get up out the bed to go to the bathroom.

Ring! Ring!

Rox ignored the phone, and went to the bathroom.

"Oh, ouch!" Rox felt like her whole insides were coming out. She changed into some sweat pants and a t-shirt. She knew that her girl's or Carl would be calling, so she wanted to be ready. Walking back into her room.

Ring! Ring!

Damn, this damn phone is still ringing.

"H-e-l-l-o Shoot."

"You finally answered, huh?"

"Who is this?"

"It's me! B." Rox was now silent, with a smile from ear to ear. "Hello....you there?"

"Um yes...um I'm here," Rox said, while grabbing her chest and sitting on her bed.

"Well what's up?"

"Nothing, I'm chillin."

"Um, I was wondering what you had planned for tonight?"

"Um is that right?"

"Yeah, you were in such a hurry this morning, did you get to school on time?"

"Yeah I made it."

"Why you say it like that?"

"Oh, cause it's been a rough day." Rox said, while checking her tone.

"Well I'll make it better for you...if you want."

Rox giggled and talked to Brian for about an hour. He let her know that he was into the detail business. He fixed cars up and that's where the name came from. Rox felt so stupid, because she thought his business was a beauty shop. The name throws a lot of people off, but that is what he wanted. Being though his shop is the first of it's kind, he still had a lot of business.

Brian was a die hard hip hop fan. Rox was really into R&B. She loved hip hop as well, so that was one thing they had in common.

Rox was really feeling him. He was 19 and had his shit together.

He informed her that he had graduated from Washburn High School, a year ago and it was very important that she stayed in school. Although she was gonna do that anyway's, she felt good about him being concerned.

"Okay, well I'm gonna get off the phone, so I can get dressed."

"When you gonna call me back?"

"When ever I can," Rox said, smiling and twirling the phone cord around her.

"Okay then fresh water, I'll be calling you then." Click.

"Damn" Rox said, looking at the phone then hangin up. What was all that about? Rox looked through her closet and pulled out everybody's clothes and looked over all three outfits. Rox made alterations to her outfit and knew that Angie, Mo and Darlene would love them.

Rox thought of not giving Darlene her's, because she was sick of her sneakiness. Rox replayed all of the events of today and remembered what Denise said about how Darlene is supposed to be her friend. If Darlene had Denise thinking they were cool, then Darlene had been telling Denise her business all along.

Rox ain't no fool. She knew how to play Darlene close. She was gonna use her for everything she could, and then it was over. Rox looked over the naked photos and nasty panties that were left in her school bag. She shook her head and giggled while lookin at her and Carl freakin each other down in the car. Then it was a picture of her with her face frowned up and holding onto Terrance. To Rox, it didn't look like she was doing anything bad with Terrance, so she would get her lie together for Carl and her mother.

"Knock knock."

"Come in."

"Where are you at?" Ms. Vicki said, while looking around the room.

"I'm in here Mom." Rox said, while straightening her closet out.

"You know we are going to dinner later with Mr. Davis and his daughter." Rox forgot all about it. With all the things that went on, she sure wasn't up for no family gathering. Rox didn't want no problems out of her mom, so she just agreed to what she was saying.

"Okay Mom, but I have to be done by 9:00, because we're dancing at the club tonight."

"What dance? What club? I thought that was next month?"

"Nah, you know the Hip Hop Shop."

"Over on Selby?" Ms. Vicki broke in.

"Yes Ma, but I'll be..."

"No. I don't want you around all them dope dealers, pimps and guns."

"Ma, I won't. We're just gonna dance, hang out and den I'll be home by 12:00." Rox was looking at her mother for approval.

"Okay, I'm gonna trust that you do what you say, but I want you here at 11:30." Rox was pissed off. She didn't argue, but she wasn't coming home at no 11:30.

"Okay Ma, whatever."

Rox rolled her eyes, and continued to clean her closet out. Before leaving the room, Ms. Vicki reminded Rox that she wasn't getting away with what happened earlier.

"Rox, you should be careful about dancing, because you haven't recovered from that abortion. It's only been a couple of hours."

"I'm fine Mom, it don't hurt anymore."

"Well I want you home early so we can talk about these pictures of you being naked...."

"Mom, I'm cool okay?" Rox broke in, she was getting real irritated by her mother. Why was she all of a sudden concerned now?

"Look, don't get flip with me. I'll smack the mess out of you. I don't care about what happened to you earlier, you better check that attitude when you're talkin to me! You hear me!" Let me check my attitude, so she will quit trippin.

"What girl..." Ms. Vicki said, while snatching her by the arm.

"I didn't say nothing Mama, please...I don't feel like arguing okay?"

"Well you just make sure you don't talk back."

Ms. Vicki left Rox alone, so she could get herself together for tonight. She went to her closet and pulled out a long fitted mint green dress with gold buttons. It had a nice half cut jacket to go with it. She then went to get her shoes. Ms. Vicki was sharp in her day. In high school, she won best dressed, and most likely to succeed, even though she had a daughter at 16, she always made it her business to dress to impress. She pulled out her gold open toed high heeled sandal's, that strapped up her ankle. To top it off, she pulled out her round gold earrings that had diamond studs at the end, with a matching gold purse. She never had to teach Rox or Lili how to dress. They just picked it up on their own. Even though Lili did the wrong things by stealing everything that wasn't nailed down, in a department store. Rox on the other hand, was a straight A student with plans and goals.

Rox didn't know it but Ms. Vicki had plans of taking her money, that she had been saving since Rox was a baby, to help her with her dream to be the first black woman to own her own floral company in Minnesota. She wasn't gonna make her daughter go to college but she was gonna encourage her to go or at least do something positive.

As positive as Rox always tried to be, people still tried to steer her in the wrong direction. She knew everybody was jealous of her. Why? What for? She had everything that anybody else had, shoot- most people had more.

Rox, Ms. Vicki, Mr. Davis and Latasha all went to Red Lobster. They all laughed and got to know each other. Tasha was 11 years old, so she acted as a young girl would. Giggling at everything somebody said, ordering food that she didn't know what it was, just looking at the picture and saying she wanted it. Boy, she was irritating Rox.

Rox kept checking the time. It seemed like 10:00 was taking so long to come. She already had a plan to leave from the restaurant dressed, so she would not have to go back to the house. She was gonna have her mother drop her off at Angie's, because she lived on Laurel Avenue and that was right by the Hip Hop Shop. Rox was gonna tell her mother that she was spending the night at Angie's because she had a big house with a lot of food and her bedroom had a canopy bed with a day bed for Rox to sleep on. She also had a bathroom connected to her room, with a jacuzzi in it. Just relaxin in Angie's tub, made Rox happy, shoot she now had to convince her mother.

"Ma, um...I'm having a good time and I appreciate you for bringin me out to eat, but I got to go." Rox knew that her mother was gonna be mad, but she had to play it cool.

"Oh no, where you going big sis?" Latasha said, while putting her hand on Rox's shoulder.

"I'm going to dance at this party tonight." Rox shifted in her chair to face Tasha, so she would shut up. This girl was very clingy. I guess that was because she was an only child. Rox didn't have no time for baby-sitting. Ms. Vicki continued to talk to Mr. Davis and ignored Rox' statement.

"Mom, I need to go. Angie and them are waiting on me." Rox seen that this was the perfect time to get her mom.

"Okay girl. I said you could go."

Ms. Vicki was still into her conversation with Mr. Davis. He seen that Rox was in a hurry to leave, so he decided to intervene.

"Rox honey...you go and have some fun okay? We'll all be at home when you get there." Rox lit up like a Christmas tree. She was beginning to like him even more. Ms. Vicki knew that Rox was taking advantage of the situation.

"No, we will drop you off, but you will be home by 11:30."

Rox' smile turned to a frown, but instead of making a incident in front of them, she decided to be cool.

"Um Mom, I need to spend the night at Angie's okay?"

"Why do you need to spend the night at Angie's?" Ms. Vicki was getting a little edgy.

"Because she has a jacuzzi and it's real comfortable over there, plus her mom and dad won't be home. They went out of town on a business trip."

"Oh, what kind of business do they do?" Mr. Davis was now concerned about the parents not being home.

"Oh some Fortune 500 company, that her dad is part owner of." Mr. Davis wasn't gonna make Rox upset, so he decided to keep his comments to himself.

"I guess you can go, but you will be back home in the morning."

"Yeah, I can sleep in your bed huh?" Tasha said, while hangin on to Rox' shoulder.

"That's cool, just don't pee in my bed." Everybody at the table laughed. Tasha chuckled and added "I'm too big for that sis." Mr. Davis added in "I trained her not to do that long ago."

Rox gave everybody a hug and left. She caught her a cab to Angie's house just in time. It was now 10:30 and the girl's were supposed to dance at 11:00. Everybody was there waiting to get dressed. Rox had all the outfits in her bag. They were stuffed in, so they had to iron them. So everyone wouldn't argue, Mo decided to iron while Rox took a quick shower. Darlene and Angie did everybody's hair.

"What color shoes is everybody wearing?" Rox yelled out from the shower.

"Damn Mo, I only brought my shell toed Addidas and some white pitty pats." Darlene looking at Mo, while her and Angie combed their hair in the mirror.

"I ain't wearing no pitty pats man, all that money your mom and them be having, yo ass out here wearing pitty pats girl!" Angie now turned, looking at Darlene with the curling iron in her hand.

"Nah, I just brought them to kick around the house in."

"Then why you bring them we gonna be looking cheap in front of them haters?"

"Oh yeah, well I guess I wasn't thinking." Darlene was saying while tryin on her Addidas.

"Now you see what happens when you don't think." Angie continued to comb her hair with an attitude. Darlene didn't know that everybody was fed up with her deceitful actions. Everybody knew that Darlene was plotting against Rox, but she was too slow to figure out that everybody had figured her out already.

"Yo Rox, come on. We all ready and I got your Addidas' out already." Angie said, while knocking on the bathroom door.

"Yo Rox, you hear me?" Rox was tryin to get the blood out of the shower.

"Yeah, I'm comin. I'm just cleaning up my mess." Rox had started hemorrhaging, from not resting. She knew that she should of not had her butt out of the house. It was time for her to really feel it. Rox put on a pad just in case any accidents tried to happen. Fly girl's always had to be prepared. Rox couldn't risk herself being embarrassed again at all.

"Ya'll all look real happy," Rox said, while putting on her shoes. "Yeah, we will be, when we whoop these hoes in this competition." Angie said, while slappin Mo's hand.

"I know girl, I want that "G" dat they giving us." Angie said, while helping Rox pull her shirt over her head. Rox looked at everybody with a smile.

"What....oh we got that easy." Rox feeling a good whiff of energy on her body, after the thought of money went through her body. That was always a good way to get somebody's mind off of stress. Especially when you weren't use to having any money. Everybody headed to the car.

"I'm getting in the front," Rox said, while running past Angie and Mo and hitting them on their butts.

"Stop you hoochie." Mo said, while chasing Rox to the front seat. "Get her Mo! Whoop her butt!" Angie yelled, while laughing at Mo and Rox chase each other around the car.

"Ya'll come on and get in, it's already 11:00." Darlene said, while sitting in the driver's seat. Rox ran and made it to the front door, jumped in and slammed the door. Mo flopped down in the back seat next to Angie, and out of breath.

"Huh huh woo, shut up Darlene, you just mad dat nobody don't play with your butt." Mo said, while breathing all hard. Angie started laughing, and slapped Darlene upside the head.

"Yeah buster, just shut up and get us there now!"

"Stop playing shit!" Darlene said, with an attitude, and started the car.

"Oh girl, chill so we can get this loot." Mo said while turning up DJ Quik's "Bitch betta have my money". Everybody started bopping their heads to the music.

Rox had to get her routine together for the $1,000 dollar plan. She recounted the dance steps and made sure she didn't get her group steps mixed up with her drill team dances. Rox had it down, and she was gonna do a head stand and then flip into the splits.

Rox started laughing out loud real hard and yelling "Yeah yeah!" Everybody in the car thought she was crazy.

"Yo, what's up with you yelling girl?"

"Yeah, I can't hear the music." Angie and Mo were saying, while playfully shaking Rox from the back seat. Darlene just looked at Rox like she was crazy and pulled into the dusty parking lot, across from the building where they give parties. It was upstairs from a community center that taught boxing during the week. It also had a dental office next door.

Some stupid crack heads use to try to break into those offices, while standing in line for the party. What were they gonna do with boxing equipment or dental scalpels and false teeth? I guess a crack head will try and make anybody buy anything, shit.

"Damn it's packed up in there." Rox said, while dancing around and shaking her butt. She didn't realize the eyes on her when she did that.

"Yo baby, do that shit again." A loud manly voice said out of a crowd of dudes, that were waiting to get into the party.

Angie, Mo and Darlene stood in line while looking at the crowd of dudes that had their eyes all on Rox. All the females in line turned their nose up at Rox, while she danced her way up to the front of the line.

"They think they're the shit....stank ass hoes." One dark skinned female said.

"Yeah, dem hoes better not be pushin up on my man, or some ass gonna get whooped." Another girl said to her. All the dudes in line heard the hoochie looking hoes in line hatin on Rox, so they chanted her on. One dude was whistling and all the others started, "Go Roxy, it's yo birthday!"

Mo, Angie and Darlene clapped and chanted their girl Rox on. Rox's head started spinning, so she ended her little dance with a quick jumpin jack, then landed down on one knee and shouted yeah.

Everybody laughed, and told her how good she looked. Rox jumped right in front of the line that was wrapped around the corner. Everybody was so into the dance that Rox just done that they didn't see her walk right in. Rox grabbed Mo, Angie and Darlene by the hand and pointed towards the stairs.

"Come on ya'll." Rox laughed while they all snuck past everybody and made it up the stairs towards the DJ's booth.

"Yeah, see ya'll was sleep on me. Ha ha! I told ya'll I had a plan!" Rox yelled to them over the music.

"Good one young one." Angie and Mo said at the same time and dancing to the music.

"Yeah, you got it, Rox," Darlene said.

"I'm bout to check into the DJ booth, cause I'm feelin it, ya know!"

Chapter 7

Hang It Up

    Rox danced all across the floor. While Darlene was talking to the DJ, to give him their music selection. Angie and Mo made their way through the party. It was all kinds of ballers there. One baller in particular, was eyeing Monique. Angie seen him peepin Mo out, so she made Mo walk his way.
    "Yo, Mo girl, you see that boy watching you?" Angie said to Mo, while tilting her head in the crowd of ballers.
    "Yeah, girl...stop looking at them!"
    "Well why don't you say something to him?" Angie was now dancing to Terry Riley's "Rump Shaker."
    "He better come say something to me shoot, you know I don't be sweatin no dudes like that." Monique said through her teeth, while dancing from side to side.
    "I'm bout to make some moves and see what done feel off up in here."
    Angie made her way through the party, dancing and snapping her fingers and leaving Mo standing there to fin for herself. Mo and the baller kept eye contacts, but neither one would make their way over to each other. Mo decided to look through the crowd for Rox, because it was almost time for them to dance.
    The DJ just made an announcement for the Booty Shaker Contest. Like they all had figured. It was about 5 groups signing up to get in on that thousand dollar prize, plus if they did something original, then they would get a bonus.
    With money on her mind, Mo had to find her girl's. As Mo started making her way through the party, she seen Rox coming out of the bathroom, holding her side.
    "Rox! Rox! Over here!" Mo was yelling over the crowd, and holding up her hand. Rox couldn't hear her that clear, but she kept looking around. Mo seen Rox looking confused. Mo made her way through the crowd and grabbed Rox by the arm.
    "You okay young one?" Rox face turned up while she held her stomach.
    "I'm cool, but I'm cramping and bleeding." Mo started sweating. She knew that this wasn't good for Rox, but she wanted that money.
    "Do you think you can make it through the dance, so we can get that "G'?"

Rox didn't want to let her homegirl's down, especially Mo, because she knew Mo had her back.

"Yeah, I can, but we got to go as soon as we finish." Monique half way smiled, and held her hand.

"I got you, young one. We are out as soon as we finish."

Rox and Mo made their way to the dance floor where everybody was gathered up to watch the contest. Rox pointed towards Darlene and Angie. They started waving their hands so Rox and Mo could see them.

The St. Paul Get It Girl's were gonna go first that was Darlene, Angie, Monique and Roxane. The DJ made the announcement for their entrance, and Rox started it off. Angie, Mo and Darlene stood behind her and did their thang. Rox did her pop shake around in a circle, flipped on her hands and did a split. The crowd went crazy. One dude yelled out, "My money is on her! Yeah $500 on her!" Rox heard them yelling, while she held her stomach. The crowd went crazy and joined in with him.

"Yeah, I got a hundred!" Then another one yelled.

Angie, Mo and Darlene clapped and jumped up and down and hugged each other. Rox was bent over throwing up. Angie noticed Rox bent over in the corner, and made her way through the crowd to Rox.

"What's up young one, you did great!" Angie said, in a nervous tone. Rox didn't respond at first, cause she was still spitting and tryin to get herself together.

"I'm cool, I just want to win the money for ya'll okay?"

Angie was mad at Rox. Angie didn't need no money and she knew that Rox was only tryin to win that money for herself and Mo. Darlene and Angie always had money, so winning wasn't a big deal for the doe, but it was for their reputation.

"What you mean girl?" Angie said, now wiping Rox' face. "Your health is more important girl." Rox leaned against the wall, with her hand on her stomach and one on her head.

"I know a...I...can make it, I just wanna win." Rox was beginning to feel dizzy. "Go get me some water and I'll make it. I promise we can leave after we win, okay?" Rox said, while looking up at Angie.

"Okay, I'm gonna go get Mo and D, so we can leave right after we win okay?" Angie said, while frantically walking into the crowd to look for Mo and D.

Angie squeezed through the crowd, and made her way over to Mo and D. It was so packed in there, that the floor was shaking. At one point, Angie felt like the walls were closing in. She thought Rox could die, from the symptoms she was having. Angie found Mo and D and told them it was time to go. They convinced her that it was about 10 minutes left, and the judges would make their decision. Mo and D went and kept an eye on Rox, while Angie went to get her some water. Angie made it back with the water, to calm Rox down.

"I'm fine. Ya'll go up to the DJ's booth, and stand so ya'll can get my "G"." Everybody started laughing. Even though Rox was in so much pain, she still had money on her mind.

To give them confirmation that she was okay, Rox guided them to the DJ's booth, so they could collect their money. Rox was sure they had won that contest, like they always do. That made her smile a little, even though she was still in a lot of pain.

She sat down at a table across from the DJ booth, in plain view, so her girl's could see her. She didn't realize that some people from school were looking at her, whispering and pointing. One dude pulled a picture out and showed it to two girl's that were sitting at the table. One girl started laughing very loud and yelling "Nasty, super freak, super freak!"

Rox heard all of the statements, but didn't realize that they were talking about her. At the same time, Angie came to the table to get Rox, so the DJ could announce the winner. The people had now formed a crowd at the table, while they discussed and pointed at the picture. Since Rox was sitting so close to them and now she could see them pointing at her and calling her a super freak over Flavor Flav's "911 Is A Joke", she could barely hear. She asked Angie, "Angie, do you hear and see them?"

Angie looked in the direction of the people, and seen them yelling and pointing in her and Rox's direction. Angie was pissed, because they were calling Rox a super freak. She knew that Rox was in pain and it was time to go. Angie snatched the picture out of the dude's hand, ripped it up and threw it in his face. Rox seen Angie throw something at the dude, and grabbed her arm.

"Angie girl what's wrong? Don't be trippin, you know I can't fight in this condition girl." Angie ignored Rox and charged the dude. Angie swung on him, and he ducked.

"Why you frontin on my homegirl nigga?" Angie said, while tryin to swing on the 6 foot 3 inch man.

"Yo, I'm just calling it like I seen it earlier today." The dude is now laughing, while holding Angie's hands.

Rox was helpless. She sat with tears rolling down her face, while all the people continued to call her names. Angie broke loose from his grip and started yelling.

"Any of you motherfuckers speak on my homegirl, you gonna have to deal with my mutt ass!" Angie walked off, grabbing Rox by her hand and wiping her tears.

"Stop cryin. Shit, these hoes do more dirty shit then taking naked pictures." Rox still felt like a slut and she couldn't bear the pain. She needed a bed fast.

"Angie, we got to go now!" Angie seen the look on Rox's face and she had to get her out of there. Angie and Rox made it over to the DJ booth where Mo and Darlene was singing and dancing.

"Where ya'll been!" Mo yelled, over the music.

"Yeah, we won and we got an extra five hundred for doing new shit they never seen!" Darlene said, while putting her arm around Rox. Rox was disgusted and felt some form of liquid coming out of her. She had a pad on, but it felt full.

"Yo Mo, I got to go!" Rox said while heading towards the door. Angie, Mo and Darlene started walking behind her. Darlene stopped and said "Here, ya'll head to the car. I'm gonna get the money okay?"

Angie ignored her, and kept following Rox. Mo made a detour and followed right behind Darlene. Nobody trusted Darlene, and even though Darlene had money, Mo knew that she would try to pull a sneaky move on them. The DJ was pissed, because he wanted to announce them individually, so they could get some exposure in Minneapolis. If they did, they could get more chances to compete for more money and a bigger audience.

Mo watched him peel off the thousand dollars to Darlene, then she seen three more dudes peel off what looked like five hundred from each one. That meant they had twenty five hundred dollars, to split amongst four people.

Mo felt that Rox should get the most, because she did the most work. She's the one that snuck them in the party, without having to pay the twenty dollar entrance fee, and she's the one that the crowd went crazy for. By splitting it four ways, that would mean that they would each get six hundred and twenty-five dollars. That was a lot of money, and Mo knew that Rox' dream was to be the first black owner of a floral shop in the Snelling and University area.

Mo watched Darlene pocket something. "Yo, how much you get D?" Mo said, standing behind Darlene and scaring the shit out of her. Darlene jumped back. "Damn girl! I got it. I thought you was in the car?"

Mo was irritated by D and her sneaky ass. "Nah, I had to check on our money."

"What you mean? I got it!" Mo seen guilt all over D's face.

"Well, I'm making sure."

Darlene didn't respond. She just headed towards the door. Mo followed right on her tail. As they headed out the party, Mo was stopped by the baller that was eyeing her. The unknown guy stepped right in front of Mo from out of nowhere.

"Hey, I've been looking for you." Mo was so shocked, that she just started smiling. She looked at the dude and then at Darlene, as she headed out of the door and disappeared in the crowd.

"I didn't know you were looking for me?" Mo said, while making her way towards the door. The dude followed her, because he didn't want to yell over the music. Mo felt his presence and kept walking, so he would follow her.

"Hey, slow down!" The unknown dude said, before Mo made it out the door.

Monique felt good inside, because nobody had been trying to talk to her lately. Maybe a few dudes at school and most of them were nerds or high school jocks. Mo knew that they weren't her speed. Ballers were more her speed, because she glamorized their life style.

Mo always imagined having her own crib with a dude, and getting a weekly hair and nail do. Rolling around in a Mercedes or a BMW. Monique knew rolling in a Mercedes was a dream, and the only thing getting close to rolling a BMW would be a human BMW, (Black Man Working). That was her only thought of driving one.

"I got to get to the car, my little sis is in trouble." The dude frowned and reached for her shoulder, when they made it outside.

"Yo, just stop, so I can at least tell you my name girl." Mo turned around and started laughing. The dude was relieved that he got her attention.

"What! What's up dog, holla at me! Why me? What you want?" The dude was shocked, because most girl's dropped at the chance to even talk to him, let alone for him to be chasing them down.

"Why not you?" The dude said with a wide smile.

Mo seen all the girl's that were in the party come out and watch Mo talk to this dude. Mo liked the fact that people were jealous of her talking to him. She was so into this cat and mouse game, that she forgot all about Rox being sick. Monique seen Terrance walk past him and remembered that Rox had to get home. Monique had to get his name, before Terrance came over and started questioning her about Rox.

"What's your name?" The dude grabbed her hand.

"Jay...Jay Hustle."

Monique knew the last part of his name was Hustle for a reason.

"Hum...what's up with Hustle? Why can't it just be Jay?" He started laughing at her slick confidence.

"Cause it's what I am and what I believe in, that's why." Mo was shocked at his confidence, but it turned her on.

"Well yo, I got to go but..."

"What's up Monique, where is Rox?" Terrance said, while interrupting her conversation. Jay looked at Terrance like he was crazy for busting in the middle of him and Monique. She seen the look on his face, so just to keep the confusion down, she grabbed his hand.

"Hold up Terrance, don't be coming up on me like that while I'm talking." Terrance had to keep his cool, cause he just wanted to find Rox.

"Sorry Mo, I'm just looking for my girl. I need to talk to her." Mo knew that Terrance was a little weird, but she also knew he meant well. Before she could answer, Terrance apologized to Jay for being disrespectful. Jay was cool about it, and told him no problem.

"Terrance, they are there in the parking lot." Mo said, while pointing in the direction of the car.

"Meet me over there, so I can finish talking okay?" Terrance walked off and gave Jay a hand shake before walking away.

"My name is Mo, but you can call me Monique."

"Yeah, well I told you mine, but you know you just said your name backwards." Monique was so into his beautiful brown eyes, that were sleepy like a puppy and his smooth lips that didn't have a chap look, that she was mumbling over her words.

"No I didn't." He started laughing and said "I'm a let you go." He reached out and hugged Mo. "Here is my number." Mo was confused.

"Wait! How did I say my name backwards?" He stepped back and handed her the paper with his number already on it.

"You said Mo is my name, but you can call me Monique, so I take it that it's the other way around." Mo and Jay laughed. Before Mo walked away, she wrote her number down and said "I'm gonna call you Jay, cause I'm original." He just shook his head and blew her a kiss goodbye.

Mo headed towards the car. On her way, she could see more people leaving the party. It seems that everybody was mad, because Mo and her girl's always win any competition that they get in. Mo seen Rox bent over, looking like she was out of breath. Darlene was in the driver's seat, Angie was rubbing Rox' back and Terrance was standing at the car, saying something, but Mo couldn't figure out the words.

"You're wrong! I can't believe you done this. Why Rox? Why girl?" Terrance was standing at the car door talking to Rox. He was so upset that he was kicking rocks, jumping up and down, and causing attention, because he was yelling at the top of his lungs. Rox wasn't saying a word. She was just ready to go home.

"I'm bout to go T. I told you I had to do it, for me. It wasn't yours no way okay?" Rox wiped her mouth, and put her feet in the car so she could shut the door. Monique knew that Terrance was a little weird, so she stood in the doorway, so he wouldn't try anything.

"How do you know? Huh? You know I hit that, without a rubber!" Rox felt herself getting angry, but she had to go. She felt like she was about to die, so she started crying.

"No Terrance, you made me do it! I didn't do it cause I wanted to." Rox said, while wiping her tears.

Terrance really loved Rox. Especially since he knew she would never be his. If he could only get that punk ass Carl out of the way. He didn't want to see Rox cry anymore, so he changed his tone, until later.

"Why don't we just call you later Terrance." Monique said.

"Okay, that's cool, but Rox already said she was gonna talk to me Sunday." Terrance said while stepping back and looking at Rox to confirm his statement.

Once Rox seen him back up, she felt better. She knew she had to say anything, to get the hell away from him.

"We'll call okay?" Monique said, while closing her door and not giving Terrance a chance to cause another scene.

Everybody was tired in the car. Angie fell straight to sleep. Rox was sitting in the back seat moaning and trying to keep herself from throwing up. Monique rolled the window down from the front seat. She felt better, once the air got on her. Monique watched Darlene drive.

"What? Why you looking at me?" Darlene started getting nervous, because she knew that she pocketed some of the winnings. She didn't know if Mo noticed her slide some in her bra, so she would wait to see.

"Why you guilty or somethin? Huh?" Monique said, while turning towards her.

"No! Guilty of what? Shit for what?" Darlene said with a frown on her face.

Monique didn't answer. She was just gonna wait until they made it in the house. Darlene took her time parking the car. Monique turned and woke Rox and Angie up. They both were so tired, that they forgot their shoes in the car, while they walked to the door barefooted.

"Come on Darlene, and bring all the money too!"

Darlene was so irritated by Monique's statement, but she kept her cool. She helped Rox up the stairs while Angie opened the door and Monique grabbed all of everyone's belongings out of the car. Monique made it in the house with everyone's bags. Rox was running her bath water. Angie was in her mom and dad's bathroom taking a shower, and Darlene was on the phone.

Monique walked over to the dresser where Darlene's purse was, and started going through it.

"What you doing girl?" Darlene said, now yelling. She quickly hung up the phone, and walked over to Monique.

"I'm checking to see if you cuffed our loot." Darlene was pissed. She snatched her purse out of Mo's hand, looked at Mo with a evil eye and said through her shut teeth, "I said I got it. I'm gonna split it up in morning, when everybody is up!" She pushed past Mo, and walked to the downstairs bathroom, and left Monique standing there looking foolish.

Monique went to the bathroom, to check on Rox. Rox had been hemorrhaging a little too much, so she decided to elevate her feet on Angie's futon bed, that she had for company in her room. Usually, Mo would sleep there, and Rox would sleep in the opposite direction on Angie's bed, and Darlene would sleep on the floor. Not tonight, shoot, Rox had to get comfortable herself. Mo didn't mind, because she knew that Rox was under a lot of stress.

"Rox, you know that bitch Darlene done cuffed some of our loot." Rox didn't want nothing but peace.

"Nah, she ain't girl, shit, she got her own money...her damn parents are loaded with that Indian loot." Monique watched Rox drift off to sleep, with her last comment. She didn't want to bother her, so she went looking for Angie.

"Angie, when you gonna be done?" Monique said, while knocking on the door. Angie was already lotioning down and on her way out the door. "In a minute."

Monique went back to Angie's room to look through Darlene's bag. Darlene was in the bathroom downstairs. Mo knew that she would be gone for a while, because she always took long in the bathroom. Her hair alone took about 30 minutes to wash, because it was so long. Angie walked in the room while Mo was tearing the room up.

"What you doing Mo? You making a lot of noise, while Rox sleeping." Angie set her stuff down. She was getting ready to lay down after she pushed Mo's feet out of the way.

"Go to bed Mo!" Angie said, while pulling the covers over her.

Now that Mo was calm, she had to make her plan. As she laid in the bed and watched Darlene come in with her purse in her hand, and pj's on, she watched her go to check her bag and put something in it. Darlene walked to the middle of the floor, to make her a pallet. She didn't know if anybody seen her pocket the thousand dollars that she put in her bag. So she decided to play it cool.

"Goodnight my homegirls."

Angie and Rox were out cold, but Mo was laying there watching D, but decided not to say nothing, so she would take her ass to sleep. Mo's plan was to hang it up with Darlene for good.

Chapter 8

Party Too Hard

It was 12:00, and everyone was still sound asleep. Monique tossed and turned all night. She went from thinking about Jay, to thinking about how sneaky D thought she was.

Mo finally got up out the bed, and headed towards the bathroom. She looked at the blinking light on the answering machine, and knew that everybody was blowing Angie's phone up, for a reason. Mo knew that one of the messages had to be from Terry.

Her and the girl's had missed practice. Even though Terry knew that the girl's had the dance down pat, she still wanted them to come through, so they could teach some of the other girl's how to dance.

Mo walked to the bathroom, and stepped over D on the floor. She moved her leg, to make sure she was sleep. She then took her bag and pulled it in the bathroom. She pulled all her things out of her bag. Razors, 2 wife beaters, men's drawers, soap, 2 pair of panties, lotion and two pairs of socks rolled up. At first Mo didn't think that she put the money in there, but she had to triple check. She took the bag and shook it up and down. All of the change and make up fell out of the purse, making a loud crashing noise to the floor. Mo opened the door to see if anybody woke up. Everybody was moving around, but no one got up. She had to make her move fast. She put all of the stuff back in the purse. Looking the drawers up and down checking them for stains, and laughing at herself. The socks were the last thing she put in the bag, and she felt one was heavier than the other. So she opened each pair. Bang! Boom! Bam! There it goes, the extra "G", that D had cuffed for herself.

Mo was furious as to why? Why would Darlene do this? She had everything a 17 year old could want. Her mother was a full blooded Indian, so she got at least thirty thousand dollars a month, from the government. They always made sure that Darlene had everything she needed. Her mom made sure she had five hundred dollars a month, and gave her access to all of her mom and dad's credit cards. She got a brand new car every year, since she was 15. She has a closet that any teenager would dream of. The only thing that they require her to do is keep her grades up and stay in tune with her Native American Culture.

Mo played it cool. She walked out the bathroom and everybody was awake. D had her face towards the wall, talking on the phone. Angie was helping Rox get out of the bed.

"Good morning wiggle." Angie said while passing Mo, to get to the bathroom.

"What's that?" She said, laughing at Angie, who's head looked like cat's were licking on it.

"You! That's who, with all that moving in the bed last night."

Mo just laughed, because she didn't want them to know why she was so restless last night. She waited for Rox and Angie to go to the bathroom, so she could confront D. Mo watched D while she had her back turned towards her.

"Yo Darlene, get off that phone so I can holla at you!" Mo was talking to D's back, as she ignored Mo's statement. She didn't want to dis D while she was talking to one of her boy toy's or even Tobby. Her hustlin boyfriend that had full control over Darlene's mind sometimes. Whenever he did spend time with her, it was on his terms, only never on her's. So every chance she got, she was going to cherish it.

"D you hear me, so get off the phone. We have business to talk about."

Darlene now irritated and looking up at Mo now and rolling her eyes. She stands up and stretches.

"Yo, boo I'm gonna call you back when I get home okay?" I guess the person she was talking to didn't want to get off, because she didn't move.

"Get off now, for I hang that shit up." Mo said, up in her face with her demon breath all up in Darlene's face. D was so disgusted by that smell, that she jumped back.

"Wait girl, he's telling me somethin."

Mo had to laugh, not only at her stank breath, but for the fact Darlene was tryin to stall her. She knew Mo peeped her game and was tryin to get that money out of her. Mo made a mad dash to put her face and breath in check. When she returned, Darlene was sitting on the floor watching TV, Angie was in her shower and Rox was heading to the guest bathroom. Mo was ready for whatever.

"Yo D, where is the loot, so we can split it up." She looked up at her.

"I got it right here." Darlene handed the money to Monique. "Damn Mo, why are you trippin?"

"Yeah Mo, we're gonna split it four ways, chill." Rox was saying, as she sat down on the bed. Mo didn't say a word, she just counted the money out on Angie's bed. Angie now returning from the shower.

"What's up ya'll?" Everyone said a dragged out ha. Angie seen the response and seen the looks on everybody's face. Mo was finished counting the money.

"It's only fifteen hundred bitch!" Mo jumped up from the floor, socking the shit out of Darlene. Bam! Bam!

"Dumb bitch! You shady hoe!" Darlene didn't have a chance to respond. She tried to defend herself, but Mo was screaming and landing hay makers all upside her head.

Angie reached out to break them up, but Monique was swinging like a mad woman. Rox sat on the bed and screamed, "Kick her ass Mo! Yeah big sis, whoop that hoe!" Rox was punching her fist to her hand and laughing. Even though Angie felt the fight was accurate, she didn't want Mo to kill her.

"Stop Mo, you gonna kill her." Angie was now pulling Mo off Darlene.

"No, this hoe was tryin to jew us." Mo was saying, while backing off and kicking D in the butt. Darlene was holding her head and stomach, crying and tryin to explain.

"I was gonna give the extra "G" to Rox....I wasn't gonna steal nothing." Everybody in the house stopped to look at Mo with guilty eyes.

"Nah, nah hoe, you was gonna cuff our shit with your shady ass!"

Mo said, while charging at Darlene again.

Angie stood in front of her to stop her.

"Sit down girl, chill out!" Angie was now pointing for Mo to sit down next to Rox. Mo was disgusted, thinking what have I done, nah, she was stealing.

"You wasn't gonna give Rox shit....you don't even like Rox. You're jealous of her." Rox broke in, "Yeah, you're jealous. You was gonna jack us like my sister said!" Rox pointing in Darlene's face. Darlene was crying, and no one cared, except for Angie. Mo was looking back and forth from Rox, Darlene and Angie.

"What? What the fuck ya'll looking at me for?" Everybody kept quiet, while Mo walked around the room yelling.

"Ya'll stupid! You feeling sorry for this hoe...shit, we keep feeling sorry for her ass!"

Rox was ready to get in the shower, so she could go home. Ms. Adams didn't want Rox to go anyway. Her mother knew that she could cause injury to herself, from all that moving around.

"Mo, chill...chill sis." Rox grabbed Mo's arm, and sat her down. When Rox stood up, she had blood coming out of her shorts.

"Yo, are you bleeding girl?" Mo said to Rox, as she tried to sit Rox back down. Everyone looked at Rox.

"Yes, you are bleeding." Darlene said, now standing next to Angie. All of the attention left Darlene, and went back on Rox.

"I'm okay ya'll...I guess from all the stress of the pictures with Carl, and Terrance. Angie calling herself a mutt all the time is making me hemorrhage. It makes me mad when you say that racist shit Angie."

Angie started crying. Rox felt sorry for her, even through her pain.

"Don't cry Angie. I'll be okay." Rox said, while hugging her.

"Yeah, we'll put Rox in the tub and call Ms. Adams okay?" Mo said, while wiping Angie's tears. Darlene felt out of place, while she watched how close they were.

"I'll call Ms. Adams okay?"

Darlene walked over to the phone to call. Angie walked Rox to the bathroom, to help her get in the shower. Monique got all of Rox' stuff, and ran to the basement to wash Rox' clothes. When she returned, she seen Darlene sitting on the bed next to the money. Mo was still upset, but she let it at ease for now.

"What you doing with the loot?" Darlene sat there, quiet for a second and looked at Mo.

"I'm gonna give Rox my cut."

"Why now? Because I caught you tryin to cuff that "G'?" Darlene didn't say nothing, because she didn't feel like fighting.

"No, I wasn't cuffing shit Mo." Darlene said, as she walked back to the phone, while rolling her eyes at Mo.

"Whatever girl, I know you was, but I'm gonna let you slide." Darlene started crying.

"Yo, here goes the note that Ms. Adams had me to make for Rox, until she get's here." Mo felt a little bad for her, so to make her stop cryin, she pulled the "G" out, pushed Darlene in the head and said "Quit cry baby... you give that to Rox and let her know what you are gonna do for her."

Darlene was still mad at Mo for fighting her, but she just wiped her face and went to check on Rox.

Angie helped Rox out of the bathroom, when she was finished. Rox felt a lot better, but knew that she needed to be at home in her own bed. Everyone else got dressed and waited on Ms. Adams.

Angie put her Guess jeans on with a Mickey Mouse shirt and jelly bean sandals. Monique had a long halter dress with a light yellow head band and matching sandals, with her all white Liz Claiborne purse. Rox was uncomfortable, and just wanted to go back to sleep. Darlene was always the one with the most clothes, even though her and Angie both came from money. Darlene did the most shopping. She had on Palimeto jean shorts, with a Gucci shirt and Gucci flip flops and a matching bag and sun shades.

Ms. Adams made it. Everybody walked Rox to the car, and put her stuff in. Darlene stood there and explained to Rox what her plan was with the loot. She gave Rox twelve hundred and fifty dollars. Rox lit up like a Christmas tree.

"Thank you girl!" Rox was happy and almost fell down, while tryin to hug D. "What's all this for girl?" Rox said, while now sitting back in the car and looking at the money. Ms. Adams was looking confused.

"Yeah, why are you giving her all that money?"

"Because she deserved it...she's the reason why we always win."

Ms. Adams was a little proud of Rox. Even though she was a mess at times, she still was a great influence, even on people older than her. Darlene felt good giving all of her earnings away. Rox was always the one with the plan. Every since they all been hanging out, Rox had the mind to do whatever she wanted to do. Everytime they rode down Snelling Ave. the girls would always go in and out of the expensive stores, dreaming of all the things they could do and be.

Rox had to watch from the side lines, while Angie and Darlene bought all the expensive clothes, but her and Monique had to put their's on lay-a-way, or go to the sales rack. Rox told them that since there was only black restaurants in the hood and no black owned stores, she would one day open up her own floral shop and name it after her great grandma.

Even though Minnesota has had more people of color invade the state, there still was a shortage of black owned businesses. Nobody in the hood had the idea of a floral shop. Rox did, and knew that she could capitalize on it. Black people are sometimes scared to try ideas, because they don't wanna fail, but we always overcome failure and get back up and try again. She always encouraged everyone to follow their dreams, every rich person either mastered somebody's idea better, or stole an idea from someone that never followed through on their own.

Ms. Adams was quiet on the drive to their house. She was upset that Rox could of killed herself. Rox knew she was mad, because she was speeding through traffic.

"Mom, why are you so quiet? Huh?" Rox turned towards her mom.

"Just thinking Rox, that's all."

"About what?"

"You girl, and what is going on with your sister." Rox didn't want to open up the can of worms, with her sister, so she tried to change the subject.

"Have you talked to Mr. Davis this morning?"

"Yes, he's at the apartment now...waiting on us."

"Is his daughter there?"

"Yes she is, and she cleaned your room for you."

"Oh that was nice." Rox turned to keep looking out the window. She was just ready to get in the bed.

Once Rox and her mom made it in the house, everything was cool. Her mom and Mr. D wanted to talk about the events that happened the day before, but Rox wasn't up for it. She walked right past Mr. D, and headed to the bathroom to check herself. Once out of the bathroom, she went to her room to pull off her clothes and get in her bed half naked.

"Hi big sis...I cleaned up for you." Tasha said with a big smile across her face.

"You did. Thank you." Rox was thinking to herself, she better not have moved my stuff around, cause I got things to do and people to see later.

"Oh well, I put all your papers and hair products over there." Tasha said, while pointing to the dresser.

"Aight, I'm gonna go to sleep, so wake me up in two hours okay and don't let nobody bother me."

Tasha tucked Rox in the bed, and turned the TV on for her. Rox was a little excited about her soon-to-be younger sister. The girl had her back and barely even knew her. She would make sure that in the future she would treat her very well.

Rox went on to sleep and slept longer than she wanted to. Tasha wanted to wake her up like she was told, but Ms. Adams instructed her not to. The phone rang in Rox' room, and Tasha went to answer it. It was now 6:00 and it was late. She remembered that Rox said she had something to do. Tasha answered.

"Rox get up!" Tasha said, while shaking her.

"What?"

"The phone is for you, it's your cousin Kane." Rox was wide awake, ready to talk.

"Why you didn't wake me up girl?" Rox was saying and snatching the phone out of her hand.

"Your mom said don't....and to let you sleep." Tasha said, with a sad look and walking to leave the room.

"Hold on Kane." Rox said and reached for Tasha. "I'm sorry okay? I didn't mean to snap kay? I'm take you with me tomorrow before you go home."

Rox said, while patting her on her back. Tasha smiled and said "Okay Sis." Rox got back to her conversation.

"What's up cuz? When you get out?"

"Yesterday and I got something for you." Rox was so excited about her cousin being home. He had to do that half way house and he didn't want to deal with nobody while he was in there.

"What you got for me?"

"Just a little something for holding me down and keeping your mouth shut."

"Oh you know you family, so I wouldn't say shit." Rox was now remembering the nightmare from five years ago.

"Well I don't wanna be on this phone, so I'm gonna halla at you later okay? Hey wait! How's my Aunt Vicki doing?"

"Oh she's cool...bout to get married."

"What? To who?"

"This dude seems cool...that was his shorty dat answered the phone."

"Yo word. Um if he makes her happy don't cause no problems for her girl."

"Boy please! I ain't, I'm cool. I just don't wanna move over south." Kane was a little excited about that.

"Over south word....damn I'm cool with that."

"Yeah you just wanna meet some hoochies over there huh?" Both of them busted out in laughter.

"Yeah that's cool too, but it might be good for a change." Rox was tryin to get herself ready for that change.

"Change is good cuz, change is good!"

"Aight, I'm be hollering at you okay?"

"Aight, bye cuz."

"Yo, don't say bye girl...that means forever and not later." Rox started laughing hard. "That ain't funny girl."

"Okay, see your crazy ass later!" Click.

Rox got up and headed towards the shower. She looked around the house and nobody was there. She was happy about that. She thought her mom must of taken Latasha and Mr. Davis home. Damn that's the phone ringin Rox said to herself out loud in the shower. She heard a voice say "I'll get it!" It sounded like it was two people talking at the same time.

She hurried in the shower and checked herself to make sure she wasn't bleeding. She had a light flow going, but knew that she had to take it easy because she was in so much pain the night before. Rox made it out the shower and headed to her room.

"Who was that out here talking?" She said, while walking into her room. "Oh shit...who let you in my house?" Rox yelled, half dressed and holding the towel up to her.

"I did Sis. He said he just had to tell you something." Terrance stood there looking Rox up and down in her bra and panties.

"Yo, why you keep poppin up over here boy?" Rox was pissed off and rolling her eyes. "Tasha get my black shirt and Adidas shorts out my closet and iron them for me okay?"

"Sure Sis." Rox waited for Tasha to leave the room.

"Wait, let me explain to you."

"Nah, nah slick, you ain't my man."

Terrance got mad and slammed his bag down on the floor. Rox jumped back, and changed her tune.

"First of all, I ain't say I was your man, and I ain't tryin to be girl."

"Yo, then why your ass following me to the party and poppin up at my house and shit?"

Rox and Terrance went back and forth about why Terrance was there and why Rox hasn't called him or been over to tutor him. Rox was a little scared of Terrance, because he wasn't no chump at all. He would pop a nigga in a heartbeat. He started walking up on Rox with blood in his eyes. He was about to slap the piss out of her.

"Sis I'm done....so you can get dressed now." Tasha said, while walking straight in the room.

Rox was glad she came in. Normally, she would of snapped on anyone just walking in her room, but she was glad that this little girl, who would have normally gotten on her nerves, had now saved her day.

"T, you need to leave."

"Why? I ain't gonna hurt you." He said, while walking up to Rox in her bra and panties. He was licking his lips with lust, instead of anger. Just that fast, it turned Rox on, but she couldn't. Not in her mom's crib, not in front of this little girl, and most of all, not after she just had an abortion yesterday.

"Sit down boy. I have to put my clothes on."

Rox pushed his long body down, while she turned her back to him and put her clothes on. Terrance watched her as she bent over to put her legs in her shorts. He let out a little chuckle and looked at Tasha, who wasn't leaving the room under no circumstances. She looked back at him and put her hand over her mouth and pointed.

"What's so damn funny?" Rox turned and looked back and forth from them.

"He was laughing at your butt and I was laughing cause you got a snuggy." Tasha said, while falling out laughing. Terrance just stared at Rox with a smile.

"Yo, my mom will be back and I told you I can't have no boy's in my house while she's gone okay?"

"Yeah, I know. I'm gonna leave, but you better be at my crib Monday, since you don't have school no more."

"Oh I thought you wanted me to come tomorrow."

"Nah nah slick, I'm gonna give you a chance to rest." Rox thought that last statement was a little weird the way it sounded.

"What you mean rest?" Rox frowned at him, with her hand on her hip.

He stood up and gave her a hug, kissed her on her forehead, and said "You're gonna need it." Rox thought crazy thoughts in her mind, while he turned to walk out the door. Tasha was right on his tail. "Wait Mr. T, you forgot your bag." Tasha ran towards him, with the bag, so she could lock the door.

"It's for Rox baby girl." He said, while patting Tasha on the head. "This is for you, for letting me in." He handed the happy Tasha a fifty dollar bill. Her eyes lit up with joy.

"Oh this is too much man you are the bomb!" Tasha jumped all around

Rox, who was now at the door making sure that the door would get locked. "Why you give her all that money boy? She's a little girl!"

"Stop hatin and take her to buy her some candy." Slam!

Rox made the apartment shake with that door and Tasha instantly stopped jumping.

"What's wrong Sis?"

"Nothing." Rox walked over to the couch, to turn the TV on. "Where did my mom and them go?"

"To the grocery store." Tasha knew Rox wasn't in the mood. She wanted to cheer her up. "Here, look in the bag and see what you got."

"What bag?"

"The bag that Mr. T brought you." Tasha held the bag in Rox' face.

"Get back, it might be some stuff in here for teenagers only." Rox said, while scooting away from Tasha.

"I've seen everything before. I'm 11, I know a lot."

"Huh...you do huh?" Rox was shocked, but she wouldn't let Tasha know it. This little girl was impressive.

"Yeah and I know how to keep my mouth shut Sis."

Tasha had a serious look on her face, while kicking her feet on the couch and twirling her money in her hands. Rox looked in the bag. It was a Nike duffle bag. She was impressed by it, cause he wasn't getting it back. It was perfect for her drill team outfit and a good overnight bag. He had some Krispy Kreme donuts and a quart of skim milk that was now leaking a' little, from when he dropped it. She then pulled out a pair of purple Guess jeans with a matching shirt and a pair of Chuck Tailor gym shoes.

This brought a smile to her face, because Terrance remembered when she argued with Darlene about borrowing the money to get this same outfit to wear to the Hip Hop Shop. As she sat the stuff to the side, a card fell out, and Tasha snatched it before Rox could and jumped up and started reading it out loud.

"This was a little thank you cause I know you haven't been feeling to good, plus I appreciate what you have done for me, because of your time spent tutoring me, I will pass on to graduate. Thank you, much love T."

Rox snatched the card out of Tasha's hand and started laughing.

"Right smart butt."

"I told you I wasn't no dummy."

"Okay, you got me sold." Rox said, with a big smile. She put all the stuff in the bag and put it in her room. When she returned, she watched Tasha enjoy the show 'Punky Brewster' on TV. She sat down and watched it with her. It was getting late, so she knew calling Carl would cause a problem, so she thought about Brian.

"Tasha, who was that who called when I was in the shower?"

"Oh, I almost forgot...actually, two people called." Rox looked.

"Who was it?"

"Yo home gurl Mo said call her when you can and some boy named B."

Rox was so excited, she didn't even realize that she was supposed to call him earlier, but had forgot. She enjoyed the idea of him sweating her. She knew it was some untold secrets about him, but she didn't want to pressure him, so he wouldn't get turned off. She enjoyed dreaming of him. He was an older dude, with his own business, so that meant a whole lot. Maybe he could help her get her own business or at least give her some tips on how to run it.

"Here Sis...you uumm...I dropped this when I read the card to you." Tasha now holding the money that fell on the floor. Rox looked a little surprised, because her thoughts were now about Brian.

Rox counted the three hundred and fifty dollars and put it in her pocket. She had plans to save that too. She now had sixteen hundred dollars, so that would be her start.

Rox knew that her mom had money in the bank for her, but she knew she wouldn't tell her how much. Ms. Vicki always felt like if she knew, then she wouldn't work hard at anything, and would use the money as an excuse not to work hard at her education.

Rox got up and made a phone call to Mo, to let her know that she was okay. She informed her of Terrance and his stalking behavior, but that he also left her some loot and some goodies.

He gave Rox the money for the abortion, but since her mom put it on her insurance, then she just kept the money for herself. Mo let her know that Terrance was crazy and eventually Carl would find out about her sexin him. Rox wasn't tryin to hear all that, so she told Mo she would get up with her tomorrow, so she could call her new freak B.

"Yeah girl, cause I've been talking to my new freak Jay Hustle, that I met at the party." Mo said, before hangin up.

"Cool, well I'll call you in the morning after I talk to Terry okay?"

"Oh girl, she ain't mad. She just wanted to make sure we was okay cause somebody was fighting after we left."

"ammi, I wonder who that was?"

"I don't know, but I'm glad we was gone."
"Yeah...me too."
"Okay, call you tomorrow." Click.

Chapter 9

Drama Queen

Ring! Ring! Damn, this boy is taking too long to answer. I'm gonna let it ring.
"Hello."
"Hi, can I speak to Brian?" Rox was interrupted by Tasha. "Wait girl, hold on."
"Hello."
"Oh, I'm sorry. Can I speak to B?" The voice was very familiar, but she didn't know.
"Yo, what's up beautiful?"
"Hey stranger."
"Nah, yo ass been M.I.A."
"What you say?"
"Missing in action girl."
"Oh, ha ha, I'm a little slow this Sunday morning."
Rox and Brian had a good conversation. He informed her that his phone was being transferred to his mom's house, because his business was closed on Sunday. She was excited to talk to him, being as though Carl had been ignoring her from all the rumors somebody was already spreading.
"Yo, I wanna take you out."
"To where?"
"Your choice."
"ammi...let's see. It depends on how much money you got."
"I can handle any price....Water."
Rox giggled off the sound of that. She was getting wide opened off this nigga and he knew how to play her too.
"Water huh....yeah, Red Lobster, dats what I'm talking bout."
"Bet dat. I'll scoop you up Tuesday night."
"Bye beautiful."
"Nah, that's your name."
"Thank you, I'll make sure I'm looking fresh for you."
"Cool, cause you know who's on my arm has to look right."

"You know I will...bye." Click.

Rox was cheesing from ear to ear. She pulled all her stuff out for church. Tasha was almost ready and waiting on Rox to pick out her outfit. She showered, put on her sundress and lace up sandals. She felt good, so she decided to call Carl, since she hasn't heard from him. She hesitated at first, because she assumed that he probably was with that bitch Denise, since she did bust those damn pictures out on the last day of school. Rox had to laugh at herself, while she dialed the number.

Ring! Ring! Ring!

"What's up?"

"Is that how you answer a phone boy?"

"Ah..um yeah, I do."

"Well you need to change that nigga."

"What the fuck I tell you about that nigga shit."

"Oh yeah, if I get use to saying that then white folks will thank they can say it."

"Yeah, yo hot ass listened to something huh?"

"I always listen to you baby."

"No yo ass don't and you think your slick. You think I don't know about you fucking that nigga Terrance. Yeah, I'm cool on you."

"You what nigga? Cool on me...naw, I'm cool on yo hoe ass, fucking that punk bitch Denise now."

"Whatever, you just mad cause she pulled your hoe card."

"Nah, I pulled her's and whooped her ass in front of you."

"Whatever, like I said, I'm cool on you. I love you but I'm cool."

"You ain't cool nigga, yo ass frontin. You're whipped now and yo ass ain't going no where!" Click.

Rox was frustrated, her and Carl always got into it, but he never wanted to break up with her. She had it out for Denise and any other woman that he chose to fool with. Just because she was cheating and knew he was, she wasn't letting him get away with it. She felt good, cause she wasn't really bleeding anymore. Even though her period would be off balance now. She decided to take the birth control pills, so she wouldn't get pregnant again and her period would come when she wanted it to.

Ms. Adams, Rox, Tasha and Mr. D all went to Pilgrim Baptist Church.

The service was good. Everyone seemed to be thinking they were going to the club instead of church. It was like 90 degrees and it was only June. People had their breast out, open toed sandals, gator shoes and strap up dresses, with their backs out. She half way paid attention to the preacher and the other half was her and Tasha laughing at all of the hoochies tryin to find a man at church. When the preacher pointed Rox out, she was so embarrassed. Her mom made her get up and go.

"Yes Sir."

"How old are you young lady?"

"15."

"Well you have a calling on your life and if you don't choose the right road, then you will be put in the pits of hell."

"How do you know?"

"Our Lord just called on me to speak this to you young lady."

"Okay."

"You can go back to your seat."

Rox was half upset and half ashamed. As she walked to her seat, she could feel all eyes on her. She noticed people from school, that she knew was looking because of those pictures. When she made it back to her seat, Tasha was pointing and teasing her.

"Shut up." Rox was mad and rolling her eyes at her mom and Tasha.

"Who you telling to shut up girl?"

"Her not you." Rox said, while pointing at Tasha. She was pissed off and kept looking at the clock. She wanted church to be over now.

It seemed like an eternity that church just wouldn't end. After church, a couple of people came up and hugged Rox and told her to take the advice for good and not worse. She felt better that everyone knew how she felt, but she still felt a little funny.

Rox thought about all the things she had done in such a short time. She thought about the slick talking, the sex she was having, the abortion and now the juggling of men. Maybe God was tryin to tell her something. She even thought about what that lady was telling her in that restaurant. She knew the Lord was speaking to her. Even though changing wasn't in the plan right now, she would eventually.

Ms. Adams and the new family went out to lunch after church. They had a good time and all got a chance to know each other better. Tasha and Rox got pretty acquainted when her mom and Mr. D went out for a talk the other night. It would take much for them to get to know each other anyway's, because they were closer in age.

Mr. D told Rox about the neighborhood. It was by a park called Powderhorn, and in the summer they have a lot of activities going on. The people were all cultures, black, white, asian but mostly indians. When he said that, she instantly thought of Darlene. He let her know she would be going to Roosevelt. It was kind of close to the house, but that was the district she was in.

Everybody left the restaurant on full. Rox wanted to take a little nap before she got up with her girl's. Damn, she was more sleepy now that she's not pregnant than she was before when she was.

"Rox, what are you going to do today?"

"I don't know Mom, since you had me at church and eating all day today, I'm gonna get some rest." Ms. Vicki just laughed, and let Rox get in the bed.

After her nap, she called up her crew. She decided to call Darlene, since she was the one that hooked her up yesterday.

Ring! Ring!

"Yo, whad up?"

"Who's this?"

"Dis Angie...you did call my number girl."

"Oh shut up. What you doing?"

"Chillin here with Mo and D."

"Oh, that's who I was looking for."

"You wanna holla at her den?"

"Nah, you'll come scoop me so we can go looking for a job."

"Aight, we'll be through in a minute young one."

"Aight, hurry up!" Click.

Rox changed into some comfortable clothes. She thought about how boring it would be all summer, without having something to do. Rox' plan was to get a job and hold it down for three more years, when she graduates from high school. She would open her floral business and go to college part time, just to satisfy her mom and make a fool out of her hatin ass sister Lili.

"I'm bout to go home Roxy."

"What girl? My name is Rox, Roxane, water or young one."

"Well, I'm gonna call you Big Sis Roxy."

"Naw!" Tasha slapped Rox playfully on her arm and ran out to the car. Rox laughed at her and walked to the front of the house to wait for Angie to come get her.

"Where you going?"

"I'm waiting for Angie to come get me so we can go look for a job tonight and the rest of the week." Rox knew that since her mom was on her way out the door, that she didn't have time to argue with her.

"Well I'm glad you're looking for a job....I want you to have some stability in your life young lady. You're gonna make something out of yourself."

"Yes Mama I know....I am okay."

"I'm gonna let you hang out this summer, you just have to be more responsible okay?"

"Yes Mama, I will be!" Ms. Vicki and Mr. Howard were on their way out the door.

"Oh yeah, did you take your birth control pills today?" Rox covered her mouth with embarrassment and rolled her eyes.

"It's okay baby, you don't have to be ashamed." Rox was relieved.

"Yes Mom, I did." Rox kept her head down, so she wouldn't have to look at Mr. Howard.

"See ya'll later."

"Call me when you get to Angie's."

"I will Mom."

"Roxy, you can call me sometimes too....you are going to be living in my house."

"Okay Mr. D."

"Have a good time, and I hope you girls find a job."

"Thank you...bye." Rox locked the door quick, and sat down to call Angie, to see what's taking so long. Ring! Ring! Ring! Nobody was at home, so Rox waited for about 10 more minutes. Honk! Honk!

"Get out here girl, let's go!"

"Yeah, it's six already and you know it's Sunday!"

Rox ran out the door, down the steps, and to the car.

"Get in the back Mo."

"Right girl, this giving you your way is over young one!" Rox slapped Mo playfully in the head.

"Come on, come on Big Sis, let the young one in the front!" Mo got out the front to let her in.

"Damn Rox, you been moving around with energy, since you got that abortion."

"I know. I go to the doctor Thursday."

"Good, cause you was jumping around a lot."

"I know, but since I've got some rest I'm cool."

The girl's all laughed and talked about the days of events, that had been going on. Mo made fun of Rox, because she always thought of a better way to do things. Darlene wasn't really talking and Angie kept turning "Freaks of the Industry" up as loud as she could. She didn't want to hear Mo and Rox go back and forth. In between Angie switching tapes, Darlene just had to be noisy.

"A Rox, have you talked to Carl since you been to the doctor?"

"Yeah, this morning."

"Oh, ya'll still together?" Rox stopped playing with Mo and frowned Up.

"Why you in my business?"

"Oh...It's like dat? I was just asking." Rox didn't say nothing at first.

"Yo Rox, you haven't been talking about him lately." Mo said, while turning to her.

"Well so what, I don't wanna talk about him." Rox rolled her eyes and looked out the window. Darlene started laughing, but kept her eyes on the road. Angie changed the tape to MC Lyte's "Cha Cha Cha". Rox got hyped and was in the party mood.

"Yo, let's just swing by Arby's, Hardee's, Micky D's, Subway, and Burger King." Rox was yelling over the music. Darlene bust up laughing. Angie turned the music down.

"What's so funny?"

"Ya'll crazy, I ain't working at no damn fast food place."

"Yeah, how may I help you?" Mo joined in, pointing her finger at Rox.

"Well I'm working anywhere....shit I don't know about ya'll, but I got three years to come up with the loot to open my business."

"Yeah, I guess you're right, I only have a year." Angie said, while taking her serious. Mo and Darlene stopped playing and everyone went into deep thought.

After they rode around and put in applications up and down University Avenue. They were hungry from smelling all that food. Angie had to remind Rox that she would have to boost her age up to make herself going on 17 instead of 16. She didn't care, cause she knew her cousin Kane knew somebody who could hook her up.

All the jobs told the crew that they would get a call back in about a week. Rox had to get her birth certificate from her mom, but Angie, D and Mo all had their info in their purse, so all the manager's at each job, checked it out right on the spot. Things like this, made Rox think that maybe she should hang with younger people, because she was moving too fast. Nah, she couldn't, cause she was already use to her girl's, that always had her back.

"Don't trip Rox, baby you are determined, so you will get you a job." Angie could tell that Rox was a little sad, by everybody else getting a okay on the jobs that they did check out. So to change things, after they got some grub, they were gonna swing through the Club Library downtown St.Paul.

"Nah, ya'll know they ain't gonna let me in." Rox said, pouting.

"Yes they are. You know your ass will come up with a trick." Darlene said, while pulling into the barnyard pimp palace "Kentucky Fried Chicken".

Everybody was glad to see some food. Everybody got out the car.

Angie went up to the counter to get their food. Rox was so hungry. She had a breast, wing, barbeque chicken strips, a large pop with side items and a strawberry parfait. The crew was so into slamming their meals, that they didn't even say a word.

"Whooooo- wee, that shit was the bomb!" Rox made her way to the bathroom.

Monique knew her girl was not feeling good about Carl, so she joined her in the bathroom. Darlene's greedy ass thought they was all still at the table, cause she never lifted her face up from eating.

"Ah....Angie girl, you think Carl broke up with Rox?" Angie was shocked by Darlene's comment.

"What makes you think that?"

"Cause she always talks about Carl."

"So! She just didn't want to talk." Angie started looking at Darlene funny, while she wiped her hands.

"You know he been with Denise lately."

"Oh word, how you know?" Angie was getting pissed, cause she knew Rox didn't like Denise because of Carl.

"Cause Denise called me from his crib."

"Why is she..."

"Hey, ya'll ready to dip?" Rox said, while coming back from the rest-room dancing around and ready to party.

"Yeah, what ya'll out here talking about?" Mo said, while helping them get their trays off the table.

"Nothing." Darlene quickly said, before Angie could answer. Angie grabbed her tray, and headed to the car, looking at Darlene with evil eyes and bumping into her.

"Yeah, nothing."

All Rox could think of in the car, was how to get in this party. It would be the jam of the summer. The local DJ had a plan, a school ending party every year, just to kick the summer off. They thought since it was downtown, that a lot of kid's wouldn't come. That wasn't the case. When they pulled up, the line was all the way in the parking lot and in the street.

It was a big club, inside of a cave. It had video games and pull tables. Sundays was teen night, so the bar was filled with virgin daiquiris, and every kind of soda pop you could think of. By it being in a cave, it had a lot of dark spots in it. Bam!

That was Rox' plan. When security checks her girl's in, she would slide past them and go straight to the check in counter. Angie walked straight up to security, acting like she had a problem with somebody in line. Mo and Darlene was arguing with everybody that jumped the line.

"Hey! Where you think you going?" Rox tried to ignore him and made it through the crowd, to get her ticket. It was five people ahead of her, so she had to duck behind some girl, with weave standing just as tall as her frame.

"Hey...hey!" The security spotted her. Rox jumped right in front of two people that were pushing and going off. Rox had to think fast.

"Yo chill, y'all I'll pay your way." That shut the two girl's up.

"Yo, block me, so he won't make it over here." While Rox paid her way and their's, the security guard seen her pop her head back up.

"You! I see you....ay you got to go!" Rox ignored him and started walking off.

"Ay... Ay ....let's go now!" Rox wasn't having it. Whether she had to fight this dude or what. He grabbed her by the arm. Rox snatched back.

"Yo chill D-Bol damn!"

"Nah, you think you're slick."

"Slick how? I paid my way in." Rox was now flashing her ticket in his face and with her hand on her hip. The bouncer was really checking for Rox, but knew that she wasn't eighteen, so he had to check his self.

"You know what? I'm gonna let you in, but I know you ain't eighteen."

Rox just laughed at him, and gave him a sexy smile, hoping that he wouldn't ask for no id. Angie, Mo and Darlene rolled up and seen him check Rox.

"Yo, what's up?" Angie was saying and stepping in the middle of Rox and the bouncer.

"What's up young one? He set trippin or something?" Mo was saying, while pointing at him.

"Nay ya'll, I'm straight, right?" Rox said, while stepping back.

"Yeah she straight, but ya'll better stop walking up on a grown ass man like that." The bouncer said, while walking away and leaving Rox relieved.

"Ay...I'm bout to get my shake on." Rox walked off ready to kick it.

The girl's all made their way to the dance floor. The party was super packed wall to wall. Mo left the dance floor to go check herself in the bathroom. On her way, eyes were watching her more than she thought. Jay Hustle was there, with his crew, and had spotted her.

Darlene was stopped by Denise on her way to the bar, to get the crew something to drink.

"Hi Darlene, why haven't you returned my calls?" Darlene was shocked, cause she wasn't expecting to see Denise.

"Oh, I'm with my girl's."

"So, yo ass always talking shit about them, but now they your friends huh?" Darlene didn't know if anyone heard, cause Monique was slowly approaching them.

"Bitch fuck you! You ain't my home girl!" Darlene said, while pushing Denise. She pushed her back in the face and said

"Fuck you! You watch, I got something for your ass!" Denise walked off.

"Hey, what's wrong with that stank ass hoe?" Monique asked.

"Shit...I don't know, probably mad cause Rox finer than her."

"Umm huh, that's right." Rox said while dancing from side to side.

Rox knew all along that Darlene was talking to Denise, but she was gonna use her just like Denise was using her. She knew not to tell her none of her business.

"Hey baby." A voice said, while Rox, Angie and Mo stood there talking and dancing. Rox turned around.

"Who are you?"

"My name is Jay." Rox was looking up and down like he was a piece of meat.

"thmull...Um excuse me." Monique was looking dead at them.

"Oh, I'm sorry, is he talking to you Mo?"

"Yeah I was." Jay said, while holding Rox by the waist.

"My fault, you are fine though....but I don't like my friend's man." Rox started laughing.

"I'm gonna leave you here so ya'll can kick it."

Rox grabbed Angie's hand and stepped back to Darlene that was holding their drinks. Everybody was shouting in the club "Go school, it's over it's over it's over!" That kept Rox hyped up. She was feeling good. She had forgot all about Carl until she seen Denise.

"Come on Angie, I'm going to find Carl."

"Don't be trippin girl."

"I won't, come on."

"You promise...cause you know you ain't healed from that abortion."

"I promise, I won't."

"Okay, let's go!"

They made it through the crowds, went into the game room and then to the pool room. As they approached the room, it seemed like it was a "couple's only" room. Everybody in there was all cuddled up in the corners, or on the pool tables kissing and rubbing. Angie spotted the back of Carl's coat and knew he was out of line. Rox had not seen him, so Angie didn't want her hurt.

"I'm tired...let's go."

"Why you in such a hurry to go girl?"

"Cause everybody got a man or two and I don't."

"So what! I know I ain't...but I still ain't even had nobody holla at me lately."

"That's why we're here girl." Rox was now hugging Angie.

"I know, but we need to go cause I'm sleepy." Rox turned back around.

"Is that Carl over there Angie?" Angie was so nervous she knew Rox was gonna snap.

"Yeah, Rox that's why I wanna go."

"You wasn't gonna tell me...NO could you!"

"No...ah...oh...I was gonna tell you just not here, not now." Angie was hugging Rox so she wouldn't look that way. Rox was flaming hot. She was ready to run right up on him and punch him in the back of his head.

"Wait young one, don't embarrass yourself girl." Rox ignored her and made her way over to him, with Angie on her tail. Angie was grabbing Rox, but she pushed her out of her way.

"Hey! What you think you doing boy?" Rox was standing right behind Carl cursing and causing a scene. He was so into cupping Denise's ass and kissing her, that he didn't know Rox was behind him this pissed Rox off, so she kicked him.

"Ouch! What the fuck?" Carl yelled out, while breaking his release from Denise. When he turned around and saw Rox, he thought he saw a ghost.

"How you get in here? What your young ass doing here?" Rox pushed him in his face.

"I got in cause I'm a smooth bitch now!"

"Yeah, you think so huh?" Carl said, while running through the party and leaving Denise and Rox standing there looking stupid.

"What you looking at you old hoe!" Rox started towards Denise, when Angie grabbed her.

"No girl, you don't wanna get kicked out, cause you won't get to come back."

Rox got herself together, so the bouncers wouldn't trip. Angie and Rox went looking for Mo and Darlene. When they rolled up on Mo, she was all cuddled up.

"Yo Mo, I got heat. Let's dip." Rox said, while tapping Mo and pointing at Darlene. She was hot. She didn't give nobody a chance to respond. As she made her way to the door, Rox got scooped up by the bouncer that didn't want her in there.

"Hey, put me down!" Rox was kicking and screaming.

"Yeah, put my people's down!" Mo, Darlene and Angie was pushing on the guard and yelling at him. Jay Hustle stepped right in front of him.

"Put her down, man." Jay put his hand right on dude's face, so he couldn't see.

"Aw...aw..okay." He put Rox down.

"You got to go...you're going to jail." Everybody was looking and pointing. Rox was scared and embarrassed. She started crying.

"What am I going to jail for?"

"A man named Carl Watkins just made a complaint against you...saying you assaulted him." Rox was really going off.

"What the fuck! That's my man!" Angie grabbed the dudes hand, while he was holding on to Rox. Mo, Darlene, and Jay wasn't there, so they didn't know.

"Well he has a witness...some woman said you hit her too."

"Oh my God! I can't believe this...Angie help me!" Angie had to think fast. Jay tried to bribe the dude with a hundred dollars.

"Yo Dog, let her go...I'll give you a c-note." He was thinking about it, when he seen Jay pull out that fat knot of nothing but hundreds. Mo had to take a triple look, thinking "Damn this nigga is paid Darlene."

Darlene's eye's were glued to the knot, that was falling on to the ground. Darlene reached down to pick up the few hundreds that hit the floor. Handing it back to him.

"Damn, you can bail this whole place out, if you wanted to." Jay just smiled, took the money and faced the dude.

"What's up? You gonna get my girl's homie out of this jam or what?"

"I need more den that, since I see you got it." He continued out the club, with Rox crying and tryin to explain herself. As she walked out, she noticed Carl and Denise talking to the police and pointing at her.

"You bitches!" Rox yelled, while getting in the police car. She didn't have on no hand cuffs, cause the female cop wanted to question her. Rox calmed down, to explain herself and the bouncer stood outside the car tryin to persuade the cops to let her out. Carl was shouting at Rox.

"I told you I was gonna get your slick ass!"

Denise just stood there holding on to Carl's waist and pointing at Rox, laughing. Rox thought her world was coming to an end. Her mom and Mr. Howard would be pissed off. After about thirty minutes of persuading the police, they let Rox out the car and wrote her a ticket for causing a disturbance. The ticket was bogus, but they had to do something, because they were called out for something. Jay had passed three pigs and the bouncer two hundred dollars to let her out. Angie had told the pigs that Carl started it with her and he hit her. Rox now seen him and Denise explaining their way out of not going to jail. She just wanted to get away from the pigs and everybody.

"Thank you Jay....you didn't even know me and got me out of this shit."

"It's cool girl, you just watch yourself with that nigga!"

"I know he's a punk ass bitch Rox!" Mo said, while grabbing Jay's hand. She was so embarrassed for her. As they all exchanged hugs, Rox slid over to Carl before they got into the car to leave.

"I hope you die bitch!" Rox said and tried to spit on him.

"Fuck you! Don't wish death on me bitch." Rox ignored him, and got in the car.

"I'm done ya'll. I'm chillin on that drama queen shit."

Chapter 10

Stressin'

It had been a long weekend. Roxane was going to get her a job. She started off by calling all of the places that she put an application in to. Clarks Submarines had called Angie back. McDonalds and a telemarketing place had called both Darlene and Monique. This was very discouraging for Rox, being that it was her idea anyway.

When she called Hardees, the manager told her that even though she's fifteen, that she could work, but not past 8:00 pm. This was music to her ears. Rox had it all planned out. She would go to work for four hours a day, and still have time for a social life. She had to fit dancing in always, because that was her thang.

Ring! Ring!

"What's up, dis Brian and I'll call you back if you leave a message." Beep.

"Yeah, you know this is fresh wa', so hit me back when you can." Click.

"Damn, I thought he would of called me by now." Rox was saying to herself. She was so excited about the job, that she just had to tell somebody. "Mama! Mama!"

"What? Why are you yelling?" Rox was now running from her room, to the living room.

"I called Hardees, and they gonna give me a job!"

"Oh really now."

"Yeah, and I don't even have to lie about my age."

"Good. See what God will do for you, when you give him some time and visit his house?"

"Yes Mom....I know." Rox saying, while putting her eyes in the air.

Rox continued to dance around and call everybody, to tell them the good news. She called up Mo, Angie and Darlene and put them all on a three way. The girls was happy for her. They made a deal that they would get their schedules at the same working hours, so they would still have time to spend together.

"Okay, I'm gonna call ya'll later to come get me when I get off."

"Cool, I get off at 4:00 and you know we got practice."

"I know Angie, I'll be ready."

"Don't you have to go to the doctor?"

"Nah, Darlene with your nosey ass....I went yesterday."

"What happened?"

"Nothing Mo, I'm cool...I'm taking the birth control like I was told." Beep! Beep! "Hold up ya'll, my lines clicking."

"Hello."

"I need to speak to Roxane please."

"Who is dis with all that proper shit?"

"Ha ha, funny you must not be use to nobody treating you like the freshness that you are huh?" Rox was embarrassed. This was an older dude, so she had to get on her game.

"Hold on Brian." Click. "Hey ya'll, I'm gonna wait for ya'll to come pick me up."

"Alright, we'll be there."

"Damn, ya'll sound like a choir."

"Ha ha ha...bye girl."

"Holla!" Click.

"Brian?"

"Yeah, I thought yo ass was gonna hang up, you took so long."

"My fault boy...I ain't take that long."

"Aight girl, I told you about that name shit. Boy, nigga, that's not my name. It's B or Brian I told you."

"I'm sorry Briaaan....now is that better?"

"That's cool."

Rox let him know about everything that was going on in her life. He felt like her story was like a soap opera. They made plans again to see each other. He felt that she should get the feel of work before she went out with him. He was glad to know that she was a young girl on her grind. That sassy attitude turned him on.

"I like talking to you...everytime I hear your voice, it makes my dick hard." Rox started smiling from ear to ear.

"Hum....we wouldn't be doing none of that no time soon."

"Yeah, that's what your mouth says, but I'll make yo body say something else."

"Whatever."

"Aight, we'll have this conversation Saturday."

"Aight, I'll call you then."

"Cool." Click.

She got dressed, made herself something to eat and watched a little TV before work. Right before leaving, she got a call from Terrence, that upset her. She shared her good news with him, but he just made her feel stupid.

"What you working at Hardees for? Yo ass could make more money giving me some of that good pussy or hustling on the block."

"What...stupid."

"I ain't stupid...shit your ass got some good shit...I'll pay you." The thought rang in her mind, but she was still independent and wanted to make a difference to herself and Mom, so no she wouldn't sale herself.

"Nah, baby I'm cool on that shit Terrence."

"Yeah, you keep dreaming about dat big business you want...hum, yo ass will change yo mind." She wasn't having it, but the thought stuck hard in her mind.

"I got to go T."

"When will you be home? You know yo ass didn't help me with my finals like you said you would."

"You passed didn't you?"

"Yeah, I did."

"Well den, I helped yo ass enough. Shit, I didn't want yo ass tryin to take my pussy again."

"Take it? Girl please, you know dis dick was good." She didn't say nothing, she just sat in silence.

"Yo, you still there?"

"Hum...yeah I'm here." He just didn't understand she just wanted to be his friend. He was fine as hell, but she knew his ass was a stalker and it would lead to problems down the line.

"I got to go to work now." Rox was irritated by this conversation.

"I'm gonna..." Click. Rox cut his ass off in mid sentence.

She made it to work, tried on her brown pants, tan shirt, brown hat and black Adidas. All the people that worked there was pretty pleasant. One girl went to her school and Rox knew that the girl wouldn't bring up those pictures, that she was ashamed of.

"What's up Rox?" She turned around, while she put the fries in the fryer.

"Hi...how you doing?"

"Girl let me show you how to do this." She stepped to the side, so she could show her. The girl showed her how to make the fries, burgers and work the ice cream machine. She got the hang of it immediately. She worked so hard, that it was time for a break.

"Come on, you can eat for half off."

"Good, what's your name again?"

"Tara."

"Thanks Tara...I was really hungry."

Rox made it through that hard day of work. It was ten minutes to four, and that meant it was time to go. Since it was summer, she could work up to ten o'clock. She didn't want her day wasted, because of her new friend and dance practice. She decided to tell her manager that she would take the same hours as Tara, nine to three. She would then have time to get herself together, in the morning. She also let her boss know her goals and that she wouldn't give her any problems, especially since she had a mission to accomplish.

Rox put her clothes in her locker and made her a quick chicken sandwich and fries. Tara was about to throw away some food that sat for too long, but Rox decided to take it to practice with her.

"Bye everybody. I'll see you tomorrow."

"Okay, have a good day." Everyone said all together. She was excited about the environment. Rox made her way to get on the bus. Somebody in a red Monte Carlo was following her. She kept looking back but she couldn't tell who it was. She stepped up her pace. Even though it was daylight, it still didn't matter about somebody tryin to snatch a young girl.

She made it to the bus stop, where there was about seven people standing there. It was three old people, two women and one man, just minding their business. There was also three dudes about her age, with headphones on their heads and one girl that looked to be a little older. Rox was bobbin her head from off the dudes headphones, while watching them slap box each other. All of a sudden from out of no where... Slap! Slap!

"Oh...ah...what the..."

"Yeah, you thought I wouldn't catch yo ass, huh?" Rox turned around to Carl slapping her from behind.

"Stop Carl! I'm not bothering you, so leave me alone!"

"Yeah dog, chill...dog hitting on a girl man."

"Shut the fuck up nigga!" Carl pulled his gun out and pointed it at one dude and socking the shit out of the other dude.

"Carl please! I don't know them. They don't have nothing to do with it!"

The older women were scared and holding their purses and sitting in silence. The other dude tried to talk to Carl, but he pointed the gun at him too.

"You get your ass in the car...now!" To make this all go away, she did as she was told.

"Now yo ass will know not to get in nobody else's business." Crack! Crack! Carl bust the dude right in the head with the butt on the gun.

"Quit Carl, I'm in the car, damn!" Rox sat in the car yelling.

When Carl got in the car, he pulled off just in time, before the police caught him. Rox seen the people pointing at the car, trying to get the license plate number. They didn't get it like she hoped, because police kept driving past them.

Carl kept tryin to talk to Rox, but she just sat in silence. They made it to Carl's house and she refused to get out of the car.

"Get out bitch!" She reached over and locked all of the doors.

"What the fuck you think that's gonna do...stupid!" Carl yelled and pulled the keys out of his pocket, while showing her his gun in his waist. When he got the car opened, he snatched her out of the car by her hair.

"Ouch! Stop!" She screamed and kicked as he dragged her in the house. Nobody was there, so he dragged her to the basement, instead of his room. She fought, even harder, but she had no luck. After he threw her down on the couch and went to get some rope to tie her up, she reached for a lamp and hit him with it. Crack!

"Ah....dumb bitch!" He slapped the spit out of her lips.

"Stop! Carl, please!" He ignored her pleas and made her strip butt naked. She took her time and dropped her clothes to the floor.

"What are you going to do to me Carl?" Tears was streaming down her face.

"You'll see." Carl stared at Rox, with evil eyes watching every move she made. He was so upset, that he wouldn't answer the phone.

"I'm naked, now what?"

"Oh...you wanna still get slick at the mouth huh?" He reached for the scissors that was on the table, grabbed her by her hair, and cut a chunk of her ponytail right off.

"No....no..please don't do this!" He slapped her.

"Shut the fuck up! Shit, you think this hair is everything!"

"It is, it's mine!" She cried out.

"Get on that couch and spread your legs!" Rox looked at him like he was crazy, shaking and shivering.

"You heard me!" He pointed at the couch with the scissors. She did as she was told. He stood in front of her and stripped down to his socks.

"Shut the fuck up with all that crying shit!" He pushed her legs open wider, with his rock hard dick and jacked off. Rox cried even harder. Even though this was the man she had once loved to death, it was now turning to hate. When he came, it went flying right on her face and stomach. She turned her face in disgust. She made sure it didn't land in her eye. Carl laughed at her, while she squirmed and made faces.

"Why are you doing this boy...I thought you was cool on me?"

"I didn't tell you to talk...you talk when I tell you to talk." She knew him well and that meant that after his first orgasm, he can go all day, like a trucker.

He grabbed a towel and wiped his self off. She cried harder.

"No, I'm not clean...I just got off work...let me get in the shower." He ignored her and took the same towel and tried to wipe her off.

"Ugh...yuk boy..stop!" She cried even harder. He was acting like a mad man. He got on top of her, lifting her legs up high, then dove right in. She was numb the whole time. Carl sexed her every which way, for about three hours and still wasn't tired. He was pissed off that she wouldn't respond to him, so he bent her over the table. She thought he was gonna hit it from behind. He tricked her by licking between her butt crack and inserting his finger inside of her.

At that moment, only then did she loosen up and feel pleasure. When he felt her muscles relax, he forced his whole ten inches up her butt. Scream! Scream!

"Oh my God! Please stop!" He ignored her.

"You know this is what you want...you love this dick."

"Carl I'm sorry...you're hurting me...please!" Thank God that her angels must of heard her, because as soon as he pumped about three times, a voice rang out.

"Who's that down there screaming?" Carl froze.

"Oh shit." He pulled it out, and she had blood mixed with cum running down her leg. He still held on to Rox' body, but she was trying to get away from him.

"It's me Mom...ah..ah it was Roxane playing." She couldn't get away from his grip.

"Are you okay Roxane?" Carl turned her around and gave her an evil eye. Out of fear, she took up for him.

"Yes Ma'am, I'm okay." Rox was still crying.

"Well Carl you need to get up here, because the police are here to see you." Rox was relieved and broke loose from his grip. She picked her clothes up from off the floor.

"Stop cryin baby...I just love you so much."

"Leave me alone, Carl please."

Carl ran up the stairs and talked to the police. He told the okie dokie about them having the wrong description and that the Monte Carlo he had just bought and that they were bothering him because he was black.

They left without any problems, but told him that they would be back, if they find out he's lying.

After telling his mom a made up lie that he put together as he talked, he ran back downstairs to Rox. She was in the shower, on full blast like a sauna. She wanted to wash away all of the sex that was forced upon her. Carl knew what he did was wrong, but he wasn't gonna admit it. Knock! Knock!

"Yo Rox, get out that shower!"

"Leave me the fuck alone, before I tell your mom and the police what you did...bitch!" Carl stepped off, he was nervous thinking that she would tell. He started getting her clothes and put them in the washer. He always bought her new clothes, so she had a change of clothes there. Ring! Ring!

"Hello can I speak to Carl?"

"This is me...who dis?"

"This Monique nigga, and I know you did something to my sister...where she at?"

"Shut up dumb hoe!" Click.

Carl ignored the phone, because he knew it was Monique. Rox finally made it out of the shower.

"What you looking at?" Rox rolled her eyes, while sitting down to relieve herself.

"Here, I bought this for you." Rox snatched the tennis skirt, shirt and matching Nikes out of his hand, without talking. Ring! Ring! Ring!

"Get the phone stupid! You think it's yo hoe Denise?" Carl ignored the phone and Rox, but he stayed close by, so Rox wouldn't try to get it. Whoever it was kept hanging up and calling right back. Rox put on her clothes and wrestled with Carl for the phone. She snatched the phone from Carl. "Hello!"

"Oh my God! What are you doing Rox?"

"Nothing...this dumb..."

"Give me that!" Carl snatched the phone back from Rox. Click.

Rox continuously slapped, kicked and punched Carl. He wouldn't hit her back, because he knew that he was wrong. He tried hugging her, but she wanted no affection. She yelled and screamed, but his mother never came to the door, to help her. She tried kicking him in his balls, but couldn't.

"Stop Rox! I'm sorry okay?" She cried and screamed, until she got tired. The phone was still ringing. Carl knew that if he didn't get Rox out of there, that the police would be there and his football career would be over. Ring! Ring!

"Hello."

"This is Ms. Adams Carl...is Roxane there?" Butterflies shot straight to his stomach.

"Yes Ma'am...ah..ah she's here." Carl wiped away Rox' tears and handed her the phone.

"What is wrong with you Roxane...it's ten o'clock and nobody has heard from you."

"I'm sorry Mom...I'm on my way home now."

"What are you crying about? Why did it take him so long to answer that phone?"

"I don't know."

"Something's going on...Monique said Carl beat you up with a gun and made you get in the car."

"No Mom, he didn't. I'm okay."

"I can hear in your voice that something is wrong. You missed dance practice and your friends are disappointed in you."

"I know Mom...I'm sorry, I'm on my way home."

"Okay, I'm giving you thirty minutes or I'm calling the police."

"Okay, I'm on my way."

"Put that boy on the phone." Rox handed Carl the phone. By the expression on his face, her mother must of told him something, because when he hung up he ran straight to the car telling her to come on.

On the way home, he tried to convince Rox that he still loved her, but he was jealous of her because she was spending too much time with Terrence and her friends. He felt that she had sex with Terrence and didn't know who that baby was by and that's what made him act that way.

Rox loved him so much, but it wasn't okay that he raped her. In the hood, dudes would call this gangstering her out her pussy, because he was her man and she knew him, but in reality, it was rape. She never responded to his plea. She felt good that he was nervous about going to jail. They made it to the house.

"Are you gonna tell everybody what I did?"

"Yep." Rox slammed the door and ran up the stairs to her house. Her mother was sitting in the window waiting, so Carl just skeeted off. Rox had no intentions on putting him in jail, because a part of her still loved him. She had to get her lie together for her mom.

"What's up Mom?" She said, while walking at a fast pace to check her messages in her room.

"Wait young lady...." Ms. Adams was right on her heels. "You don't come in here like that, and I've been worried sick about you."

"Why Mom? I was coming home."

"Yeah I know, but I haven't heard from you since this morning and Monique...."

"She what Ma?"

"She called here saying that Carl kidnapped you and put a gun up to your head, forcing you in the car!" Rox was pissed at Mo for getting her mother worried.

"Ma, I told you I can handle myself....I'm cool okay?" Rox looked at her mother for assurance.

"Okay, but you better not scare me like that...I even called your cousin Kane."

"Oh goodness, Ma for what?"

"Because he was gonna go look for you for me."

"Ma, next time don't jump the gun. The boy just got out."

"So! Family sticks together, you know that."

"I know Ma."

Ms. Vicki left her room and closed the door. Rox went straight to the bathroom to take a bath this time. She washed Carl off of her again. The pain in her butt wouldn't go away, so she just put more hot water in the tub every time the water got cold.

After she finished in the bath tub, she gave Brian a call. He was beginning to give up on her, because he felt like she was avoiding him for some reason. She assured him that she wasn't and that she would make it up to him when they have their date.

The rest of the week went smoothly. Rox got the hang of things at work and the bosses were already talking about moving her to the drive thru window. Mo, Darlene and Angie had already started with high positions at their jobs. I mean, how high of a position can you have at a fast food restaurant? I mean if you ain't a part of the franchise, then your title ain't really standing on nothing. Rox enjoyed the job, but long term definitely wasn't gonna be an option.

Practice and work was definitely keeping her busy. She only got about six hours of sleep a day and this worried her mom. Like always, she convinced her mom that she was fine and that on Sunday's after church, that she would sleep in.

It was two days before the fourth of July, and the girl's had a week and a half left before Rondo days start. As the days approached, Rox was nervous. She knew that she could battle anybody and win. These groups were from all over though, and she wasn't sure of how they do it in their city. They told her that she was confident that her girl's would win and even if they didn't then it was okay, the point was to show the heritage of our culture and how talented we are. That enforced her to be a better woman.

They were having a contest on the 4th at the Taste Of Minnesota. You had to go to Oxford Recreational Center. Darlene went to sign them up, because everyone else was at work. Ring! Ring!

"What you doing Angie?"

"Nothing, painting my nails."

"Oh, did you sign us up for the competition?"

"Nah, but Darlene did."

"Um."

"Why you say it like that?"

"Cause you know she don't like me for real."

"So what, she gonna have to deal with you if she wanna hang with me."

"I know that's right girl."

"Mo ain't off work yet, but you need to come over so we can practice a new routine okay?"

"Cool, come get me."

"I'm gonna stay here so I can wait for Mo to get off...catch a cab, I'll pay for it."

"Okay." Click.

Rox thought about the routine that they were gonna do. Even though the prize wasn't much, it would be a lot of white people there and plenty of out of towners, so the recognition would be good.

Rox made it over to Angie's with a change of clothes. She was off for two days. She called Brian up, to tell him her plans. He told her that he was gonna swing by Angie's to watch them practice. Ding! Dong!

"Who is that?" Rox looked out of the window while Angie ran downstairs to get the door. It was Mo and Darlene.

"Hey ya'll, what's up?"

"Hey my young one." Mo said, while giving Rox a hug.

"What's up girl?" Darlene said, while slapping her lightly on the shoulder. Rox gave them the full run down about what Carl did. She made them promise not to tell the police. She just wanted it over with him.

"Damn young one, you have really been through some shit girl." Darlene saying, while looking Rox in the face.

"Yeah, I know one thing, I told his ass he better chill before I have my man Jay handle his ass."

"I know that nigga Kane is a nut about you...shit, he better not hear about it."

"Nah, Angie my Mom already told him." All the girls looked at her and said

"What did he do?"

"Damn, ya'll sound like a choir."

"Ha ha ha!"

"Yo butt still silly after what you been through."

Ding! Dong! Ding! Dong!

"Damn, who is dat on my damn door bell like they crazy?" Angie said, yelling out the window. Everybody looked to see who it was.

"It's B, is Roxane here?" Everybody started smiling at Rox.

"Go get the door scary." Mo was pushing Rox to the door.

"Wait girl, how do I look?" Rox did a double take in the mirror, before she headed to the door to let him in.

"Hi Brian." Rox put her hand out to greet him. He grabbed, hugged and kissed her all at once. She was turned on, but this was their first encounter, so he had to slow up.

"Yo, ya chillin boo?" She released from his grip.

"Oh, my fault, I was just happy to see you."

"That's cool...we have time for that later."

"Okay,,,,ah, my boy is in the car, can he come in?"

"Yeah, tell him to get out in this neighborhood...shit, they might call the police cause you black and have a Benz."

"Ha ha, you ain't got to tell me twice."

As Brian told his boy to get out, Rox ran back in to inform the girls that he brought a friend and the dude was fine. Milk chocolate skin, asian eyes about 6 feet and charcoal black hair. Everybody was eyeing him, but he was turned on by Angie's boldness.

After everybody seen he wanted Angie, Mo and Darlene backed off, being as though they had a man.

"Ah, I forgot my music." Everybody started checking their bags for a tape to dance off of.

"Yo, I got ya'll!" Coop ran outside to the car, with a bag full of tapes for them to practice to. They looked through them while Coop and Brian drank sodas and ate their turkey sandwiches that Angie made them. The girls practiced, got their routine together. Coop and Brian were impressed by Rox' talent and encouraged her to do it professionally. "I love to dance ya'll, but I'm gonna be a florist."

"Dat's cool girl...do you."

"Yeah, cause as long as it's funerals and weddings, you never go out of business."

Chapter 11

After a long night of laughs and dancing with her girls, Brian and Coop, Rox needed some long rest. She decided to spend the night at Angie's, because her parents weren't home. They were out of town on business, as usual, and this meant that it was kick it time.

The next morning, everybody got up for work. They wanted to put in extra time, so they would have some money for the Rondo day's event. Tomorrow was the fourth of July, and the next day they would be off.

"Hi, welcome to Hardees, may I help you?" Rox was on a roll. Tara had showed her how to work the drive thru. She wanted this position so badly, because it paid an extra 75(. That meant she would get $4.50).

"Yes, can I have a monkey shake, a nigger sandwich with cheese, and a large order of white folks fries." Rox was pissed off at this statement and thought she was hearing things, so she asked the male voice to repeat himself.

"Yo Tara, come listen to the mother..."

"Noooo, you don't want to get fired Roxane, so handle this like a woman." Rox got herself together before she had a race war of words with this unknown male.

"I'll get that for you Sir, just pull around."

"Ha ha, that's right, call me Sir, Hazel." As Rox stood there with steam shooting out of her head, Tara decided to deal with the customer, so Rox could calm down. Rox agreed but she had to see the face of this man.

"Hi Sir, I couldn't get that quite right, could you please repeat it."

"You dumb half bred bitch, you can't do shit right!"

"No Sir, I just didn't know what a nigger sandwich was because I don't know what a nigger is."

"You know, cause your half of it."

"Oh my God, Mr. Mackman you let this ignorant motherfucker say this.... oooh wait till I..."

"No no Roxane, it was a joke to test...."

"To test what Mr. Mackman? To test what!" Rox cried hysterically. She couldn't believe that the man who lend his house out to her and her friends, who would snap out if someone said anything about his wife and daughter, was letting this go down.

"No..no baby, don't cry, please, it was all a joke."

"This is no joking manner Mr. Mackman. I'm telling...."

"No! Please Roxane, don't tell Angie..."

"Fuck her, man she knows white is pure. It's superior. The black man will never make it without a white man in front."

Rox and Tara was in tears. "Fuck you!" Slam!

Tara shut the drive thru window, to console her friend. Mr. Mackman pulled off, so the situation would disappear.

"Stop crying Roxane, girl this stuff happens all the time. You have to know how to deal with people in a business where you're gonna be dealing with customers."

"I know, but I know him Tara. It's my friend's dad girl."

"Well you know prejudice is in people's soul. You can see a whole person for what they are, through their eyes."

"I know, my Grandma use to tell me that and I believe that."

Tara went on to give Rox good advice. She told her that she should hold off on telling Angie, until they had their competition complete. Rox agreed and out of guilt, Mr. Mackman would probably try to explain his self to Angie and Mrs. Mackman first, before Rox could get over there to tell them.

The rest of the day went well. The boss told Rox that someone named Brian would be up there to get her after she got off work. This made her work even harder and put a smile on her face. After Rox prepared to leave, Tara was counting the register, with the manager.

"My ride is here, so I'll see everybody Monday."

"Hold up Rox...can I get a ride with you?" Rox sensed something was wrong by the look on her face.

"Yeah, I'll wait at the table." Rox waved her hand at Brian, to let him know she was coming. As she sat there to wait, a crowd of people had entered the restaurant. Rox seen Terrance, and so did Tara. She was rushing her boss to count the money, because she thought it would be drama if Terrance seen Rox with Brian. As Tara headed for the door, she felt someone grab her arm.

"Yo, where Roxane...don't she work today?" Tara didn't look at him, she ignored him and headed for the door. Rox was already in the car honking the horn and headed to leave the parking lot.

"What took you so long girl?"

"See that dude? He was asking for somebody and I just shrugged him off." Tara was now pointing, and Terrance stood there and made his finger like a gun and pointed it at the car, while they drove away.

"What's up! How was ya'll's day?" Coop said, while sitting in the back seat with Tara.

"Fine." The girl's said together. After Brian dropped Tara off, Coop was asking Rox all kinds of questions about her.

"Make up yo mind boy....you was just chillin with Angie the other day, now you wanna holla at my girl Tara."

"Yo, chill. You hollering at my boy so yo pass to keep that on the hush you dig?"

"Whatever boy, I know you better not try and play Angie, cause she's my peoples, you dig?"

Brian took Rox and Coop over to Angie's house. Mr. Mackman wasn't there, but like Tara told her, she wouldn't tell her nothing about it. Ding! Dong!

"Yo Angie, it's Rox, let me in!" Rox looked through the window and seen Angie on the phone, so Darlene opened the door.

"What's up ya'll?"

"Hey D, Brian and Coop want to take us to get something to eat."

"Cool with me."

"Ask Mo and Angie do they wanna go."

"Yo, let's go downtown Minneapolis to get something to eat." Brian said, while taking a seat on the couch. The girls was excited, because they never go to Minneapolis for anything.

"Where we going?" Monique said to Coop, while putting her purse on her shoulder.

"This cool Chinese place called Nakins and if that ain't cool we'll go to the Japanese Steak House."

"Damn, is that your favorite place to take chicks, cause you smiling hard as hell." Ha ha ha, everybody busted up laughing.

"Quit trippin girl, and go get in the car."

"Yeah ya'll, I'm bout to go to the car."

"Me too."

Angie and Rox got in the car. Mo and Darlene had to call their men, to tell them what they were doing. Brian, Coop, Angie and Rox was deep into their conversation the whole ride to the restaurant. Darlene and Mo was just enjoying the free ride and meal.

When they made it to the restaurant, it was packed. The waiting period was about forty five minutes to one hour. Darlene and Mo decided to go check out downtown Minneapolis, because they had only been there about three times in their life. Angie and Rox was entertained by Brian and Coop. They barely heard them say they were gonna do a little sight seeing.

"Yo, Darlene let's go to the Express."

"Okay, I got like five hundred on me that Tobby gave me, so let's just spend it."

"You ain't said nothing but a word girl." Mo slapping hands with Darlene. The girl's went to the Express, County Seat, Lady Foot Locker and Daytons. They tried on everything from shoes to make up. Mo was so excited about the fine men that she seen, so her and Darlene made a plan to come visit downtown Minneapolis at least once a month, with the girls. The dudes they met along the way let them know that Saturday's was the day it's usually packed. They were geeked to tell Angie and Rox.

"I want to go to the men's Gap Mo, so I can buy Tobby something."

"What?"

"I need to grab Tobby a fit or something."

"Why you buying that nigga shit? You...."

"Chill with that nigga shit Mo, that's my dude." Monique now rollin her eyes and putting her hand on her hip.

"I can't tell...shit, you be mad at his ass one minute for not spending no time with yo ass, then you be geeked when his ass give you chump change in his book."

"Shut up Mo." Darlene turned to walk away from Mo. She was hot on her heels, because Darlene knew her way around and she didn't want to get lost. Darlene went in to find him a nice shirt and a pair of pants. Since Mo had to be there, she decided to help her homegirl out.

"Look D, here goes a nice brown striped shirt with some corduroy's... and you can get him some light brown timbo's to go with them." Monique held it up to Darlene, for her to see.

"Yeah girl, that's cool....now let's go cause I know Angie and Rox is probably eating."

"I know we been gone for about an hour and a half."

"Oh my God! We got to go Darlene!" As Darlene paid for her stuff, she kept hearing a familiar voice. Mo didn't pay attention to Darlene stopping. When she finally turned around, she noticed Darlene snapping out on somebody, so she ran back in the store.

"What's up D? You got beef?" Mo said, while throwing her hands in the air. Mo looked at her friend and followed her lead.

"Girl, this bitch ass Tobby came rollin up in here with this bitch!" Mo looked over and seen Tobby and some girl that looked like a younger version of Pam Grier. Mo knew that Darlene was intimidated by her beauty. The chick was thick, with long hair. She had on some DKNY jeans with the matching shirt, boots, ski jacket and head band. She had her shit tight, looking like a walking label, topped with diamonds.

"I'm bout to murder both these punk bitches." Darlene charged Tobby first, while Mo told the girl she better kick back. The girl wasn't no punk though, so she swung on Mo.

"I know yo ass didn't!" Slap! Slap! Boom!

"Help me! Help!" Mo started screaming for Darlene to help her.

"Yeah baby, beat that ass!" Tobby yelled out, while holding Darlene, so she couldn't help her friend.

"Let me go Tobby...you bitch!" She did everything she could to help Mo and get away from Tobby. He pulled her hair and bent her arms back, in a double chicken wing. (This means holding her arms up from behind and putting his arm under hers and his hands, behind her head. Then taking her legs and spreading them while he put his in between hers, so she couldn't move).

Darlene was so pissed off that she cried. Mo and the girl was all over the floor, knocking clothes down, rolling around. The security guard told them if they didn't quit, they were going to jail. That made Mo stop, and the girl was so tired that she stopped without a problem. The guard told Tobby to release Darlene or he was going to jail. As soon as he let her go, Darlene put on a performance of a life time.

"Call the police now!" She yelled and cried. "He got dope on him!" Everybody looked at Darlene, but the guard grabbed Tobby. Mo knew this was wrong, and her friend was jealous.

"No I don't bitch, you just mad cause I'm with my other hoe!"

"What nigga...I ain't yo hoe!" The girl went crazy and started snapping. "Nigga you see if I carry any of your dope any more bitch!"

She spit at Tobby, and this pissed him off.

"Oh, you dat dumb?"

"I ain't dumb, I was just getting mines."

"Sir, come with me." The guard tried to grab Tobby, but he "pow", right in the mouth, he stumbled back and fell. Tobby took off running.

The girl, Darlene and Mo left out the store talking. When the guard finally got up, he ran towards them. "Where did he go?"

Darlene and the girl had calmed down a little, and didn't really want to get him into trouble, so they gave him the wrong directions. The police was all over. People were looking at them like they were stupid, because they seen them fighting, now they were all talking. Mo and Darlene walked the girl to the bus stop. When they made it back to the Chinese restaurant, Rox and Angie was still being entertained by Brian and Coop. They had ordered some food for them, but it was getting cool. Monique was hungry, but Darlene had an attitude and Rox wanted to know why.

"What's wrong D...you look like a puppy that can't find his way home." Brian and Coop bust into laughter. Darlene rolled her eyes at Rox so she didn't press anymore.

"Damn Mo, slow down girl." Mo looked up at Rox and continued to slam her plate.

"Uumm, damn these egg rolls are the bomb!" Mo had a greasy face and offered Darlene some.

"Girl eat something...and get you another man."

"No, all men are dogs, fuck it...I might start fucking girls." Coop spit his pop out across the table and laughed so loud, the whole restaurant looked at their table.

"Chill Coop...you causing a scene." Brian said, while patting him on his back.

"Thank you. Sorry dog." Coop got his self together, while Angie, Mo and Rox looked at Darlene like she had just been shot.

"Are you crazy...you freak!" Rox was pissed off.

"Nah, you trippin girl...just get another man and get over it." Mo said through a mouth full of food.

"Are you sick in the head?" Angie checked Darlene's head.

"No, I'm just sick of these stupid niggas."

"So you sizing every man up in the same category girl?" Brian now has a frown on his face and looking at everybody.

"No, but with all the stuff I seen my mom, Rox, Mo, Angie and myself go through, it has made me wanna try something else."

Everyone looked at Darlene crazy, but they felt sorry for her. Mo cleaned her mouth and explained to them what just happened. Even though Rox and Angie wasn't buying it, they felt it was a little more to why there friend was all of a sudden talking about being gay. Darlene was a freak, but she was so boy crazy. Her mom and dad would flip and not accept her ever being with no damn women.

"Damn girl, you are so pretty, why would you be so in love with a nigga you barely even see anyway?"

"Well Coop, every man don't have your morals dog! I guess I was so high off him being the biggest dope boy in town."

"So that would make you go as low as a woman girl?"

Coop was disgusted. Brian just sat and listened. He didn't want to make his opinion on the situation, because he still had to win Rox' heart. On the ride home, everyone was real quiet. They listened to Brian's music selection the whole ride.

"Where we going? You getting off on the wrong exit." Rox started getting nervous, thinking that he might be tryin to pull something. Her thoughts were quickly erased.

"I'm taking ya'll to my shop, so you can see how a real baller does it." Rox and the girls lit up.

"Yeah, he wants to show off." Coop said, while slappin Brian in the head from the back seat.

They made it over south to Brian's shop. Like Rox thought, it was tight. He had a car wash with high tech wax jobs and every kind of rim you could think of. It was a man's playground, when it came to cars. He showed her how to measure car tires and which ones look good on which car. He let her know when he buys her a car in the winter, she would have to keep it clean because the salt will eat up her paint job.

He showed the rest of the place off, and Coop cracked jokes about how Brian first started with washing cars every weekend in his uncle's garage, to make money for his football uniforms. His uncle told him he is to never work for nobody, and to make his own way in this world legitimately. He made sure that he listened to his uncle, and came up with the idea of a detail shop and also a car wash, that way if nobody wanted a detail job or rims, they could just get a simple car wash.

Brian and Coop decided to give the girl's a little Entrepreneur 101. They were all impressed with the information and events of the day. Darlene was mad at

Coop, because of the advice he gave her. He didn't care, so he kept taunting her.

"So you still thinking of being a dyke....ha ha ha."

"Fuck you nigga."

"Yeah, you would probably like to, but I'm doing yo girl or...oh, I should say I wanna do her."

"Chill Coop. Leave her alone."

"Nah, Angie she weak as hell if she wanna go to women that...."

"No, you didn't listen to what I said stupid. I said I should not I will."

"Nah, if you thought about it, then you either did it or wished you did it."

"Whatever....I'm ready to go."

"We bout to leave, quit trippin." Rox said, while entertaining Brian. Nobody wanted to believe that Darlene was gay, except Rox. She now confirmed the fact that Darlene was definitely jealous of her, for a reason. Yeah, she wanted to be Rox in more ways than a friend.

On the way home, everyone was quiet except Coop of course. He got to telling us about the different hoods we drove through, in South Minneapolis. The bloods resided in the 4th Avenue area. The vice lords resided in the 19th and Park Avenue area, closer to downtown. The crips and gangsters were basically anywhere they wanted to be, but most of them resided over north. Me and my girl's witness gang bangin in our hood, but it was nothing about colors really in our hoods. It was about who was making the most money in this area, or who was gonna take over.

Ever since the crack era, people from Chicago, California, Detroit and Milwaukee have come and invaded Minnesota. A lot of nigga's didn't appreciate it, and wasn't allowing it, so from then on, the murder rate in Minnesota has been out of control. As Coop and Brian told them more and more stories, they sounded like cousin Kane. He felt the same way, about niggas coming from another state and tryin to take over. This was the first time Rox learned that Brian wasn't a punk at all. She seen his stash spot, that had two 9 milly's and a hand grenade. That shit looked like they were going to war.

Everybody was sleep by the time they made it to Angie's house. Rox woke them up and told them they would be in, in a minute.

"Come here." Brian said, while reaching out to hug and kiss Rox.

She was intertwined with him and moved up in his lap. It felt so good, to her that she had to stop.

"What?...What's wrong baby?" She moved back off him. "Girl come back here." He reached to grab her back.

"Wait Brian...." She put her head down. "Um...we can't do this here... in this car....nah dog, I don't get down like that." He smiled at her, and put his hand on her face.

"I respect you for that...it just felt good. I'm sorry." He kissed Rox and told her he'll get up with her tomorrow. She had to remind him that they had to go dance at the taste, because a lot of people were gonna be there.

"Cool, I'm gonna meet ya'll out there when you page me."

"Okay baby." Rox seductively kissed him, while reaching in his pants to see what he was working with. He grabbed her hand.

"Don't do nothing that you ain't ready for."

"Ha ha....you're right." He watched Rox while she was getting out the car.

"Tell Coop's ass to come on and you have sweet dreams Water!" She looked back with a smile as wide as a Lincoln Continental.

"I will, and you have sweet dreams about me cutie!" She made it into the house. Like she thought but hoped that Mr. Mackman wasn't there waiting for her to come in.

"Oh...ah where's Angie and them?"

"They're in the basement." He was looking at Rox pitifully, hoping she would break the ice. She couldn't forgive him so easily, so she just decided not to bring the issue up.

"Are they sleep?"

"Angie and the dude Coop are awake, but Darlene and Monique are asleep."

"Oh thank you sir or should I say master...ha ha ha."

She shot right past him and told Coop that Brian was about to leave him. She got into the shower, prayed and went to bed. As she laid there, she thought about how she felt about Mr. Mackman. She couldn't get it out her head, as bad as she wanted to, she couldn't shake it.

It was twelve o'clock and they had to be at practice by eight. She got up to read the Bible and fell asleep on Isaiah. The next morning they all got up and made it to practice on time. Terry was happy to know and see that Rox was ready to go.

When they made it down to the taste, it was a lot of white people there, but they were ready to see some dancing. The groups that were performing had nothing on Rox and she knew it.

"What's up Fresh Water?" Brian kissed Rox from behind. She jumped.

"Oh boy....um...I'm glad to see you made it." She embraced him and kissed him back. Jay was there to cheer Mo on and Coop was there of course to cheer Angie on.

"Baby this is Jay Hustle." Rox said, while pointing at Jay.

"What's up my brother?"

"Cool....cool." Jay said, while giving Brian and Coop a manly handshake.

"Oh come on ya'll, we're up." Rox gave Brian a kiss for good luck. The crowd went crazy when Rox twirled around and did the splits. Like always, they won.

The crew got to eat all day for free and got plenty of offers to take their routine on the road.

Chapter 12

Mad Love

It's been about two months that Rox been hangin out with Brian. She was waiting patiently, for him to ask her to be his girl. You know girls in the hood don't never ever ask a man to be his girl. "Shit", if he don't ask then everybody is just left out there to assume.

Work was becoming a bit much, being as though she had a homie, lover, friend, practice, church and work. Her mom always told her that she didn't have to work, as long as she did good in school, she would provide her with everything she needed.

"Wake up Rox, someone is at the front door for you." She rolled over and looked at her mother like she had three heads.

"Who is it Mom? Dang!"

"Get yo butt up girl." Her mother snatched the covers off her. "Your butt been asleep since you got off work yesterday."

"Okay, okay...Mom." She went to the shower and got herself together. "Hum, whoever that is is gonna have to wait...shoot, I got to get my breath straight, before I get up in somebody face." Rox said to herself, as she showered.

After she was finished, she didn't even realize who it could of been, but she was in for a surprise. She walked into the living room with her mom, grinning from ear to ear.

"Oh shit, what is this...a set up?" She said in her mind, while she looked at the situation in front of her. "Mom, come here." Rox tried to go hide in her room, but she knew sooner or later she was gonna have to come out.

"I'll call Kane! He'll know what to do." Ring! Ring!

"Roxane you have company out here. It's not nice to make people wait." Ms. Vicki thought it was so funny that Rox had two of her men waiting in the living room for her.

"Kane."

"What girl!"

"I need your help!"

"This early?"

"Yeah boy...wake up please, so I can tell you what's going on." Kane sat quiet for a minute, while he rolled away from the female he hit last night.

"Run it down young one, cause this ass that's in my face is looking really good right now."

"Okay okay, I have two dudes in the front room and I don't know what to do."

"Is that it girl? I thought you really had a problem."

"It is boy! Do you know Terrance is crazy!"

"Who's that? I thought Carl was your man."

"Roxane!"

"Okay Mom, I'm coming!"

"Hello."

"Yeah...sorry, I'm still here Kane. What should I do?"

"Pick the one you like the most and tell the other nigga to step."

"What if they get to fighting."

"Tell them niggas I'll handle my business with them, if they disrespect my aunties house. Now let me get back to my pussy....love you." Click.

She was nervous before making it to the living room. To her surprise, Brian and Terrance was sitting there like they were old buddies, at a class reunion.

"Good morning my beautiful Water." Brian reached over and gave Rox a hug and kiss on the cheek. Ms. Vicki was enjoying herself, to see how this would play out.

"What's up Rox?" Terrance said, while sitting still and watching Rox hug on Brian.

"What's up ya'll? What brings both of you here so early?" She said, while looking back and forth at the both of them.

"Um, I came to take my girl to breakfast." Rox turned and looked at Terrance with an evil eye, waiting on an answer.

"I came to tell you that I have to go to summer school, but I did pass on to the twelfth grade."

Brian was holding in his laugh. He knew that his game was wack, and he didn't have a chance with Rox, if his life depended on it.

"That's good...but I know you've been in summer school for at least two weeks, so you could of been told me this."

Brian watched as his girl handled her business. Even though he was a little jealous, because he didn't know if Rox had been seeing this dude or not. He would hope not, because she hadn't gave it up to him yet and he wanted it! If not for life, at least for one time.

"I'm sorry...I didn't know you had a new man in your life, plus you've been at work a lot." She was really pissed off now. Not only did he pop up at her crib, but now he was trying to dry snitch.

"What! Let me tell you something!" Rox got all up in Terrance face, while he was seated next to her mom. "I told yo ass before not to pop up at my crib at no time. You keep acting like I'm yo girl!"

"But, I thought...."

"You thought what nigga? I don't like you at all. I got a man, right here!" Rox now pointing at Brian. "He's mine, so don't disrespect him, me, my mom or my house."

Terrance was so embarrassed, but what could he do. He loved Rox, but she didn't feel the same, but he had a plan. He wasn't about to let his girl get away from him.

"I'm sorry, it won't happen again." Terrance got up to leave. Rox stood there next to Brian, with her arms crossed. Ms. Vicki stood up to watch Terrance leave.

"You're one lucky man." He said before leaving out the door.

"Whooo, I'm glad that went smooth." Ms. Vicki said, while smiling and going to her room. Before she made it to her room, she turned around. "I love to see my daughter with a gentleman Brian."

"Yes Ma'am, I know....and I'm nothing but that. Don't worry, I'll never hurt her."

"Okay, I got my eye on you!"

Rox and Brian laughed and joked about both of their past. She decided to lay some things out on the line, since he was calling her his girl. He told her about his old girlfriend that use to wanna fight any girl that he was cool with. She was so jealous of a customer one time, that she followed the girl home, keyed her car and rims up, just because he gave her a discount. After that incident, he put a restraining order on her and she finally left him alone. That had him shook up for a while, until he finally bumped into Rox.

They left to go to Perkins to get something to eat. She wanted to take him to The Soul Food Joint, but it was too early for that kind of food. As they sat down to eat, she told him all about Carl and Terrance. She held back on the fact that Carl and Terrance had both raped her. He listened to her story, and loved her even more. He was turned on by her independence. He never heard anybody as young as her talk about wanting their own floral company.

Her story lead him to believe that Terrance was gonna be a problem. She tried convincing him that he wasn't gonna be a problem, but Brian knew better. From that day on, he was never gonna be caught without his heater.

"Baby you know it's my birthday next month." Rox said, with her pretty eyes, while he was driving.

"I know beautiful...how old will you be?"

"Don't play boy...sixteen." She said, while playfully hitting him in the head.

"I know baby...I got something real special for you." He leaned over and kissed her on the head. She didn't know that he was just about to cut off all the girl's he was fooling with.

"Yeah, well I hope you let yo hoes know it's my time now, and they can step." He laughed at Rox and was wondering did she know about all his women problems. He didn't want her to know nothing.

"Chill baby...let's go to the mall."

"I'm with it."

She didn't know she was in for a surprise. He was about to make her his wife, but first he will test her to see if she was down for him. In their way to the mall, he stopped by his house to pick up his 9 mil gun. He had a stash spot, so the pigs couldn't find it.

As they got out to go in the mall, Rox was nervous, because she seen it sticking out the side of his shirt.

"What you got that for?" She questioned, while walking into the mall.

"What's what for?" He's now smiling and putting his arm around her. He kissed her on the lips and said, "It's just a little protection for you ...Water...quit trippin."

"I ain't...I just need to know what's up with you? I can't have my life in danger." She was worried that he could be wanted by somebody. She didn't want no accidents, like with Kane. She didn't want to go through all of the pressure and interrogation for tryin to cover up for another mistake.

"Your life will never be in danger...when you're my girl. You're mines...you got that?" He frowned and grabbed her by the arm, to let her know he means business. She must think I'm some lame ass nigga.

"I hope not." This boy is a rough neck, just like I love them, but I can't let him know this. I got to at least make him wait until my birthday or I might make him wait 6 months.

"Baby you want these shoes right here?" She was in a daze, thinking about this man that was in front of her. He shook her arm.

"Baby look." He held the shoe in her face.

"Oh...I'm sorry, I was just thinking."

"About what?"

"You baby!" She smiled and kissed him on the lips. They walked the mall and bought everything in sight. He bought four pairs of Nikes and her four pairs to match. He took her to the Dayton's Oval Room. She had no clue to where she was. Rox thought it was a dream. They sold everything from ballroom dresses that cost $20,000 to ski jackets that cost $300. He told her it was on him.

She thought the Nikes was enough for her, but he wanted her to feel good about being with him. They left the mall and went back to his house. This made Rox a little nervous, because she knew he was gonna try and hit. This wasn't gonna happen today, but she didn't want him to take her whole wardrobe away.

"Come in here baby." Rox left out the living room.

"What's up?"

"Girl...come over here and sit next to me!" He grabbed her by the waist and put her on the bed with him. It was about to go down and she wasn't gonna let it. He started off licking her in her ear and rubbing her breast. He told her to lay back and relax. When she laid back, he clipped her bra off with a pocket knife. As he rubbed her breast, he planted soft wet kisses slowly down to her navel. As she spread her legs, he stuck a finger in her and slowly stroked it.

"Urlimmi...ah...oooh...please stop." She moaned, as he continued. Sliding her panties halfway down, she grabbed them.

"Chill baby, it's enough time for this...baby!" She said, while looking into his eyes.

"What you mean...your body is saying yes, but your mouth is saying no." She looked off to the side.

"I know...it's too soon and you won't respect me." He rolled over, and was a little irritated, but he had to understand. Shit, if she would of gave it up, I would of played her anyway!

Damn, if I would of gave it to him, he would play me. I hope he don't take my three G's worth of clothes back. Rox thought as she stood up to get herself together. She walked over to him and put her arms around him.

"Are you mad at me?" She now kissed him.

"No girl...I told you in front of your mom...I got you. I won't hurt you!"

"I'm glad to know that baby."

They left the house to get something to eat and take Rox to Angie's, so she could get ready for the Rondo Days celebration. They rode down 4th and 33rd where all the blood gang hangs out at. She watched as Brian walked up to the crowd of dudes with red bandanas, brown khaki pants and red Chuck Taylor gym shoes. She watched, while they jocked Brian and threw up gang signs. The young boy's had their hands out for money. He broke them off 20 dollars, to about seven teenagers that were bangin as well.

As Brian was walking to the car, a group of girl's that were flamed up like all the bangin niggas that hung around, they stopped for him.

He talked for a second and kept walking. One girl that looked like a reject Sheila E, grabbed him by his hand and whispered something in his ear and felt on his butt. He laughed and pointed at the car and told the girl Rox was his only woman. As they drove away, the girl was cursing and sticking her middle finger up.

The ride back to St. Paul was going one way. She didn't talk much. She let Brian do the talking. He noticed she was quiet and thought she was mad.

"Why you so quiet baby?"

"I'm just listening to you, that's all." She rubbed his hand to confirm that she wasn't mad about anything. Shit, this nigga betta know I ain't no fool by a long shot. I ain't about to let him get over on me, like Carl did. Shit, I see he's paid up and legit, so I'm at least gonna juice his ass till I get my doe for my floral shop.

She just don't know she my wifey and I got her back on whatever. She still in high school, so she won't be hearing about all the hoes I done hit in the sota.

"What you want to eat Water?"

"Stop by my job so I can get us a discount." They stopped at Hardees and like she said, they got a discount.

They road through the hood, before making a stop at Angie's house. Coop was gonna be mad, because him and Angie became inseparable. As she thought, Coop and Angie was laid up. Rox walked in Angie's room looking for them.

"Angie! Angie!" She kept calling out, but got no answer. As she looked upstairs and continued to call out, the house was empty. She knew somebody was there cause the door was open. She walked to the basement where she could hear noises.

"Slee..ummm...oooh...yeah baby." She started laughing and hoped it wasn't what she thought. She didn't want to catch her girl freakin in the middle of the basement floor. As she got closer to the laundry room, she could hear the dryer going and somebody getting some moans. She pushed the door open.

"Ooooh...aahh...girl what the!" Angie grabbed herself, after she realized Rox was in the doorway.

"Oh, I'm sorry Angie." Rox was holding in her laugh. Coop covered his head and body up, while he was on his knees. "I ain't know you had it like that Coop." Rox slammed the door, laughing and ran back up the stairs.

Angie and Coop went and got in the shower. They were a little embarrassed because Rox just caught Coop giving his girl some head. It was funny to her, because she didn't think Angie was freaky like that. Rox killed herself laughing, as she walked back to the door to tell Brian that he needs to come in.

"Yo B...baby come in ha ha ha"

"What's so damn funny, tell that fool to come on." Rox was laughing her butt off.

"Yo boy was a little busy, so you need to come in...he's in the shower." Brian came in and waited on Coop. Rox was still laughing and telling him about what happened. He laughed his ass off, cause he didn't know his boy had it in him. Coop was the type of nigga that had yo back, but always had to think before he did anything. He bragged about not ever licking on no girl unless she was his wife and she had to do him first. At this point Rox and Brian knew that they were serious and Angie must of did him if he did her.

Coop made it into the living room, with his head down. They knew he was embarrassed, because he kept his head down as he walked to the door. Rox and Brian watched him and Angie kiss at the door. They busted out laughing.

"What's so funny ya'll?" Angie and Coop said, while standing in the door way.

"Nothing, ya'll just paranoid as hell."

"Shut up, don't act like you don't do it!" Angie said in defense of her man.

"I know, quit trippin girl."

Brian and Coop left and got in the car. They road home laughing about him getting his knees dirty. Coop was still embarrassed, but stood up for himself. Meanwhile Angie and Rox had to call Mo and Darlene over. They all were off work for a couple of days and they wanted to practice before Saturday. Rondo days was Saturday and for it to be a winner, Rox had to show the girls what she had to rock the crowd.

The girl's made it over, and they all went through the routine. They were satisfied as usual, with what Rox came up with.

For the next two days, Rox went to spend time with her mom. She let her know how proud she was of her, that she kept herself busy with positive things. They stopped by the nursing home to visit her great grandma. Grandma was bedridden from brain cancer. This bothered Rox, because her grandma (dad's grandma), was a powerful woman. She hated to see her like that, but her mom reminded her that it's important for Grandma to know she is loved and when she passes on she will know that she was loved.

When they left from seeing Grandma, they stopped at the floral shop. Rox admired all the beautiful flowers. While her mother watched and picked out a bouquet for her friend that was getting married at work. As they left out the door, Ms. Vicki stopped to ask the woman behind the counter how much does it cost to open up a shop like this.

"Oh, it's around $650 a month for rent and you pay first and last months rent plus deposit."

"Oh that's it?"

"No Ma'am, you have to have at least $10,000 worth of equipment to get started." Ms. Vicki was amazed about how cheap it was. The woman gave her some information about getting started.

"What took you so long Mom? Why was you talking to that lady?" Rox was hungry and ready to go.

"Nothing baby...I was getting a little info that's all."

Rox drifted off to sleep, as she thought about what her mom was in there talking about. Traffic was pretty busy, so what would of taken 20 minutes to get home, it took about 45 minutes. Whey they finally made it home, Rox was still tired.

"Mom, I'm going to sleep, and tell whoever calls that I need rest and call tomorrow."

"Okay baby, you get some rest."

Since Rox was sleep, Ms. Vicki called all the places that the woman told her to. As she did her research, she found out that she could get grants for Rox, if she stayed in college while trying to open up her business. She decided that this would be a test for her. If she kept a 3.0 grade average, then she would help her get her business off the ground and hire her some employee's, so she could have some time for herself.

The next day was the big day for the Rondo days parade. The phone started ringing off the hook at 6:00 am. Since Rox was well rested, she was ready and prepared for the events. Angie had to inform her that Coop and Brian would be there and everybody was to meet at Terry's house at 10:00 am.

Everybody made it to the last practice and went through the routine, that Rox had for them. She was a little pissed off, because some of the girl's couldn't get it. They have been practicing for 2 months and they should of known it.

"Damn! Ya'll don't get the shit...man, I'm stealing on whoever fucks this up! All this hard work I've done to make sure we win, and on the day of, ya'll wanna fuck up!" Rox walked around saying and waving her hands.

Angie, Darlene and Monique didn't say a word. She was right. They weren't on top of their game and this might make them lose. The other girls started crying, so Terry had to step in.

"Roxane, please stop being so harsh...we'll go through it one more time and will get it...okay?"

"They better damn it....or I'm snapping!"

"Roxane, we understand that you're the best dancer here, but you need to be a team leader." Terry said, while putting her hand on Rox' shoulder. Rox got a little emotional from her statement. She did have to realize that in order for them to win, then her team couldn't be under any pressure.

"Okay, okay...chill ya'll. I'm sorry, we are gonna go over it twice and ya'll will get it." The girl's started wiping their faces and got started. After she watched each girl do the routine, one by one, they got in the van to leave. They rode the hood and watched all the cars that were in town for the event. This made Rox a little nervous. She was waiting for this day. This would bring great exposure and respect from every where.

They finally made it to the Peoples Park. It was people from every where. The parade started from Selby Ave. to Carrole Ave. Terry had to check everyone in.

"Rox, there goes Coop, Brian, Jay Hustle and Ms. Vicki." She looked around and seen everyone. Angie and Monique walked over to tell them what was going on. Rox blew Brian a kiss while she got in a last minute check with the girls.

The announcers let it be known that it was time to get started. They made it through the parade successfully. Roxanne was so proud. All the groups from the other states came and gave them their props. Terry let Rox know how much she appreciated what she has done for the group.

Ms. Vicki gave the girls a present for doing so well and Brian treated the whole drill team to all the soul food that the parade provided. Winning the competition wouldn't put any money in their pockets, but it sho gave recognition. Brian was able to see her leadership in effect and her mom and homegirls was able to see that she was a girl tryin to make her way in this world.

Chapter 13

Shook Up!

"Damn Coop, what's taken you so long?" Coop is in the parking lot of the chop shop. Brian is nervous, because he can't get caught up. His business will go down and it's too many investors involved. Brian would buy parts off of the cars that the Mexican chop shop would steal. He would tell them what kind of rims or parts he needed, then resale them in his shop. Even though he didn't have to do this, he felt that people in corporate America robbed the poor to get right, so he felt he had to take back what they owed him and his people already.

"Yo Coop, I'm bout to leave yo ass." A short Mexican comes walking out with an older woman.

"Amigo chill, he say he coming."

Brian was irritated and turned his music back up. As he sat in the car, he kept seeing a man in a Ford Taurus circle the alley. This was making him nervous, because don't no white people be in this neighborhood, this time of night. Honk! Honk!

"Yo Coop, I'm bout to leave yo ass!" He could see Coop talking to the Mexican and exchanging money. He kept his eyes from the transaction, to the white man. As he seen Coop coming to the car, the man was speaking into a walkie talkie. Coop is now running to the car and Brian makes a u turn to face the street. Coop jumps in out of breath.

"What took you so long man?"

"Chill, I was looking at all that ammo they had."

"Look at that car." The red Taurus is now following them.

"Right there stupid!" Brian is pointing at the car, while speeding down Lake Street.

"Damn dog, is dat the dic's?" (Detectives)

"I don't know, but I'm bout to lose him." Brian is doing bout 60 in a residential area. He's going in the opposite lane.

"Whoa...damn boy, you almost hit that lady! Boy...ha ha!" Coop thinks this shits a joke.

"Yo is he still on us?" Brian looks out his rearview mirror. "He's back a little, but dip through 4th Ave." Brian comes to a yellow light.

"Go boy go! Ha ha..."

"Shut up with dat shit man!" Coop is killing his self laughing. "Shit ain't funny man, I ain't going to jail dog." Brian doesn't want to go to jail. This could sure nuff send his ass to Stillwater, for a long time. He couldn't be away from his baby Rox for a 3 to 9.

They've been doing good for these last two months. She's been practically living at his house anyway. She told him that if he ever goes to jail behind some bullshit, then she ain't waiting. She felt that the only way anybody should be locked up, is for taking someone away from somebody or for taking one for somebody. She felt Brian was bullshitting with that petty money. Shit, the shop alone grossed $75,000 a year. She saw no reason for him to be hustling stolen car parts and guns on the side.

Rox constantly put in his head that slow money is fo sho money. If you're patient, you will always get what ever you want in life. Benefitting off of somebody else's hard work will never make you rich. If you don't have a rich heart, then your brain will have broke thoughts and you will be broke forever.

He loved and respected the fact that she was younger than him and so smart. She learned all she knew from her cousin Kane. When Rox was about 10 years old, Kane and her were on their way to their grandma's house. This was a hustle infested area. If you didn't sale something, boost clothes, or prostitute on University Ave, then you had no business in this area. Rox watched all of these things growing up. Kane never wanted her to get unfocused, so he always spent time with her because Lili mistreated her.

When they made it to grandma's, they could hear a lot of yelling and the sounds of guns going off.

"Oh! What's that noise Kane? Why are all them people in the back yard?" They started walking faster. Rox started crying, cause she could feel in her gut that something was wrong with her grandma. She started crying.

"Stop crying like a punk...girl." Kane said, while wiping tears from her face. She had to play hard in front of him . He never allowed that sissy shit, as he would say. "You don't even know what's going on...ain't nothing wrong with Grandma..."

Rox stood in front of the gate, while Kane moved through the people. She asked everybody what was going on and they said somebody was shooting up grandma's house from the inside. All they could hear was screaming, but they didn't see nobody. When she seen Kane kick the door in, she went in with him.

"Stay at the door Rox, and tell somebody to call the police." In this hood, nobody called the police, cause they took their time about coming. "Nah, I ain't leaving you." She stayed right on his heels, as they moved to the upstairs bedroom, where the noise was coming from. As they got closer to the door, they could hear their grandma's boyfriend's voice. Rox instantly started crying.

"Stop that shit girl!" Another gun shot went off. Boom! Click! Click! Boom! Rox jumped back, and Kane pulled his gun out.

"Stop crying and go in the bathroom and call the police!"

"I ain't leaving yo side Kane!" In a light tone, Kane instructed Rox to hold on to his waist. He kicked the door in. Boom! He scared the shit out of their grandma who was tied up and had blood rushing out of her head.

"Grandma you okay?" The man turned the gun towards Kane.

"Run...baby Kane....run!" Kane rushed the man and knocked him down. His gun flew in the air and Kane's slapped against the wall and went off. Boom! As Kane fought the man, Rox untied her grandma. They both rushed to try and break it up. Kane grabbed the shot gun off the floor and blew the man's stomach right into the wall. The impact of his body hit the wall so hard, that he was stuck in there.

The house was a bloody mess. Grandma said he was fighting her because she put him out for having a prostitute suck him off in her house. She said she came home and it was a house full of people smoking dope. He was in the corner of the basement getting sucked off and grandma beat him in the head with the gun. Everybody ran out the house and left her. Her head was bleeding because he hit her with the buck shots of the gun. He put holes in the windows and walls of the house.

The police took Kane to prison because the people in the neighborhood said Kane always stirred up trouble. They were scared of him. They told about Kane having a gun on him when he walked in the house. Rox took the gun and hid it. Every since that incident, Rox had nightmares and has never really been able to get over it. Sometimes, she would break into a sweat and recite Bible scriptures.

Monique and Jay Hustle had been kicking it strong. She had moved in with him. He had a lot of haters and people call the police on him constantly. Monique had numerous women call her house and appear at her door. One girl some how got on top of their roof and videotaped them having sex. Mo was pissed and told his ass he better pay her whatever she wants. The woman sent a letter saying she wanted 20 g's or she'll destroy everything. Jay said fuck her. You can't hustle a hustler. He told that hoe to stand on the corner and sale them, cause she'll get more. Mo was tryin to get him to make the girl lower her price, but she was Jay's ex so she knew that 20 g's wasn't shit to him.

After that, Mo came to the conclusion that Rox had done it and made it through that, so she could too. Everyday Jay would leave the house to give everybody their daily work. He would give his workers their work and let his hoes know how much money they had to bring in. Mo kept her a job. She was now working at a daycare center. Being around children on a daily basis made her want children more. She stopped taking her birth control pills and convinced Jay they didn't have to use rubbers. This was totally against his rules, because he already had five kids by three different women.

Mo didn't want marriage, she just wanted a baby. One day after work, she noticed a discoloration in her pee. She was excited and ran to her closet, got out her home pregnancy test, a glass of water and the phone. She drank the water and about 20 minutes later, she took the test. To her surprise, she was pregnant.

Ring! Ring!

"Hello."

"Yeah boy....oh..ah Rox, guess what?"

"What girl...damn, quit yelling in my ear!"

"Oh...I'm sorry, I'm pregnant." Rox sat quietly for a second.

"Um...didn't he say he didn't want no kid's girl...damn, the nigga got enough." Mo's attitude changed completely. She thought Rox was hating on her.

"So what bitch, I want one."

"What the fuck you just call me?"

"You heard me Rox!"

"Nah, I don't think I did."

"Yeah, you been acting real fake since you moved to Minneapolis. You just hatin on me and mines." Rox was pissed off. She couldn't believe that her best friend, sis, homegirl would say such a thing.

"First of all hoe, I have no reason to hate on yo dumb ass."

"I ain't dumb!"

"Like I said, dumb ass, me and my man are doing fine. We don't bother nobody and I'm working on me...I'm tryin to have something in the long run, unlike you."

"I'm have...." Click. Rox just cut her off, she didn't want to argue with Monique anymore. She cried her heart out and hasn't heard from her since. That was a year ago. Last thing she heard, Monique had a beautiful little boy and Jay put her and her baby out. He found him another young girl to put up with his mess and organize his illegal business.

Darlene eventually went back to Tobby. Everyone knew that she was gay, but her homegirl's wouldn't believe it. Tobby had her so strung out, that he had her doing threesomes with any and every hoe that was willing. Darlene had all that money, so she would persuade hungry college girl's or stripper's to do it. Tobby would tape Darlene and all of her acts and play them for his homeboy's.

One day, her and Tobby were visiting her mom at work. As they left, they bumped into Denise. Unknown to Rox and crew, Denise and Darlene use to freak each other. Darlene is the one who gave Denise the idea to tape Rox while her and Carl was in the car doing it.

"Hi baby....where you been?" Denise reached out and grabbed Darlene's ass. Tobby was turned on, but Darlene's mom was pissed off. Her mouth dropped to the floor.

"Bitch, don't you ever disrespect my mom." Darlene charged Denise, and started whooping her ass. Tobby and Mrs. Longtongue tried to stop Darlene, but she wouldn't stop. She beat her ass so bad that the people in the office had to call the police.

Darlene went to jail, and was ordered to never come back to her mom's job. Tobby bailed her out. He convinced her to make and sell XXX tapes full time, instead of college. Once Rox heard all this, she never wanted to hear from her again.

Cousin Kane was mad Rox moved in with Brian. Every time he called, she was gone with him. He had to realize that his baby cousin was growing up. When Rox did catch up with her cousin, she had to hear about the daily drama of the dope boy's and their blocks. Kane had drug business on lock. Of course he had numerous women and that brought hella drama. He told her he had a baby girl and two more on the way. He kept telling her that it was getting hot for him around there and he had plans to open up a beauty shop and restaurant, so all his hoes can work for him. He thought he was such a pimp, that Rox was scared he would get Aids. She tried convincing him that he couldn't have wild sex like you could back in the day. He would soon find out.

Mr. and Mrs. Davis were doing good for themselves. They had a small wedding and Brian was invited. Her mom was happy now that she wasn't living in sin, with Howard anymore. Rox didn't really want to abide by his rules, so instead of upsetting her mom and disrespecting Mr. D., she would spend the night at Brian's, if her and Brian hung out late. Like always, her mom was so lenient that Rox never felt like she had any parental guidance. This is not a good thing for parents to do. But of course, Rox appreciated it.

Lili was still hating on her little sister. Sometimes for money, she would convince Brian to buy her stolen clothes for Rox. Once Rox found out, she cut that shit short. Lili got mad and called the police on Brian, and gave them a bunch of lies. They raided his house and business. Luckily, nothing was there and nobody went to jail. Brian was so mad that he was gonna pay somebody to kill Lili. Rox convinced him that even though her sister was shady, she still was family and didn't want her dead. Brian still wouldn't let that shit ride, so he paid his cousin to slap her in her mouth.

One day, when Lili was on her way to her kid's school, a girl walked right up on her and asked her did she have clothes for sale. Being the greedy snake that she was, she took the kid's into the school and went straight to the trunk. As Lili showed her whole trunk to this unknown woman, she got beat over the head, with a crow bar, bleach thrown on her, and all of her clothes stolen back from her. Now she had to deal with her wounds burning, from the bleach. When Rox found out from her mom, she played it off. She was so glad that Brian didn't kill her, but she did feel that Lili deserved what she got.

Two Years Later

"Brian wake up!" Rox was mad, a girl was at the front door for him. "Brian, get the fuck up now! You got me fucked up nigga!" Rox continued to beat Brian across his head.

"What girl? Damn!" He got up and rubbed his eyes. "What girl...shit!" He scratched his head and felt his dick.

"Get your hand out yo pants nigga, cause it may have got you in trouble."

Brian laughed a little.

"What you talking about?" She grabbed his other hand and lead him to the door. As he stomped through the house towards the door, he could feel in his gut that something wasn't right.

"Hold up, I got to pee!" He tried to cut to the bathroom, but Rox wasn't having it.

"Nah nigga, you bout to get to this door now!" She swung the door open and bam! There stood his old girlfriend, Leanna.

"What the fuck you doing here?" Brian had not brushed his teeth yet, so his breath was on fire. Rox had to get back from the smell.

"I need to talk to you." Leanna said, while trying to push past him and Rox.

"Hold up hoe, you ain't coming up in here!" Rox stood next to Brian, with her arms folded.

"I ain't come here for no..." Bam! Pow! Kick! Rox had knocked Leanna down the step.

"Don't ever think you can disrespect me!" Rox dog walked Leanna all across the yard. He couldn't even get her off of Leanna.

"Chill Rox...come on, don't do this out here!" Whop! Bam!

"What nigga! You with this hoe? You been fuckin her or something?" Brian grabbed her from the back in a bear hug, to try and stop her.

"Let me go boy!" Rox kicked and screamed. Leanna got up and dusted herself off. As Brian calmed Rox down, Leanna pulled out a piece of paper and walked away. As she went to go get in her car, Rox picked up a rock and threw it at the car. "Bitch!"

Leanna shook her head, and pulled off. Brian picked up the paper and read it. He had his back to Rox while walking up the stairs.

"Let me see it!" She tried to snatch it out of his hands, but he wasn't having it. "Why you hiding it? You must be guilty...bitch!" Rox cried out. She knew that letter said something that wasn't good, because Brian's whole attitude changed. He didn't even check Rox for calling him a bitch. He just let her get everything off her chest.

"Come here baby..." He reached out to grab her.

"No!" She said, while wiping her tears and running up the stairs. (Damn, I can't tell her this shit...what did I get myself into...Rox will leave me if she finds out. Ah...damn, I'm gonna go to the doctor first.)

Brian sat and recited the letter in his mind. He ripped it up and flushed it down the toilet. He had to get Rox back on his good side. "Where you going...girl?" Rox ignored him and headed towards the door, with all her bags. He jumped up off the couch, and tried to grab her with that dancing devil morning breath.

"Stop...stop!" She yelled and cried out. He wrestled her to the ground, and laid on her, until she stopped kicking and screaming. He let her cry herself tired.

"I'm sorry baby, stop crying. Baby...stop." He wiped her tears, from her face.

"What are you sorry for Brian? Huh?" Rox tried lifting up, but he wouldn't let her.

"I'm sorry for making you cry. I didn't think that she would ever come back here. I haven't been with her or seen her in two years baby, I swear."

"Then why now...huh? Why would she come over here now Brian, huh?" He didn't answer right away. He kissed Rox on the lips and tried to stall her out. "Answer me Brian." He looked her in the eyes and said "cause she wants me back."

"So, you think I'm stupid huh? What was that letter about?"

"It was some old mail that was left at our old apartment."

"Yeah right boy! Then let me see it!" Brian lifted up off of her. "I threw it away." She was pissed off. What was in the letter she thought. She was going to find out soon enough. If he didn't tell her, then it must of been something worth hiding.

The next day, Brian dropped Rox off at work and made his way to the doctor. (Damn, what if I got this shit? What am I gonna do? Shit, how am I gonna tell my girl that the rest of her life will be ruined on the count of me?) Brian thought, as he pulled into the doctor's parking lot.

When he made it into the office, he looked around and noticed a customer from the shop and he didn't want her to see him. As he walked up to the counter, to check in, he could feel eyes on him, so he didn't turn around.

"Hello Ma'am, my name is Brian Walters and I'm here to check in for my appointment." He whispered to the nurse, sitting behind the desk.

"Sir you need to speak up okay?" (He went into a panic. Oh, now if I speak up, these people will know my business.) He took a quick glance behind him and seen the girl looking directly at him. Brian leaned into the desk and spoke, straight into the woman's face.

"Can you hear me now? I said my name is...."

"Step back sir, I understand." She felt a little uncomfortable with Brian all up on her. She knew that when people came in to do an HIV test, that it's a major secret.

"How long do I have to wait to see the doctor Ma'am?" He was so nervous and wondered if all these people have to be tested as well.

"Not long Sir, just have a seat over there." She pointed at the only available seat, right next to the girl from the shop.

"Thank you Ma'am."

As he walked to his seat, his feet felt like something was weighing him down. Oh no he thought as beads of sweat formed on his head. She's about to say something oh....

"What's up B?" He turned to her.

"What's up?" He didn't want to look her in the face.

"What's wrong? Oh....I know you don't want no one to know your business huh?" The girl sang out, with a smirk on her face.

"Nah baby girl, that ain't it....I'm just shocked to see you here." She laughed hysterically. "What's so damn funny?" She covered her mouth, and kept laughing.

"You dog....you funny as hell." Brian just knew she knew why he was there.

"You trippin girl." He rolled his eyes and kept quiet. He hoped and prayed that she didn't know what was up. Damn, I hope she's here for the same reason, that way she won't be telling nobody I was in here.

As he looked back over, a tall light skinned man with gold teeth approached her and kissed her on the lips. Damn, that ain't her husband. He thought, as the man took a seat and she sat on his lap.

"Next!" The doctor yelled, from the back. The girl stood up, with this dude, and they proceeded to walk to the back.

"Yo B." He looked up at her. "Yo, don't tell my husband you saw me here and I won't tell yo crazy ass girl I seen you."

He laughed at her, while she walked away from him. Brian watched her and dude walk to the back. He remembered that she has a husband and a son. Damn, hoes are slick round this place. Damn, she must be getting a pregnancy test.

"Mr. Walter's, we're ready to see you."

Brian's heart dropped to his feet, but he was ready to conquer whatever his situation would be. It just had him shook because he didn't want to hurt his fresh water.

Chapter 14

Hot Water

Ring! Ring! Ring!

"Um, I don't want to get up. Hello."

"Yo, get up nigga, it's time to get them results."

"Who da fuck is dis?" Brian was just coming out of a sleep. He figured it was Coop's crazy ass. He told Coop that the doctor gave him two weeks, before the results would come back.

"Me nigga! Who the fuck else you tell yo damn business to?"

"Shut up man...I'm just rollin over." Brian rubbed his eyes and gave Rox a kiss.

"You want me to come get you or what?"

"What time is it?" Rox began to wake up, she wrapped her legs around him.

"Make love to me baby." With all the emotions going on in his mind, he still had to play it cool with Rox, so she wouldn't suspect nothing. "Yo! You still there man? Get up, it's 6:00 am!"

"Damn, alright nigga, come get me at 8:30." Click.

Brian was walking on egg shells. His mind was going crazy, because for some reason, he didn't want to do it to Rox. Even though it wouldn't of mattered, because if he gave her HIV, the damage was done.

"Did you hear me baby....I need you inside of me now."

"Okay hold up, I got to piss."

He went to the bathroom to look at himself in the mirror. His body was fine like a top athlete. His muscles were nice and firm and his skin was smooth like a newborn baby. Damn, it don't look like I got no damn AIDS.

"Baby I'm waiting, shit."

"Oh...I'm coming." He gave his self one last check and said a prayer. "Jesus Christ my Lord and Savior, please give me a pass Sir. Don't let any sickness come between me and my baby, please. I know she's the one for me and I promise Lord that when I get these results back, I won't ever do anything careless. Amen."

He made his way back to the bed. Rox was stretched out butt ass naked and rubbing on herself. This made Brian stand at attention instantly. Her words alone made him get brick hard.

"You know the dick is fire in the morning." He laughed to cover up the pain.

"Yeah, so let me shoot my flames in you baby." Brian started by kissing Rox softly all over her body. Doing this made him get his mind off of his results. He did his usual sex session with Rox, but he just wasn't into it like she was.

"Uh....oooh...uh Brian, baby....ba...aby, I'm bout to...cccu..cu.. ..cum!" He pulled back, so he wouldn't nut in her. All they needed to add to the bad news was a baby.

"What the fuck is up Brian!" She was flippin out. All he had to do was tell her, but he couldn't.

"Chill Water...damn, I didn't want to cum in you."

"Why the fuck not nigga? You been nuttin in me since you met me nigga!"

"Well I wanna wait till we get married." She was pissed off. The worse thing you could do was fuck with a girl's emotion when they're in the middle of a good nut.

"Get the fuck off me!" Rox kicked him off of her. Boom! Bam! He rolled over and laughed all over the floor.

"Ain't shit funny...I'm gonna get yo ass back!"

Rox ran to the bathroom to get ready for school. Brian got up off the floor and went to the shower downstairs. Under the circumstances that Rox knew nothing about, the sex seemed to be pretty good for a morning quickie. Brian stood in the shower for what seemed to be forever. After the change, Coop was outside yelling. It was 9:00 am and Brian's appointment was at 9:30.

Honk! Honk!

"Come on nigga, I got shit to do!" Coop was yelling over Jay Z's Money Cash Hoes. As Brian heard the rhymes, it made him think of Jay Z's protege that said sex is a weapon, since it's deadly I'll shoot. That had him in a deeper thought. If he passed this on to his girl, it was going to add salt to the wound.

"Yo baby, I'm bout to finish up these last finals and I need some money for gas."

"You got money in your purse."

"No I don't boy! I don't get paid until Friday."

"Look in your damn purse." Brian was headed towards the door. He had put $500 in Rox' purse last night. He been doing a lot more lately, to cover up the pain and guilt of what might come in the next hour. As he stood in the door and told Coop he was coming, Rox opened her purse.

"Oh boo...you know how to cover up your fuck ups don't you?"

"Nah, I just know how to look out for Water." Brian smiled and skipped down the steps, to get in the car. Rox grabbed her stuff and was in such a hurry, that she almost forgot to lock the door.

"Damn B, wait!"

"What's up? I got some shit to do with Coop." She was now in his face.

"Damn, you was gonna leave without kissing me?" He put his arms around her waist and palmed her fatty and planted a long soft kiss on her.

"Come on nigga." Honk! They were broken by Coop's ignorant ass.

"Damn nigga, I can't kiss my girl?"

"Yeah Coop, you just mad cause Angie knows you're fucking with Tara."

"Yeah cause yo big mouth ass told her." Brian sat down in the passenger seat.

"No I didn't, you told on yourself, dummy."

"Alright, enough with this political shit, we got to dip Boo."

"Okay, well this weekend we going to Arnella's cause Kane is giving a party for his crip homeboy's, so we got to be there to rep."

"What!!! You know I don't get along with them like that." Rox frowned up because even though Brian don't twist with Kane, she was hoping they could kick it a little.

"Well I'm going and it's for my family." Brian had to get to the doctor, so he just agreed for now and decided to talk about it later. "Smooth...I'll see you when you get off work."

"Bye big head." Rox pushed Coop in the head, while they drove off.

Brian thought about what the doctor might say. He tried hard to think about if he used a rubber with Leanna. "Damn!" he thought out loud. Coop was pulling into the doctor's office again. As they pulled up, Brian saw the girl from the shop again as Coop parked. "Damn!".

"What nigga?" Coop said.

"What?" Brian said with an attitude.

"What....what...damn...damn...damn. ha ha ha." Coop always took shit as a joke and at this time, it wasn't no laughing matter.

"Ha ha ha mothafucka, shit ain't funny." Brian raised up out the car to walk in the office for his appointment. At the same time, the girl walked in with them, by herself.

"Um, it's funny seeing you here again." Brian wasn't going to answer her at first, but he had to remind his self, that she kept her word, about not telling Rox. He kept his as well. Then it dawned on him. Damn, she must be in here for the same results.

"Yo B, ain't that homegirl dat comes in the shop with her dude?" She turned around.

"Yeah dat's me...what?" She stood there with her hand on her hip. Coop was caught off guard, and put his head down.

"Chill Ma, he just remembered your face." She smiles and walked off to check in.

Brian and Coop sat down to wait for Brian to be called. Brian sat and prayed, while Coop looked at the paper and watched all the men and women come in, to get checked out. Coop was being messy. He knew that this doctor's office was right outside the hood, and everybody ran there, so nobody would know their business.

"Mr. Walter's....Brian Wal.."

"Yo, I heard you Ma." Everybody in the room looked at Brian as he walked to the back, like he had weights on his shoes.

"Chill B, it will be cool." Coop put the paper up and continued to read.

"Hello Mr. Walter's, you're here today for your results."

"Yes Sir, and if it's bad news just lay it on me." Brian had prepared his self for the worse, like he always did in life.

"Well I'm gonna tell you like...."

"Doc, go ahead, tell me damn."

"Well just listen..."

"Doc." Brian began to stand up and raise his voice. "Doc tell me." Brian now had tears in his eyes and was shaking like a snitch in a room full of soldiers.

"Okay...okay Son, you're negative okay...now sit down." The doctor was a little shaken by Brian's attitude. He had seen people do all kinds of things when it came to their results. This was the first time that someone put fear in his heart.

Brian began to smile and wipe the sweat off his head. As he sat down, he thought hard about God and the prayers that he said, over the past two weeks. "Thank you Lord!" Brian began to pray out loud, jumping up and down hugging and kissing the doctor.

"Calm down Son....I need to tell you something." Brian's smile went straight to a stern look.

"What's up Doc? You said I'm negative." Brian didn't understand that when you get a HIV test you had a three month window.

"You need to get tested every three months, for the next year, if you had more than one partner."

"I've had the same girl for the last two years Doc, and I can say Sir that I've been faithful."

"Okay, that's good Son, but are you sure she's been faithful?" Brian thought quietly for a second.

"Yes Sir, I know she had been on lock for two years."

"Okay, well then I'm going to give you a word of advice." Brian sat down, because he knew he was in for a lesson.

"You need to stay spiritually connected to the Lord. If you're not married in the name of the most high, then he may not hear your prayers next time." Brian thought about marrying Rox ever since he laid eyes on her, but he knew that fornication was a sin, just like the rest in God's eyes so it was time for a change.

"Thanks Doc, I'll remember that." Brian headed for the door.

"Hold up Son." The Doc gathered all of the HIV information he could, along with every STD info he could find. Brian chuckled a little, while looking down at the rubbers the doc just passed him.

"What's funny Son...just because you got out of this one don't mean you'll get out of the next one."

"Nah Doc." Brian began to shake his head. "What am I gonna do with them small rubbers?"

"Well I figured you needed something to cover that loose pole up." Brian busted out in laughter. The doctor had to laugh at himself as well. "Thanks Doc, but I need jumbos baby."

"Sorry my brotha, but we don't supply magnums." Brian laughed, and walked out with the info in his hand. Everybody that watched him walk pass didn't matter now, because he felt like a nigga getting outta jail after 20 years.

"Yo ass happy nigga....what's up?" Brian didn't say a word, he just walked to the car. "Yo man, what's up? What did Doc say man?" Brian sat down and began to roll him a blunt.

"Yo man, I ain't pulling off until you tell me what's up!" Brian laughed and turned the music up.

"Yo, man chill...he said I'm negative."

"Well she ain't."

"Who nigga?" Brian and Coop sat and watched the girl from the shop run to her car crying and screaming. Everybody from the doctor's to the nurse's tried to calm her down. She jumped in her car and burned rubber.

"Ha ha ha ha...damn!"

"Whooo...wee...she mad as hell!"

"I know, them results must of been the wrong one for her."

Brian had to think back on the conversation he had with that girl. He assumed that she was getting a pregnancy test, but the way she ran out of that building, hollering and screaming, seemed to be a positive result. Oh well, maybe now she would stop being so scandalous.

Coop kept quiet the whole ride home. He was glad to know his boy didn't have that shit.

"What's up man? I....I know yo ass is happy as hell."

"Yes Sir....I sho am homie, now pass that shit."

"Hold up, let me babysit for a minute."

Brian dozed off in front of the house, while the music blasted through the speakers. Coop smoked and smoked, until he dozed off. Brian headed in the house to check the messages. People had been coming by all morning, to get their cars checked on. Uncle Tate and Mrs. Walter's had the business together, when Brian was gone. It was pretty busy, because of the weather. Everybody came right before the summer, to get tires and detailing. It was always cheaper around tax return time. Brian knew he could capitalize at this time, and that's usually what made him happy.

Under the circumstances that just had taken place, he still was a little depressed, about the every three month check up he would have to take. He went back and forth with himself, about calling Leanna. He wanted so badly to rub the results in her face.   If he was to call, then she would be messy and tell Rox. How would he explain his reasons for talking to Leanna?

Ring! Ring!

"B-Boy's Detail, how may I help ya?"

"I'm calling for Brian Walter's."

"Hold please." He almost lost his breath. Damn, I was just thinking about this hoe. Shit, I can't believe this hoe called, knowing my girl is always here.

"Yo Mom, answer the phone on line one."

129

"Huh?"

"Please Mom, take this call and say I'm not here okay?"

"Gotcha baby." Mrs. Walter's answered. The look on her face gave it away. She closed her eyes and kept one hand on the phone and one over her mouth. Brian was nervous, because he didn't want his mother being worried about him having HIV.

"Okay baby, and if there is ever anything you need, just call...okay I'll tell him you called." Click.

"What happened Mom....what?" Brian knew damn well what was wrong, but he had to play it off. If his mother knew what he knew, she would make him have a discussion with Rox.

"I need you to tell me what's going on." Brian put his head down and waited to get his words right.

"Now, Brian."

He started off by letting her know that he never cheated on Rox. He told her that he went and got tested, but was negative. She informed him that Leanna never told her all of that. Even though she was relieved that he wasn't positive, she felt that he shouldn't of kept it bottled up. She encouraged him to inform Rox of the details, if he had nothing to hide.

"Mom no....I can't do it."

"Why not baby...if you let her know, then later on in your relationship it could come up and she won't believe you."

"I'll think about it later."

Brian walked off to get his self and thoughts together. He went back and forth about how he would tell Rox. He really didn't want to go to the party that her cousin was giving. Even though Kane was a good dude, his boy's might not be. When gangs hang around each other, sometimes situations happen out of control. Even though it might do him some good to get to know her family a little more, the idea of partying with the unknown, was a little unusual.

Brian decided to take a run around Powderhorn Park. It was cold as hell out, but he really needed to take a run. He tested his self. Run 5 blocks and walk 2, run 3, walk 1. He did this for about 30 minutes. After finishing, he made it back to the house to shower and watch a little TV.

On the other side of town, Rox had just finished at work. She only went to school half a day, because her grades were so good. That gave her time to work, until 6pm. Then she would have the rest of the day to herself. Going back and forth to St. Paul daily was a hassle, so she transferred her job to Minneapolis. Everyone would crack on her for working at Hardees for so long, being as though most of the hoochie's in her school were sack chasers.

It was the thang to have a D boy. The ladies room gossip was always about what nigga was holdin what, who was curb servin for who, or who had the flyest whip. Well in Rox' case, she didn't have to worry about the police or dope fiends runnin up in Brian's crib. That was a relief, plus her baby had much respect in the streets. Even if nigga's plotted to run in his crib or kidnap her, they would get dealt with and they knew it.

Rox loved it, she sucked it up. So many girl's were jealous of her. Everytime she went to any club or concert, her man was there faithfully. Leanna use to attend the same school that Rox goes to now. She just graduated last year, so some of her friends are still there. They always tried to make it hard for Rox.

One day, Rox was picking Tasha up from Folwell Jr. High. It was her last day of seventh grade. Rox was rolling Brian's black and gray Denali, with chrome rims. She was already nervous, because he barely let her drive his truck, without him being in it. As she pulled off from the school, she noticed a white and gold Honda following her. She didn't want to make Tasha scared, so she road around to try and shake the driver's. When she realized it was two girl's in the car, she was relieved and pulled her bat out. Tasha took notice of her getting her weapon out and looked but just kept bobbin her head to the music. She knew her big sister was crazy, but she didn't want to ruin the moment of hangin out with Rox. She slowed down at the Dairy Queen, to pick Tasha up some ice cream. As Tasha made her order for her and Rox, the Honda pulled in on the other side. The driver jumped out and ran up to the front of the truck and started blasting it with eggs. Anyone that knows anything about cars, knows that eggs will fuck a paint job up. Rox didn't know what she was doing right away. As Rox paid for the ice cream, Tasha screamed out, "Look Rox!!!! Look!"

Rox took off running towards the car. By the time she got her bat out, the car was pulling away.

"Fuckin bitches...hatin ass hoes!" Rox yelled out and made one big swing at the top of the trunk of the Honda. Even though it left a dent in the girl's car, she knew Brian wasn't gonna let her drive anymore.

At the time, she never knew who the two girls were. One year later is when she figured out it was Leanna and her cousin. The day she showed up at Brian's house to talk, is when she saw her car. That's the reason why Rox snapped out. When she took Brian his car back, she told him about what happened. He didn't trip when she told him what color the car was. It never dawned on her that that was his reason for being so nice.

Even though he was pissed off, Rox didn't do anything wrong. After talking to Brian, Rox went to pick Tasha up from her moms after work.

He was catching up on a little TV, and doing an inventory check. She didn't feel like helping him, so she told him she'll be home later and made her way to St. Paul.

Everything was the same. The local D boy's still hung out at the Pop Shop. Oxford Community Center was still backed with high rollers and curb servers. She scooped up Angie and Mo to catch up on the latest gossip.

Mo and Jay was still living together. Angie and Coop were doing okay, except for his disappearing acts, with Tara. Rox sometimes felt like it was her fault, but in another case, if Tara didn't save her from Terrance's crazy ass that day, then it would of been a problem.

Rox laughed and kicked it with her girl's, like old times. They made plans to go to Kane's party, that everyone was talking about. It was flyers and billboards up. Kane said he was gonna do it big. His flyer told people that if you bring drama, then drama will come for ya ass. The women had to be in dresses or booty shorts, and heels. The dude's couldn't wear any sneakers.

Rox smiled at her big cousin, while looking at the flyer in her hand. Tasha was excited and couldn't even go. She told Rox that the girl's in her school were going , with their fake ID's. Rox just smiled and let her know that if they get caught then they will go to jail.

This didn't mean nothing to Tasha. Shit, she was fourteen now and big thangs excited her. So just to hear the gossip afterwards turned her on. Rox promised to tell her the details.

Rox dropped Angie and Mo back off and made plans to hit the mall Friday, to pick out something to wear. Before heading back to Minneapolis, she needed to holla at Kane. When she made it to his house, as usual, it was drama.

Kane had two girl's fighting in front of the house, while his ass sat in the car smokin a blunt and listening to music. Rox just shook her head.

"What's up player." Rox was talking to Kane through the window. Bam! Bam! Bam! "Turn that damn music down."

"Oh shit....I'm sorry lil cuz....I didn't see you."

"I know yo dumb ass is watching them chicken heads over there."

"I know, I told them hoes to leave, but they won't, so I'm chillin in the car."

"They might argue all night!"

"Well fuck it....I'll go get me a hotel, shit!"

"You crazy boy...you wanna come kick it with me and Brian for the night?"

"Nah cuz, I'm gonna chill...I got to get ready for the player party."

"Yeah, everybody been talking about it."

"I know, I spent like 10 g's already and still ain't done yet. Shit, nigga's better not clown or I'm poppin their ass!" Rox laughed hard. Her cousin would still wild Bill on yo ass.

"Well, I just came to check on you and let you know me and my people's will be there."

"Cool! Tell him to bring whoever's cool, but let him know I don't want NO shit."

"Boy please, my baby don't play No games...he respects you...he wouldn't fuck up yo shit."

"Good, cause I plan on making this my job."

"Ha ha....what...your job?"

"Parties...shit, I'm good at it and I know how to do it so I can get big money for it, after that I'll move on to promoting concerts." "Give me a hug nigga...I got to go."

After the hug and kiss, Rox was ready to pull off.

"Yo cuz...come a little early okay?"

"Why?"

"So you can help me out with the door."

"Yeah, yo ass don't trust nobody with your loot huh?"

"Hell nah!" Rox rolled her window up and threw up the peace sign.

Chapter 15

Money Don't Matter

Ring! Ring! Ring!
"Hello."
"Get up hot girl, it's party time baby!"
"Um um hum."
"Roxane!!!! Get up girl, come scoop me and Angie before Coop changes his mind." Rox wasn't feeling it. It was time to go shopping, but her heart wasn't into it. She had a bad feeling ever since she saw her big cousin three days ago.

She had been having dreams of herself dying and Terrance killing her. Even though she heard that Carl and Terrance had both moved on. She still felt threatened by their presence. This party was so off the chain with promotion, that she was sure they both would be there. Her gut feeling said somebody was gonna die.

"What Coop gonna change his mind about?" Rox got up with the phone, and walked to the bathroom. Brian's voice was so loud with customer's, so she shut the door to the store. He looked back and blew her a kiss. It made her feel good to know that he was in good spirits. He really didn't want to go to this party, but he was going for her.

"Coop gave Angie five G's to go shopping, and he gave her his Lac, so we can ball."

"Word?"

"Yeah...and he said he was takin her out to dinner tonight, because he has something to talk to her about."

"Uumm...Imagine that."

"Yeah, dat's what I said."

"Well ya'll come get me, so Brian can handle his business today."

"Cool, do we got to bring Tasha?"

"Nah, we'll swing by City Center and on our way to Mall of America, we'll pick her up."

"Cool, I'm a bring Jay's daughter."

"Ah, damn girl! I don't feel like being bothered with all them damn kids!"

"Shut up, shit...I got to hold my man down, while he get's that paper."

"How many rugrats you bringin?" She didn't want to be bothered with them damn kids, because Tasha was enough. She felt Monique was stupid for being with him. He was nice and had lots of paper, but she wouldn't be with no man, that has all them kid's.

"Just his daughter...dang!"

"Ha ha...don't get hot at me girl, check that nigga for dumping them bay bays on you!"

"What! Well, I'll be there at 11:00." Click.

"Damn Mo...ha ha ha." She knew that she pissed Mo off. She had to make it up to her friend.

After showering and doing her hair, she went downstairs, to check on Brian.

"Baby, I'm going to get us some suits for the party." Brian finished with the last customer.

"What we wearing?" He's now holding Rox, with his hands on her ass. "You better stop, before you have to close the store and handle your business." Brian was cheesin from ear to ear.

"Yeah Water, I'm gonna have to be here all day. It's money to be made." Rox now steps back, because more people have entered the store. "Okay, well I see Monique and Angie pulling up outside. I need some more money!"

He made her step back in the house, so the customers wouldn't see his stack. After giving her five G's and instructing her not to buy no faggot shit, he embraced her with a kiss, to let her know he loved her. It was weird, because he didn't feel up to the party either.

This was the biggest 'shing ding', since the All Star game or the Super Bowl came to Minnesota. All his boy's were going out of territory to go to this party. Rappers and strippers would be there to perform. Nobody had ever done anything like it. By it being broadcast all on the radio, that made it an even bigger event.

"Hold up Baby, before you come in swing by Jan's Chinese on Lake and Chicago okay?"

"Ah..Baby, we ain't going to dinner with Coop and Angie later?"

"What you talking about?" The customer's were getting impatient, because Brian's sales clerk didn't know what tires fit on what car.

"Monique said...."

"What I tell you about getting in their business?"

She didn't want to upset him, so she kept quiet. "I know Baby, but I thought we were going..."

"Look Water, go handle your business and just get home as soon as the mall closes okay?" Smooch! Smooch!

"Ha ha, okay Baby!"

Rox got in the car with her girl's. The first thing Monique said was "Why you dis me like that?" She had to convince her that she meant well and that she's too good to be going through shit with him.

Rox wouldn't talk much anyway, because his daughter was in the car. You know anything you say around kids, will get repeated, so it better be the truth. They know when you're talking in code, about them and their parents! It's like kids are in their own bodies, with grown people's minds.

Rox had no understanding of Monique wanting the little girl to come anyway. Well I guess that's what people do to try and keep their man. Rox learned from her sister Lili, that having a baby for a nigga, will for sho make them run far away.

Shit, Lili has them seven damn kid's, by six nigga's and two of them are worth something and the other four ain't even worth talking about. Mrs. Vicki is the only one that helps Lili and she doesn't appreciate it. Every now and then, Rox will let them come with her and Brian. Even when the booster comes through with clothes, she'll pick them something out.

It seemed like forever tryin to get to the mall. Once they made it to Dayton's, it was hell tryin to find parking. It was close to Easter, so that was probably the reason for all the traffic. As soon as they made it inside, the little girl had to use the bathroom and then wanted to get ice cream. Angie took it all in. She thought it was so funny. The little girl was getting on Rox' nerves and she hadn't even given her a chance.

"Why you so quiet Rox, huh? Ha ha "

"Shut up Angie, you know how I feel about that little girl hangin with us."

Monique was tending to the girl, so she couldn't hear what they were saying, so she didn't say much. It hurt her feelings that Rox wouldn't be proud of her having a man. Everyone wasn't fortunate enough to get a prince like she had ran into. Shit, Monique wasn't jealous of her girl, but she did have it going on.

"What ya'll whispering about?" Angie ignored her. Rox walked off and picked up a dress off the rack.

"Ain't this cute Mo?" She knew Rox was blowing smoke up her ass, out of guilt.

"Un hun...but you heard me."

"Heard you what?"

"Nothing girl, let me see another color." Monique was playing it off for now, but she would let Rox have it later.

"They have pink and silver."

"Cool, I'm gonna try on the silver."

After looking around The Oval Room, the girl's headed towards the kid's section. Rox let up off the little girl, because she wasn't complaining at all. She was doing everything they said. She took a liking to Rox, probably because she didn't like her at first. She had to kick herself in the ass, because she was real childish for not liking a kid, just because the daddy was cheating on her friend.

"Baby, is it anything you like?"

"Yeah Roxy, I want that." The little girl pointed to the gumball machine. It was displayed in the middle of the floor, in the kid's section. "That's it Baby?"

"Yep!" Damn, that was simple. Rox started to like her so much, that she even thought about babysitting sometimes. Then that thought went quickly out the window.

It was going on 2:00 pm. After hitting Footlocker and Charles Men's Wear, Rox picked Brian a Versace shirt and some gator shoes in case he wanted to get fly on them. She had to pick Tasha up and head to the Mall of America. They slid over to Lake Street, to see if she could find a fly suit to match his.

After hitting the hood store, they went up on Lake and Hennepin. This was the bourgeois area, and if you didn't look like you were gonna spend some money, they sure would let you know it. Nobody in the car wanted to spend all their money on one thing, so they headed to the big mall. The only thing about shopping out there was you was sure to see everybody out there. Rox was trippin, cause she didn't want no one looking like her and Brian.

"Yo, let me go scoop Tasha up."

"You wanna drive, cause I'm not too familiar with your hood."

"Nah girl." Rox said, while rolling her eyes. "You know Coop's ass will kill me...plus I don't wanna hear Brian's mouth at all." Angie rolled her eyes and got in the driver's seat.

"Don't be mad shit!...I'm just saying, ya'll on good terms, shit." Angie threw her hand in the air.

"Whatever, just tell me where to go." Rox gave Angie the directions.

When they made it there, Tasha was sitting on the steps crying.

"What's wrong?" Rox and Mo jumped out the car and ran towards Tasha. "Nothing, I just been sitting here for two hours."

"Oh shit....why? Ain't school out at 2:00 pm?"

"No." Tasha had her hands folded and stomped her way to the car. Rox and Mo looked at each other and laughed.

"It ain't funny." Tasha had a major attitude. Rox knew she was wrong. It had totally slipped her mind, that she got out of school early.

"Chill Baby, I'm a hook you up when we get to the mall, okay?" Tasha just nodded her head yes.

The ride was long again. When they made it to the mall, once again, it was packed. Being as though this was the biggest mall in the world, tourist visited this place daily. This made shopping even harder. They had every store you could think of, so they would sure find something.

They walked around and ate, shopped and played video games. Everybody ended up finding what they wanted.

Angie went in the Gap, and found Coop his whole outfit. She got him some white on whites from Footlocker. He was so fine, it didn't matter what he wore, he would look good regardless.

Monique had to get Jay some ole pimp shit. He was an older player, so gators or linen suits was his forte'. When she found his outfit and gators, she was ready to go.

Rox went into Banana Republic, to find her something. She got a knit shirt and a leather vest, with a tight fitting skirt, with matching boots, that she found in Nordstroms.

The next stop was to The Limited. They had to buy the little girl and Tasha something. Angie went in to entertain the girl's, while Mo and Rox sat on the bench. Mo had to lay into her ass, for tryin to talk about her to Angie.

"So Rox, you think cause you got it going on, you better than everybody else?"

"Huh? Where is all this coming from?"

"You know...shit, yo ass got dragged through the dirt with Carl and nobody talked about your ass." Rox didn't want to argue with Mo, cause she was her dog and she was right.

"Look Sis, I'm a let you have that okay...I ain't tryin to trip."

"Good, as long as you know I love you too, but you ain't no better then me."

"Aight."

Sometimes, you just have to suck shit up. When you're wrong, you're wrong. Shit, it's hard to find friends. True genuine friends that got yo back, so when you get out of line, they have to put you in your place.

"Look what we got Rox." Both girl's ran up to Mo and Rox, to show off their new clothes.

"That's pretty...now let's eat!" They all went to grab a meal, before taking that long ride home.

After making it back to the south side, Rox had Angie make a quick stop at Jan's. Rox went in to order egg foo yung with shrimp sauce, shrimp wontons and chicken fried rice with butter fried shrimp. The food was smelling so good, that Rox had to get extra, in case somebody wanted some. She had to savor the moment. Everytime Brian said order Chinese, she knew he had something to talk to her about.

She instructed Angie to drop Tasha off first. After reaching her house, she ran in to check on her mom and Mr. D. Her mom had told her to be careful at that party. She let her know that her gut was telling her that the party was gonna get crashed. She didn't know what, but she knew it would be something.

Mrs. Vicki called Kane to have a talk with him, and told Rox about it. He insisted that he had high security and he wasn't on no gang bangin shit. He also let her know about his future plans to be a party promoter and concert promoter.

After kicking it for a minute with Mom, she went to the crib. She instructed Angie and Mo not to call Darlene. She didn't want to be bothered with that hoe. She was shady, after Rox found out that she was fucking with Denise.

They didn't entertain Rox. They was cool with that, even though they figured Rox still had feelings for Carl. He was her first love and you know what they say about your first. She let them know to be ready early tomorrow, because she had to help Kane at the door.

"Bye ya'll!" The girl's pulled off. Honk! Honk!

"Holla Baby!"

Rox struggled to get the bags in the house. Brian seen her, so he ran out to help her. "I'm glad you made it home...I got a surprise for you."

"Good Baby." Smooch. Rox gave Brian a kiss right in the middle of the side walk. They made it in the house, with about eight bags and three bags of Chinese food. They got all settled in, before Brian gave her the surprise.

"What's that smell Baby?" Rox could smell something coming from the bathroom.

"That's your love scent candles that you had under the sink."

"Ha ha, how you gonna use my stuff boy!" She had plans herself for a special night with him. I guess he beat her to it.

"Cause I can...shit, I don't know much about all that romance stuff, but I can set the mood a little." Smooch.

"Good Baby, as long as it's for me...I'm cool."

"Who else it gonna be for?" Brian pulled the three carat pink diamond out of his pocket, while kissing Rox. He laid it behind her back, so she would be surprised to see it.

"Um...this is good Baby."

"I know, put the gravy sauce on it." They both ate until they got full. Brian didn't want to eat much, because once all that food moves around in your stomach while freakin, he knew from experience, that getting your freak on after eating would cause major farts.

The night was set right. The snow began to fall lightly. After watching Belly and Streets are Watchin, Rox began to get sleepy. "Baby, where is my surprise at?"

"Right here." Brian began to kiss and caress her nipples. This is all Rox wanted. It had been a while, since Brian gave her the ultimate treatment. For a minute, he was giving her quickies, and she thought her relationship was going sour. But tonight, has proved her wrong.

"Um Baby, I need you to tell me you love me."

"Water...I wanna marry you....I wanna do big thangs."

He pulled her off the bed and made his way to the bathroom sink. He bent her over and slid in. He beat it up with force, while she tried to hold on to the walls.

"Yes....Brian yes....oooh..yes baby, I love you!" This made him real excited, but he didn't want to come yet. He pulled out and lifted her waist up to his face. His whole face was in it backwards, and Rox couldn't breath.

"Oh...Brian...oh God! Oh Baby...whatever you want Baby!" After Brian heard that, he knew that it was on. Anything he had to tell her, now would be the time to do it. He finished putting it down and putting her right to sleep.

Brian couldn't sleep. Something about this party turned him off. Trying to convince her, was out of the question. (Huh, maybe going wouldn't be so bad after all. I know this nigga and his boy's better not try no funky shit or I got something for him. Oh damn, I forgot this is my girl's cousin, I'm talking about, shit. Well, I'm just gonna stick my 380 glock in my shoe, just in case...just in case them nigga's Carl or Terrance wanna act a fool. I know them nigga's still want my girl. Yeah, they know my baby is a dime piece and she's highly educated.)

"Ha ha." Brian's thoughts were broken, as he looked out the window. Rox was talking in her sleep.

"Baby come get in the bed too."

"I am Water...just go to sleep."

"I can't, I'm cold without you." He climbed back in the bed with her, and held her in his arms, as she drifted back to sleep.

He continued to think, as the night went on. He tossed and turned, all night, with bad thoughts of Rox getting killed. When these thoughts came in, he would pray on his knees and quote Bible scriptures that all the old folks in his past taught him. After about three hours, he finally made it to sleep peacefully. The next day was a whole turn of events. They both were awakened with Angie and Coop waking them up.

"Yo, ya'll get up...shit we got to get ready!" Rox wouldn't even open her eyes, because her rest was so peaceful. It felt so good to be in her baby's arms, that she knew this was her never ending relationship.

"Shit, ya'll know how to fuck up a wet dream!" She jumped up, to get ready.

"I know, shit, how in the hell did ya'll get in here?"

"Nigga don't act...now you know I got keys." Coop stood, waving the keys in his face.

"Back the fuck up shit...I ain't even got rid of the dancin devil."

"Ha ha, I know nigga, ya'll go fix that shit, cause you're stinkin up this room, with that hot breath."

"Shut up Coop, your's stank when it ain't morning."

Angie grabbed Coop by the arm to lead him out the door. She didn't want to irritate her friend, by ruining the rest of the day. Coop was always trying to jone, and sometimes this pissed Brian off. Brian knew his boy had his back on every situation, but he would be disrespectful at times. On many occasions, Brian had to check him, about his attitude. He always dusted it off, as Brian was trippin.

Everybody got dressed to run around and do errands for the shop. Angie and Coop was all over each other in the back seat. Rox was trippin, because he had a whole new attitude. He was just with Tara two days ago. Now he was in the back seat, acting like a freshly in love man. Brian told Rox to mind her own business, so she did as she was told. Watching Coop made her sick to her stomach. She kept thinking Brian was doing the same thing. Even though she had no proof at all, it still lingered in her mind, about that letter. Bringing it up now, would ruin the day, but she just had to know.

As they approached the back of the chop shop, to pick up some supplies, Rox looked around and saw that white Honda following them. She kept watching Brian look in the rearview mirror, like he was nervous about something. She just blew it off, as him trippin. This gave her reason to question the thoughts that were in her head.

"Brian baby, what's wrong?" Beads of sweat formed on his head, as he got ready to step out the car.

"What's wrong with what?" He said, as he kissed her for a long time. She pulled back from him. She knew he was nervous about that car following them.

Slap! Slap! Slap! This stopped Coop and Angie from kissing and cuddling.

"Yo, you trippin....you better quit slapping me girl!" Brian hurried out the car and ran in the shop to see if his stuff was ready. He kept looking out the window, to keep an eye on Rox and the car Leanna was in.

"Damn...damn." Brian paid as he punched the wall.

"Yo..yo amigo, what's up with you?" The Mexican yelled, as everyone in the shop looked at Brian. Everyone drew their gun, thinking he was on some jack shit.

"Chill ya'll, I ain't on nothing....just give me my shit, so I can dip."

The convicts went back to their work, as they watched Brian through one eye. This made them a little nervous, because they knew Brian would snap at any moment. So handling business with him quick, was a must.

As he turned to leave, he seen someone walking towards the back door. Here we go again as he thought and watched Leanna come towards him. He tried to play it off and push past her, but Rox was already out the car and ready for action.

"Let me holla at you Brian!" Leanna yelled, as she tried to catch up to him. (What does this stalking bitch want? Shit, I already got the test.) Brian's thoughts broke, as Rox flipped out her six inch pocket knife and swung.

"Yo..hold up Boo!" Brian tried to grab Rox, as she chased Leanna around the car.

"Oh shit...help me!" Leanna ran back to her car, but didn't quite make it. Rox sliced her right across her left shoulder, as she jumped in her car and locked the door. Rox ran around to the other side of the car, and tried to open the door.

"Open the door bitch and fight me hoe!" Rox yelled and caused everyone in the shop to run out to watch the excitement. The men cheered on in spanish. They chanted her on, as she tried to bust her window, with a pop can. Most of the people out there laughed and pointed.

"Fuck...fuck...I'm sick of you bitch!"

"Come on Boo...let's go baby...fuck her." Angie grabbed on to Rox to put her in the car. As Brian finally got her to sit in the car. Angie went back to Leanna's car, to make sure she was okay. This pissed Rox off, because she wanted that hoe out of her life. Angie wanted Leanna to not press charges.

"Yo, roll your window down." Angie convinced her to crack her window. Leanna had her shirt wrapped around her arm, to stop the blood from flowing. One of the guy's in the shop, gave Angie a first aid kit to give to her.

She opened the door with fear, as she grabbed the kit from Angie. She tried to hurry and slam the door, but Angie's body was in the way. Brian, Rox and Coop looked on, as Angie spoke her peace.

"Yo...you know if you try and call the police, you're going to jail." Leanna ignored her and continued to treat herself. Slap! "Hey hoe, you hear me."

"Ouch!" Leanna started backing into the passenger seat.

"Chill, I ain't going to the police." Angie seen the fear written all over her.

"Why in the fuck are you stalking a nigga that don't want you?" By this time,

Angie had caught Leanna by the neck. Coop came running out the car.

"Yo Angie...chill girl, before the po po comes!" Coop grabbed Angie and pulled her away. As Angie backed up enough for Leanna to slam the door, she yelled "cause that dirty dick nigga got that package and I hope he dies!"

Angie and Coop looked at each other in shock. Even though Coop knew that his boy didn't have shit, cause he went with him to the doctor. Coop would never tell Angie or Rox, but it felt good to know Brian was HIV negative.

On their way home, Angie kept asking Coop what Leanna meant by her last comment. Brian nervously looked through the rearview mirror and watched Coop's actions. The music was so loud, that Rox never paid attention to the eye contact that Brian gave Coop. She ran her mouth, about how she knows for a fact, that he has cheated on her with Leanna.

After dropping Coop and Angie off, Rox continued to lay into Brian. Pow! Rox continued to lay into Brian's head.

"Chill...chill girl, I told your ass ain't nobody cheated on you, shit!" Rox continued to fight him and cry out.

"Yes you did....bitch you don't love me nigga!"

As Brian pulled into the driveway of the house, Rox jumped out and ran in, before the car stopped. He quickly turned the car off and ran behind her. All thoughts went through his mind, because he knew that his girl was crazy. He thought she was running into the house to get a gun, knife or bat to beat him with.

"Open the damn door, girl!" Brian stood back, to break it down. His mom was gone and the store was closed, so nobody would hear him. He made up his mind to whoop her ass, because he was tired of the disrespect.

"No bitch!"

"Girl, what I tell you about that shit...I ain't that nigga!" He started kicking the door. Bam! Bam! His foot was getting tired. "Open the door girl..." Bam! Bam! "I love you..shit!"

Rox cried out. "No you don't!"

"Stop crying, let me in so we can talk, please." He continued to kick the door and wiggle the lock. Rox let him keep beggin and when she opened it. Bloom! Bam! "Ouch....oh...oh...girl!"

Rox opened the door and he fell flat on the floor and hit his head, against the chair.

"Ha ha ha...that's what you get." She said, while pointing at him.

"Shut up."

Chapter 16

Karma Gotcha

Kane was just putting the finishing touches on the locks. He had to check out every door and window, to make sure security did their job. He was happy to look around the place, and see where all his money went. He was finally doing something he enjoyed and made lots of money.

This party would include Next, Mint Condition, Low Key and the highly anticipated rap group called Heat Roc. Even though he asked for Prince to come through, it was said by his management, that he already made promises to someone's wedding reception. That didn't stop Kane, because all of the out of town people will enjoy themselves, and bring exposure to "Shine Sota." Yeah, we up in our city just like everybody else. Garnett and Culpepper got special invites, along with Jimmy Jam and Terry Lewis. Aunt Judy use to go with Terry Lewis in high school, so she hollered at him, to inform some of his friends.

Kane started sweating bullets, because the thought of something going wrong, just wouldn't leave his mind. He laughed it off, as just nervousness or butterflies, but his gut told him different. He decided to call Rox, to see what's taking so long.

Ring! Ring!

"Yeah, whad up?"

"That ain't no way to answer no phone."

"Ha...my fault dog, I thought..."

"Chill man, let me speak to little cuz."

Brian was a little irritated, by his slick talk. "Hold on." Slam! The phone dropped, on the floor. When Rox returned, she wondered what Brian was so upset about, all of a sudden.

"Hello."

"Ah baby cuz, you was suppose to be here to help me...dat nigga got you..."

"Chill Kane, damn...shit! He ain't got me nothing! We are getting ready now!"

"What's with the flip talk?"

"I ain't flipping I'm just saying he don't disrespect you, so don't dis him."

"Okay, okay, chill baby cuz...we ain't gonna get into that..my fault, tell homeboy my fault and I'm waiting on ya'll to come through before it get's too packed."

"What! You don't got us a table for six reserved?"

"Yeah girl...now you trippin shit, don't ask stupid questions."

Rox smiled and said "Aight, we on our way."

"Make sure you tell homeboy I'm a little nervous, that's why I'm trippin, so don't take it to heart." Click.

"Damn." Rox said out loud and she walked to the bathroom to finish combing her hair.

"What's up?" Rox turned to look at Brian.

"What's up...I'm getting ready." Brian started pacing the floor, with his head down. He was contemplating on telling Rox, but he just couldn't do it. He knew it would ruin the mood. Even though Kane had pissed him off, he still held his composure.

"What boy...let it out, shit!"

"You better stop yelling at me, like I'm some fucking kid!" Brian grabbed her by the back of her neck, with the flat iron still in her hand.

This startled Rox, because this wasn't him at all.

"Stop Brian, that hurts!" She now sat back down in the chair and looked into his eyes. He took his finger and put it right in her face and squeezed her neck.

"Let me tell you something, just because I don't like hitting women don't mean I won't whoop your ass. I'm tired of the disrespect."

"Slee....ouch...." He squeezed harder.

"Yeah, and next time you ain't getting no warning..." Smooch. After kissing Rox real hard on the lips, he walked away and went outside to start the car up.

"This nigga is crazy." She said out loud, while sliding her skirt up. She knew he meant business and her attitude better change, before she loses him.

Honk! Honk!

"Come on girl, everybody is waiting on us!"

"Okay, I'm coming!" Rox ran around the house and put all her stuff away. Dudes can always put on anything and look right. Then they have the nerve to be impatient. She checked everything and put her mace, six inch knife and mini baseball bat in her purse. She knew hoes will try and test you at a party like this, because nobody was getting in with a gun.

Kane had security on lock. He even put his gun up, so nobody's life would be threatened.

Everybody was on their way to the party. Rox and Brian looked real good. He wasn't feeling up to party, until they pulled on the block of Selby Avenue. Cars were parked back to back. Traffic was thick for three blocks. Angie seen cars park on people's lawn. Some people parked in the alley ways.

Police was tight and instead of causing a problem, they took this as an opportunity to make money. 5-0 charged everybody $15 to park in the alley and the local residents charged $20. The whole neighborhood felt good for the come up, but were also afraid of what the outcome could be. It was almost guaranteed that drama would kick off in an event filled with hoodlums.

Brian parked the truck right next to Kane's Cadillac. Angie, Rox and Coop conversed and looked on in amazement, while waiting for Brian to walk from the truck.

"Hey Monique, we're over here!" Monique and Jay were walking towards them. They looked fly as hell. Jay had on his pimp suit with matching gators.

"What's up young one, you bout to break some hearts huh?"

"Your so crazy Jay...how you doing?" Rox blushed, as her and Angie gave Jay a hug. They all exchanged greetings, as they walked in the door. It was only 9:00 and it was packed at the front door.

Once they made it inside, it wasn't that many people in there. Mint Condition was on stage singing "Pretty Brown Eyes", as people sang along, while checking their coats in.

"What took your ass so damn long?" Kane said, while grabbing Rox by the neck and giving her a kiss on the cheek.

"You know I had to get cute."

"Hun...hun, I seen your old..."

"What's up cousin Kane?" Brian greeted Kane with a pound. Kane was caught off guard, because he didn't see him. Kane turned and pasted on the pound and gave Brian a hug.

"My fault for earlier dog...I'm just happy this..."

"Chill cuz, you don't have to explain dog, I know you...we family." Kane felt good about Brian's attitude. Rox and Angie looked on in shock.

Coop and Jay was happy they were in his presence. Kane was known for his willyn out on folks, so to see him calm, made them at ease.

"Yo, what was you gonna say when I walked up Cuz?" Kane hesitated at first, cause he didn't want no drama. If he didn't tell who he saw, then it would be a betrayal and his family couldn't get caught off guard.

"Oh, ah..I was just gonna tell baby cuz I saw her ex up in here."

"Who?" Brian is now sweating with anger, because he didn't have his heater on him. Rox seen his change in attitude. Angie and Coop looked at each other, in slight fear. Monique and Jay laughed, because they knew Carl wasn't gonna do shit. Every chance he got, he talked to Mo and Jay about Rox. He wasn't over her at all. Even though he went on to have a baby by Denise, he still couldn't get over her. That's why, he wouldn't miss this party for nothing in the world.

"I saw Carl checking his coat in...chill dog, nothing ain't gonna happen okay?"

"Oh I know ain't shit gonna happen...dat nigga better recognize...dis is my water, my fresh water..."

"Hey what's up Roxane Adams?"

Just like that, out of nowhere, Carl rolled up on the scene, without anybody noticing him. He had a crew of nigga's with him and they was ready for whatever. Rox didn't recognize any of the dudes, so she got real nervous. She broke out into a sweat and grabbed Brian's hand, to assure him that she was with him.

Brian grabbed Rox and kissed her and said, "she don't respect chumps that call her by her government, you dig?" Brian was pissed off, because he knew exactly what Carl was tryin to do.

"Oh...well not when I was knockin the bottom out that shit." Brian let go of Rox and started to lunge at Carl.

"Chill baby...I got this." He stood back and let his woman handle the situation. Everybody made a small circle.

"Carl Watkins, I haven't seen you in two years nigga."

"Nigga...what?"

"Yeah Nigga, I got a man...he's a real man, so I'd appreciate it if you don't disrespect my man." She turned around and kissed him. Carl stepped right up on them.

"And so yeah! It won't be for long." He threw his hands up in the air and walked on with his crew.

"Damn...Rox girl, you still got niggas hollering about you." Some girl said, while the crowd went their separate ways.

"Yeah, dat means dat pussy is the f-i-r-e you know." Another dude said, while slapping his boy's hand.

"What you say?" Rox started running towards the crowd of people that were talking about her.

"Hey chill baby cuz...damn." Kane grabbed her and told her that "when people stop talking shit about you, that's when you get upset, okay?"

"Okay cuz, I'm sorry. I won't ruin this for you."

"Thanks, now let's go kick it!" Kane gave Rox a hug and a kiss.

As he walked away from her through the crowd of people, she seen him holding his side.

"B baby! Look at Kane, he is holding himself." Brian not paying any attention, is heading towards the dance floor.

"Come on girl, I'm ready to party." He started doing the two step to Red and Meth's "I Get High."

"No, something is wrong with my cousin!" Rox stormed off, with an attitude, and headed for Kane.

"Wait girl!" Brian is running behind her, with his drink spilling all over the floor and causing people to slip as they try and see what's going on. As she made her way through the crowd, she seen Kane being held up by Darlene, while he was holding his side.

"What's up....ah...ah, what the fuck happen to my cuz?" Rox walked around hollering and screaming. As she ranted and raved about Kane being half way passed out on the floor, she didn't realize that Terrance was laying in the cut, watching the whole scene.

"Kane! Kane! K-a-a-a-n-e wake the fuck up!" Rox seen blood coming from his chest, but knew that he couldn't of been shot or stabbed, because everybody was checked at the door.

Mo, Angie and Coop made it off the dance floor. They headed towards the crowd faster, because they could hear Rox yelling and screaming. Rox was finally able to get Kane to talk.

"Baby Cuz...that nigga T walked up on me...." Kane was losing focus again.

"Wake up....what the fuck did he do to you?" Kane was losing a lot of blood and felt cold coming over him.

"Caaall the pooolice babbby cuzzz." He started blinking and sweating, because Terrance walked right up and stood over him.

"The police and ambulance is on the way, okay baby?" Rox was praying and crying at the same time. "Lord please, please let my cousin live. He just getting legit. Please Lord, amen."

She looked over the crowd and seen what Kane was so afraid of. There was the so tuff Terrance standing there, with an ice pick dangling, right in her face. Rox jumped up and charged him.

"You punk! You hurt my cousin!" She was hitting T all upside his head. He tried to make a break for it, but her grip was tight.

"Let me go bitch!" He slapped the breath out of her, causing her to fly into Brian. As she laid there trying to shake that blow off, Brian socked him in his right temple then a left upper cut to his jaw. That caused him to fall and the ice pick went flying.

The party goers ran everywhere. They seen Kane laying in a puddle of blood, as he ran the story down to Darlene & Angie, Coop and Jay fought off Carl and his crew, thinking that they were the cause of this. Carl backed up towards the door and tried to make it out, but Jay socked him in his lip.

"Ah man chill! I didn't stab him dog!" Carl holding his mouth, while Jay continued to lay hay makers on him. He tried to run, after taking an ass whooping. Jay grabbed Carl and walked him outdoors.

The ambulance came and they took Kane away. Rox made it out of her daze and still wasn't finished with Terrance. "Angie, where is that nigga T?" She looked around, to see the party damn near empty. All she could think of was how happy her cousin was to go legit.

"I'm not sure, but I know we need to be at the hospital."

"Yeah, I don't think your cuz is gonna make it...look at all that blood." Coop said, while pointing at the blood, that was about 20 feet away.

"All that came out of him?"

"Yeah girl, and my baby Jay is outside beating the shit out of Carl." Rox looked around to see all the people crowded at the door. One thing was weird, she hadn't seen Brian at all, since Terrance knocked her out.

"If Carl is outside, then where is Terrance and Brian?"

"I don't know...oh shit!" Coop ducked, while a glass came flying at him and hitting Angie.

"Oh shit!" Rox ran towards the door, as Terrance and Brian continued to throw blows.

"Didn't I tell you it was over nigga?" Blam! Blam! Brian continued to beat the shoes off T. Terrance was running around the table.

"That's why I killed that nigga....he killed my daddy!" Rox watched on, with a confused look. She knew Kane had done dirt, but for some odd reason, she didn't know what Terrance was talking about. Her and Brian both grabbed him.

"What! What do you mean, he killed your daddy?" He tried running, but Angie and Coop had him cornered in. Slap! Slap! Rox continued to slap the shit out of him.

"Your damn grandma was fuckin my daddy and...." Rox slapped him again, for disrespecting her grandma.

"Don't curse in the same sentence, when speaking on my grandma!"

She stepped back, because all this time, Terrance had been trying to get close to her. His ulterior motive was to kill her or Kane.

"Fuck yo grandma..." That's as far as the words he got, because everybody was beating the shit out of him. Coop jumped in the air and stomped him on his head. Brian kept kicking him in his stomach. Rox fought and cried at the same time. It seemed like a bad dream, that would never go away. Every time she tried to get that night out of her mind, It was still there.

The police came in and stopped everybody from fighting. Rox slid past them, so they wouldn't ask any questions. She didn't know if Brian had a heater (gun) in the car, so she made sure she was out of sight. Once outside, she seen Jay in the police car and Monique pleading with the officer to let him go.

"What's going on Mo?" She explained that Jay had beat Carl, until he pissed all over his self. The dudes he was with didn't help him, but as soon as the po po pulled up, they went to snitchin. Just like a punk ass nigga to start shit, then go tell it when shit get's hot. Mo didn't know that Jay had a warrant for gun possession and that's why they didn't let him go.

Angie, Brian and Coop made it out the party, after being fully searched by the police. Brian said that when the po po found the ice pick, it matched the same blood smeared on Terrance's shirt. Terrance started yelling and cursing about Kane killing his daddy, so that also let them know that the ice pick belonged to him.

"Angie, Rox...we got to go. I just heard them say on that cop's radio, that a victim from this party is in critical condition."

"Oh my God! I forgot all about Kane!" Rox proceeded to run towards the car, with everybody behind her.

"Come on Mo, we'll bail him out!" Mo was confused, she didn't want to leave Jay, but there wasn't shit she could do. She ran towards the car, with Jay all on her mind. Why she even bothered to love him, even she didn't know!

Brian swerved in and out of lanes, so he would make it to the hospital quickly. Angie, Monique and Rox said a prayer for Kane, while Coop directed traffic. As they approached Ramsey County Medical Center, everybody felt a rush come over them.

They watched Darlene as she jumped up and down screaming. It was like a small concert forming around her. Rox and Angie jumped out, so Brian could park. The only thing going through her mind, was why is Darlene crying so hard.

Is she fucking Kane or something? She questioned herself, as she approached D.

"Damn, she trippin Angie." She tried cooling herself, because from the look of the crowd, it seemed to be bad news.

"Um...ah Rox...homegirl, you right. It don't look too good." Rox made it through the crowd. She watched Darlene cry to God, on her knees.

"Hey Darlene, what's going on?" She grabbed her by the arm.

"He's dead! H-e-e-e i-s d-d-e-ad!" She released Darlene's arm, and fell to the ground. Angie fell to her knees.

"God Nooooooo...why?" Brian and Coop just stood there, looking at each other. Monique tried to revive Rox, she laid there, with a blank stare. Tears streamed down her face with anger, hate and confusion, on her mind. She decided that she needed to save herself. Right when Kane was doing good for himself, everything came back on him.

Karma came back on his ass. The grim reaper came stomping on his world, and took him away. She finally came to herself, when Darlene began to tell them what actually happened.

Come to find out, Terrance had been stalking Kane, ever since he's been out. Being as though Rox told Terrance everything about him, he didn't have to look far. Kane and Darlene was standing there kissing, when Kane said it felt like somebody was punching him. Darlene didn't see anybody, because it was so dark. When she finally looked around, Terrance punched him again saying "dat's for my pops...nigga!" After that, Kane buckled and Darlene caught him. She seen blood and started screaming. Kane asked her to lay him down, so he could catch his breath.

"So who said he was dead, because I just asked to be let into the emergency room and they won't give me no info." Rox said, while pacing back and forth.

"The Doctor came out and told me! Rox....we were gonna get married!"

Rox looked up with a confused look on her face. She hadn't checked her cousin out in a while. So she didn't know his business, being as though she was so into Brian and school. Damn, here it is about to be graduation in a couple of months and she just knew her big cousin was gonna be there.

Rox was so hurt that she felt it was her fault. If she would of paid more attention to the snakes that Kane told her about, then he would still be here. Brian felt her pain and gave her a hug and kiss, to assure her he was there for her.

"Why my cousin....why not somebody else? Why not   ?"

"Stop Baby...it's gonna be alright. I'm here for you okay?" Brian didn't want her feeling guilty.

"Let's go check it out."

Angie grabbed Coop and Monique by the arm, so everyone would move into the hospital. The patrons was in fear of walking into the hospital, because of the large crowd of black people. Darlene let everyone know that he was gone, so they would leave.

"Well it was a bomb party!" Some girl yelled at Darlene, trying to make her feel better.

"Yeah, it's sad he had to die, just to make us feel good." Some dude said, while patting her on her back. She nodded in agreement and walked in. As she approached the counter, she seen the doctors and Brian holding Rox.

Even though they fell out two years ago, she still loved her. Rox was gonna feel a little better after knowing that the baby Darlene's carrying, is Kane's. She wasn't as jealous of her anymore, because she would now be family.

"Did you ask the doctor what I already told you?" Darlene said, in a irritating voice.

"Yes damn it, but I had to make sure!" Rox said, yelling on her way out the door.

On their way back to the party, Rox had change on her mind. She was gonna go back to get some of the things Kane had spent his money on. She was gonna make, it up to him, by giving him a nice burial. Knowing that Darlene was loaded with loot, she thought the same thing.

By the time they all made it back to the party, everything was cleaned up. All of Rox' family was there. They had heard about Kane getting killed. The whole family was confused. After all his talk about doing the right thing, this came back on him.

The days leading up to the funeral was hectic. The police didn't have a liking for Kane, whatsoever. So Terrance was able to get out on bail. Being as though the only person that actually watched the whole thing go down was Darlene. She only could explain that she seen Terrance punch Kane. She never saw a ice pick, until he waved it afterwards. When the ice pick was tested, it wasn't enough of Kane's blood to charge Terrance. Terrance said that when he reached out to give Kane a hug, he fell into it. The whole family protested that the police do a further investigation, but it never happened.

Darlene informed everyone that she was three months pregnant. She told the story, as Rox looked on. "He saw me one day on my way to the store. He complimented me on my shape and how he heard I fell out with you." Darlene continued to look at Rox for a response, but she gave her none.

"Rox, did you hear me?" She rolled her eyes and sucked her teeth.

"Yeah girl, I heard you shit....what the fuck you want a cookie? He's gone now!" Rox stormed off, as all the family and friends looked on.

The funeral went pretty well. All the women that were involved with Kane at the time, tried to come and claim their spot. They were trying to get their greedy hands on something he owned, just to have props in the streets. Rox wasn't having it of course. Dismissing them as crumb snatching hoochies that wanted street fame.

As she laid there looking out the basement window of her grandma's house, she thought about college and how she would run her business. She knew that every year over 200 million cards were sold. Plus, 156 million roses are sold also. That meant a lot having that bit of information, because this would get her started. As sad as it was to be thinking of a business while her favorite cousin laid dead in the ground, over some hateful revenge of Terrance, she knew she had to get it together.

It would be perfect to be the first African American floral designer. Her smile got brighter as she thought about how many flowers would be sold at funerals and weddings. More funerals in the hood than weddings, but dollar signs appeared in her eyes. Her smile was broken by her mother.

"Hey you." She was tapping Rox on the shoulder.

"Yes Mom, what's up?"

"What are you thinking about...I know you're hurt from your cousin, but he'll be okay, with the Lord."

"I know Mom, I've accepted that part...I'm just trippin off the part about Terrance." Mrs. Vicki took a seat and so did Tasha and Mr. D.

"Yes Rox honey, you have to be more careful about who you trust." Mr. D said, while hugging Rox.

"I know, Brian tells me that all the time, but I would of never guessed it." They all sat and discussed how obsessed Terrance was about Rox. They still knew he still loved Rox and hoped that with him being out that he would still have the fear of Brian in him.

Mrs. Vicki still felt angry, that nothing was going to happen to him or Carl, for starting it. Carl tried to call and give his condolences, but everyone hung up in his face. Denise had the nerve to try and send a message through Darlene, but Rox cut her off at the knee caps. Stating that "yo ass is lucky I'm even fucking with yo hatin ass! Shit, that baby probably ain't Kane's! Yo ass was fucking girl's and nigga's at the same time! I told yo ass me and my peeps is gonna do a ghetto DNA, and if it don't have none of our trade marks, then you and that baby can bounce!" Darlene tried hard to keep her composure and just dismissed Rox' comments as still being hurt.

"You'll see Water...don't even trip, and when you see, don't try and apologize to me or my baby." Rox rolled her eyes, and put her hand on her hip. That water statement pissed her off. She knew damn well only nigga's call her water.

"Don't let water roll off them lips again."

"Ain't that what your a.k.a. is?"

"Yeah, but not for dykes."

Chapter 17

All Falls Down

Roxane Adams is what my name is. These were her thoughts, as she sucked up the thoughts and reality of her cousin's death. She couldn't deal with the fact that Terrance was walking around fronting, like he had not done nothing wrong.

Murder was on her mind, but she dismissed that thought. Knowing that karma would be sure to catch up with his ass. Waiting on it, was sure to be an impatient process to wait for. As she prayed, she asked the Lord to forgive her for her thoughts and she hoped Kane was up there chillin, with the rest of the family. She also let Kane know that she was sorry for not having his back. She cried over and over, with a dry throat, thinking that her knife, mace and bat could of fought Terrance off.

"Yo Baby, what are you thinking so hard about?" Rox looked up to see Brian tapping her.

"Nothing, I'm sorry...how long have you been here....I got finals to finish." She stood up to give him a hug and gather her school books.

"I've been downstairs with Moms. She's been getting your graduation ready."

"Really....what is she doing? I was gonna do it."

"Well she didn't want you to worry about it, plus her and Darlene was discussing some business proposals for you."

Her eyebrow raised at the thought of Darlene and her having any discussion with her business. Instead of being hostile, Rox decided to give her a chance. Especially now, because she definitely has the loot to help her pursue her dream.

"What, is she gone...."

"No! Water...baby, I will not let you do this any longer. You are gonna give that girl a damn chance!"

"Hold up Brian!" She has her hand on her hip. "Before you cut me off, I was just about to tell you that same shit, you was about to preach okay?" She pointed her finger in his face and causing a scene. As she seen the crowd form, she checked her attitude. "Look....look, I'm not gonna argue with you baby okay.... thank you." She reached out to give Brian a kiss.

They made their way down to the front entrance of the school. Rox called out to her mom, Darlene and Angie. It seemed as if they were up to something, because Brian yelled out that they would meet them by the cars.

She kept telling him that she had two more finals to finish, before graduation, but he ignored her. Her gut told her that she was in for a good surprise, so she wouldn't spoil it, with her being nosy.

She waited in the car patiently and listened to Dre's "Let Me Ride", off the Chronic CD. She bobbed her head and visioned herself having a floral designing company throughout the metro area. She didn't want to be greedy and jump straight out with numerous locations, so she would have one in St. Paul right off Snelling and Grand. Then she would later put one on Lake and Hennepin. Even though the north side wasn't her stomping grounds, she thought that Broadway and Lyndale in the mini mall next to Payless, would be a great location as well. She watched all of her homegirls and mother approach the car.

"What's up Roxy...Water?" Angie said, while hitting her and jumping in the back seat.

"Shit....chillin, listening to Dre and Snoop!" She didn't let them know that she knew they were gonna surprise her. Mrs. Vicki leaned in the car, to give her a hug and kiss. She let her know that her teacher's said that since graduation was only two weeks away, that she could take her finals anytime, before then.

Everyone got in their cars and went their separate ways. Brian hadn't informed her that everyone was gonna meet at the house later, to tell Rox about her surprise. She turned around to face Angie.

"So, what was ya'll in a huddle discussing Angie ?" She was smiling from ear to ear, because she knew Angie couldn't lie to her about nothing.

"Nothing g-u-r-l, you'll see!" She wasn't gonna break and tell Rox shit she thought, as Rox continued to press her.

Rox turned around and started playing with Brian. She laid her head on his shoulder, as he drove to the house. She started licking in his ear and rubbing his man hood. She's been with him for two years now, and marriage was looking real bright, being as though he has put up with her mess.

"I'd love to Water...but if you don't move your hand, I'm gonna crash baby!" Angie busted out laughing and pushed the seat.

"Ha..ha...you're fishing for everything ain't cha! Ha..Ha..ha!"

She took her hand out his pants and laughed."Shut up Angie!" She laid back and waited to get home. As they pulled up to the house, Brian stopped to let Angie jump out and run in. That was pretty odd, but she said nothing. He parked and kissed Rox on the forehead.

"What was that for?" She said, while walking towards the house. He checked the locks on the car door and ran up behind her, so he could make it to the house first, and open the door.

"Because you deserve it and I love you." He grabbed her by the face and held it, as he softly kissed her.

"Hey...hey...enough of that shit, my man ain't here." Angie said, as she clapped her hands telling them to stop. Rox laughed at her.

"You just mad cause Coop ain't got it like my baby got it."

She laughed and said "naw neva that Roxy g-u-r-l, I'm just saying ya'll gonna have all the time in the world to be lovie dubby."

"What is these indirect statements ya'll keep on throwing around?" She was more and more anticipating the surprise, so she decided to lay down.

"Angie, I'm bout to crash out okay? If my Mom calls, tell her I'm gonna come over there later." Angie laughed to herself, because everybody would be over anyway.

"Oh gurl, get you some rest."

Rox went to her room, to take a shower. She was very tired, but at the same time, she wanted to be nosy and find out what the big surprise was.

Angie and Brian decorated the house, once Rox was sound asleep. He put the ghetto lock on the door, so she wouldn't get up and start snooping.

"Put the first picture of ya'll together right there." Angie was pointing at a spot on the middle of the wall.

"Why? I was gonna put it on my door." Angie put her hands on her hips and sized up the spot. Men never know how to decorate anything. See that, Angie was right, he got the hammer and decided to put the picture in place.

"Okay, okay girl, shit....I'm gonna do it, hell, you know bout this better than I do."

Angie smiled, and started preparing the food. Brian finished with the picture and cleaning. As he walked in the kitchen, he could see that Leanna was pulling up outside.

"Yo, Angie look." He was pointing out the window to Leanna's car. Right when Angie took a look out the window....Bam! Crash! Boom!

Leanna took a brick, with a note attached to it and threw it right through Rox's car window and pulled off. Angie immediately ran out the house cursing and snapping. Brian ran upstairs to make sure Rox didn't wake up. As he hoped, she was knocked out snoring. She never snored, so he knew she would be sleep until somebody woke her up. As he made it back downstairs, Angie got started.

"Damn, that hoe won't give up. Shit....what in the hell did you do to her boy?" Brian feeling stupid and didn't feel comfortable trying to explain this to Angie, just shrugged it off. He didn't know that Angie heard her, when she flipped out at the shop that day.

"Do you still think it's a good idea to ask her to marry me?" Angie looked him upside his head.

"Yeah boy....shit, that's mainly what this dinner is for, plus she will be even more excited that my dad, Mrs. Vicki and Darlene is going to get her started on her company."

"Oh okay, well she might reject me."

He headed outside to clean up the mess. As he was cleaning, Coop, Monique, Darlene and Mrs. Vicki pulled up. Everyone parked and thought the worst.

"Did you and Rox get into a fight?" Monique questioned, as her and Jay walked towards the house. Brian ignored her and hoped Angie wouldn't say nothing. Kissing him on the cheek, Mrs. Vicki asked "where's my baby? She's going to be so happy!" Looking at Brian clean up the glass. "Oh... where did all that glass come from? Is my baby okay?" Mrs. Vicki felt something was wrong, as she looked at the brick that was thrown into Rox' windshield. Brian had to think fast, but didn't want to lie and later lose her trust or respect.

"Oh Ma, it's nothing. Somebody has been doing a lot of vandalism in the neighborhood and it seems they want to pick this house for some reason. Don't worry, I'm gonna get it fixed right now....I have a friend that will hook it right up." She didn't say a word, but she had a feeling he wasn't telling her something, but she was happy he loved her daughter, so she'll let Rox handle her own business.

"Okay baby, I'm going to go in and wait on Lili and the kid's okay... oh, is your momma in there?"

"Yes Ma, she's in the office." Brian didn't feel like being bothered with Lili and her bullshit.

"Yo Coop, take this car around the corner to Joe, so he can fix this. Tell him I need it back in about 2 hours, so he don't wake up snapping." Coop assumed what happened, so he didn't ask any questions.

"Aight dog...I see the stalker came through huh?"

"Yeah man and she's like a fuckin roach...she won't go away." Coop laughed at his comment and jumped in the car. He threw the brick out the window and handed Brian the note.

"Forgot something." He said and pulled off. Thank God the shop was around the corner, because Coop would get a big ticket for that. The note read: I-f a-n-d when-you-call your-self-havin-a-weddin-your-life-willend! Brian laughed it off.

"This Bitch is psycho. Damn! I shouldn't of never fucked with her ass!" He talked to his self, all the way into the house. Everybody was getting along just fine and he didn't wanna spoil anything. As time went on, he hoped that Coop would hurry back, with the car.

"Ya'll, I'm gonna finish the decorations, while Rox is still sleeping."

"Oh Brian, I was gonna ask, if you can go pick up Lili and my grandkids because Howard had to get Tasha and Mr. Mackman." He rolled his eyes at the thought, but knew he had to do something to make it up.

"Who is gonna finish cooking?" As he questioned Mrs. Vicki, he could see Darlene pulling up. "Oh Mama, I could get Darlene to do it, since she hasn't gotten out the car yet."

"That's fine son!" She raised an eyebrow, thinking Brian was up to something. He ran outside, to tell Darlene to go pick up Lili and the kid's. She did as she was asked, and made him promise that she wouldn't get the good news without her. He promised and made his way back in the house.

The seven carat ring he bought looked great, as he examined it, and thought about paradise with Roxane.

All of Brian's family made it. Lili and her basketball team was there, along with their close friends. Rox still hadn't woke up, with all the commotion, so

Monique put everyone in position, as Brian went to wake his beautiful water up.

He walked in his room, to find her stretched out butt ass naked, with a blind fold over her eyes and handcuffs in her hand. Damn, she was fine.

He thought, as he approached her. Kissing her and covering her with a blanket, she woke up.

"Oh my God! How long have I been sleep....I got..."

"Chill baby." He crooned and he softly kissed her on her neck and shoulder.

"I'm gonna take care of you." She didn't hesitate to let him enjoy his self, as he kissed her all the way down and stopped between her legs. After he finished, she was ready to get put back to sleep. She laid there grinding, as he wiped her juices away.

"Come on B...put it on please..." She begged, but he wanted it right. He wanted his wedding night to be special. If he was celibate for at least 30 days, he would feel more spiritually connected to God. Plus, the second accurate AIDS test would be back in seven days. That would seal their marriage of approval.

"No baby...we can...ah..ah, I have a surprise for you!" She jumped up in a rage.

"What? I'm sick of this shit! Motherfucker...you been trippin lately.."

"Excuse me, is everything okay in there?" Mrs. Vicki questioned, as she tried to shake the lock on the door. Rox calmed down and was confused. "What is my Mom doing over here?"

"I told you to put some clothes on Water....damn! Go ahead, I'm gonna find you something to wear." He put out a Roc-A-Wear valor sweat suit, with matching Nikes, and left the room. He made his way back downstairs and made everybody get quiet. As she made it down the stairs, she called out. "Brian boy.... what are you doing? Why is it so dark in here?"

She made it to the bottom of the steps and tried to turn on the light.

"Quit playin, and turn the lights on boy." She tried feeling her way on the wall, but couldn't see. Then Angie couldn't take it anymore.

"Surprise! Surprise! Surprise!" Everyone yelled, balloons went flying banners were all lit up and the kid's attacked Rox.

"Wait...wait!" She tried getting up, as they jumped and hung all over her, kissing her all over the face. She felt so good, but she didn't know what for. She stood up, to pull herself together, as the kid's ran around the house.

"What is all this for? I mean...what's going on?" She questioned, as she looked to see excitement and joy in everyone's eyes.

She saw Mr. Mackman and felt a little uneasy, but she blew it off. Darlene was standing there looking about 5 months pregnant and beautiful as ever.

"Well baby, we all are here to let you know that we are so proud of you, as a human being. You are graduating with honors and have been blessed to have a good man by your side. You want to be a floral designer, and that you will be." She looked around and started to cry.

"I didn't need all of this Mom. I'm okay with a small party...you didn't have to..."

"Oh girl, be quiet already....you never like when somebody helps you... you always help people and we just wanna show you thanks." Angie walked up and hugged her.

"So here, take this." She handed her a check for $15,000 dollars. Her eyes almost popped out of her head.

"Were did you get this from?" She said, while holding her heart and covering her mouth.

"From my Dad." Angie stated and pointed at Mr. Mackman. He stood there looking with shame in his eyes and a half smile.

"Oh you didn't have to do this." She said, as she ran over and hugged him.

"Yes I did young lady...you deserve this and please forgive me..."

"It's cool Mr. Mackman, God said 'forgive those that know not what they do.'"

"Thank you young lady." A load lifted off of his shoulders, as he thanked God himself, for Rox not telling Angie about the incident.

"We're not done yet girl." Darlene said, as she pulled out a check for $5,000 dollars and handed it to Rox. "Here girl, this will keep you busy, so you won't have time to be trippin on nobody." She laughed, and gave Darlene a hug around her neck, because she didn't want to hurt the baby.

She cried with tears of joy, as she watched her jealous sister frown her nose up. As she walked over to thank her Mom and Mr. Howard, she was greeted with more joy.

"This is from us baby." She read the notarized paper, that informed her of how much money her college account held. She had a choice to go off to college or invest her money into something that would pay off, or do both. She jumped up and down and cried.

"Oh my God! I haven't even graduated yet!" She said, while walking around and giving everybody hugs and kisses. As she hugged Brian's Mom and Uncle, she noticed that her baby was no where in sight.

"Where's Brian at?" She looked around, as everybody ate. As she walked to the door, him and Coop came strolling in. "Where have you been?" She wasn't gonna let him mess up her joy, so she held her composure.

"Nowhere...I was letting Coop in, he went to get the window fixed." She didn't know what was going on, so she left it alone.

"Oh...well look baby, I got money from Darlene and Mr. Mackman to start my own business." He was happy to know she was in a good mood.

He kissed her and said, "Everybody listen up...I have an announcement to make!" He held his hands in the air, to get their attention. He then pulled the box out of his pocket, that contained the seven carat engagement ring. Rox instantly started shaking.

"No...no, this is a dream. It...it's a dream." She was smiling from ear to ear and shaking her head. Her girl's all grabbed her and cried and laughed as well. He bent down on one knee, and did the honors, by grabbing her by the hand.

"Water, my be-a-u-tiful-water, we have been together for two years, and ever since that day I met you, I knew you were the one for me. Please be my wifey."

She was still crying and being held up, by her friends. All you could hear was sniffs and smiles.

"Yes....yes....yes...baby...I love you!" She lifted him up off of his knee and jumped in his arms. They kissed long and hard for what seemed like an eternity.

"Oh already...let's eat!" Angie said, as her and Coop grabbed their hands so they could pray.

Everyone got their grub on. Fried chicken, mac 'n cheese, greens, cornbread muffins, Kool aid and soda, along with Rox' favorite caramel chocolate brownies that her mother was famous for making.

Monique knew it would be a great idea to have colorful flowers decorate throughout the house. This was sure nuff gonna make her smile. Brian informed everybody that they needed private time together and they would have a small wedding, but a big reception. It had to be that way, so nobody would argue about who was going to be the best man or maid of honor.

Rox felt getting her own business was gonna be enough, so wasting money on a wedding, would be senseless. When it all falls down, her and Brian will be Mr. and Mrs. Walters.

Chapter 18

Claimin' Mine

The graduation was beautiful. Like everyone knew, Roxane Adams graduated, with honors, from Roosevelt High School, in South Minneapolis. She graduated with two scholarships. One was to the University of Minnesota, and the other one was to Clark University, in Atlanta, Georgia. Both schools learned of her fascination with flowers and gardening, and were quite impressed. It isn't too common for any African Americans to get involved with floral designing.

She decided to stay off campus, with her fiance' Brian, but will attend the U of M, for business management and horticulture. To make sure she received her full scholarship, she would take the 15 credits required, but would only go on certain days of the week, so she would have time to run her business.

Surrounding herself around Brian, made her want to become an entrepreneur even more. "Baby, what color do you want our wedding to be?" She asked, as they were getting ready for the wedding planner to come. Brian was discussing business with someone, in the shop.

"Hold up Water, I'll be there in a minute." She continued to clean up and prepare for company. He now was finished with the customers and made his way into the house.

"What's up?" He's giving her his full attention and looking into her beautiful eyes.

"I was asking what color do you want us to wear?" He reached out and grabbed her close, to smell her lovely scent.

"Whatever you want....just make it nice, but gangsta at the same time." He said, while kissing her.

"Oh...don't start what you ain't gonna finish." She started to pull away.

"No, I'm not gonna start Water...because I want our marriage to be right." She understood his meaning, for the Lord and so she had to respect that. Even though her pussy was saying beat it up now, her heart knew that celibacy would be the proper thing to do.

"Baby I have something to tell you, and I hope this doesn't change your mind about me." She looked directly in his eyes, and could read the worry all over his face. She longed for him to be straight forward and tell her what was going on with him, but he wouldn't. The blow wouldn't shock her, because she already knew.

"What is it B....spit that shit out!" She stepped back from him, to let him speak.

"I got tested."

"Okay and what...you straight ain't you? I mean...what?" He started sweating and playing with his fingers.

"Um...and it was...ah..negative baby." She knew all along, but felt the need to play hard even longer, to teach his ass a lesson about being careless.

"When in the hell were you gonna tell me? After I got married to you and had your damn kids boy!" He understood her anger and let her vent. "I mean, is that why that psycho bitch keeps coming around tryin to get yo ass back?"

"Yes, probably...but you know she ain't got shit coming."

She started crying, partly because she was happy that she didn't have the Monster (AIDS) and because this was her fiance'.

"Why couldn't you just tell me...it was before my time. I mean, you haven't fucked her since I've been with you?" He started crying and embraced her.

"No...Baby....I would never ever cheat on you...sniff sniff." They stood there cryin snot and booger session, for about ten minutes, until the doorbell rung.

"Oh, we forgot...the wedding planner is here!" He said, while wiping Rox' face and kissing her.

"Here...blow your nose Baby." She said, after blowing her's as well. "Here...take this tic tac, so yo shit don't be foul, while we are all up in her face." Rox busted out laughing.

"Boy! That's why I l-o-v-e you!" She reached over to put the mints in her mouth and give him a kiss.

"Thank you Baby, and my second test will be back by our honeymoon okay?" She nodded, and opened the door for the woman.

After arranging that the colors would be soft purple and navy blue, they had to decide if Monique or Angie would be the bridesmaid. Lili was out of the question, because Rox had to face it, they just didn't click. She still loved her to death and she would be invited, but she really didn't want her to participate, out of fear of her ruining the wedding. Lili's oldest kids, would be carrying the rings and Mr. Davis and Brian's uncle, would be giving them away.

Mrs. Vicki made their honeymoon in the motherland of Africa. It was an old ritual to jump the broom, and Brian felt that he has done so wrong in his life, that spending two weeks in the motherland would make his marriage last forever.

The wedding day was two days away, and everything was going smoothly. Angie informed Rox, that her parents were so happy that she decided to get married in their back yard. She let her know that she had missed her period, and took the EPT test and it was positive. She informed Coop and he's already making plans. He also confessed to her, that he slept with Tara, but Rox knew nothing about it.

Angie forgave him, because it was at the beginning of their relationship and he confessed to it.

Darlene was in charge of all the invitations and said everyone knew the directions to Angie's house.

Uncle Tate, Brian's mom and Mrs. Vicki were meeting with the people today, to pay for the building on Snelling and Grand. That would be the first location of the floral shop. It would be called "Louise Lovely Floral Designs", named after her grandmother. Once they see how the first location comes out, then they will open the Lake and Hennepin area next.

It was Saturday afternoon, and everyone was in place. Everyone cried, as they watched Rox walk down the aisle, with her soft purple dress sprinkled with navy blue pearls. Her hair was in a bun and her make up looked like she just stepped out of Cover Girl. Darlene made sure of that, and since she found her talent in it, she will be pursuing a career in that as well.

The preacher started his sermon, and everyone followed. After saying their vows, Rox immediately jumped in Brian's arms and kissed him. They danced the night away, and thanked everybody for being so patient.

Angie, Tasha and Monique prepared everything in Roxanne's bag. Making sure she had all the lingerie she could ever dream of. Tasha enjoyed herself, being as though she was 13, she hadn't seen so many panties at one time.

Lili came in to give her sister a hug and to tell her how proud of her she was. She also made an announcement, to let everybody know that the Lord has called on her, to change her life and that she no longer does illegal acts to get by, nor does she take prescription pills anymore. Everyone hugged her and gave her their love.

Brian's mom gave Rox a wedding ring, from his great great grandma, that has been in their family for years. This made her feel even more welcomed.

Just as everybody was leaving, Coop's car alarm went off. Monique and Jay were on their way to the car, so they let him know that they would check on it.

"Ooooh....what is that?" Monique pointed at the liquid that was on the ground.

"It's coming from the gas tank."

"Damn...somebody don't like Coop. Shit, they put something in his gas tank!" They both stepped closer to the car, to find a sugary residue, all over the end of the car. Monique ran back in the house, as Jay tried to clean it up.

"Yo Coop, somebody put sugar in your gas tank dog....you need to come look." Everybody jumped up and ran outside. Angie grabbed her bat and Rox dropped the train off her dress.

"Wait! Let me put my shoes on!" Rox kicked those heels off and made her way outside.

From out of nowhere, Tara and Leanna came flying from out the bushes, with paint guns. They lit everybody up, causing the older people to panic, because they thought it was really blood. Lili ran right up on Leanna.

"I'm tired of you harassing my sister bitch!" She whooped her ass, until the police came. Angie and Rox beat the shit out of Tara.

"Oh...you gonna try and team up with this hoe?" Rox said, while picking her up and slamming her. Angie was furious, because Coop was jumping up and down hollering about his gas tank and engine.

"What's wrong with you girl? Shit, you better not lose my baby!"

Everybody stopped fighting as the police arrived. Brian explained in front of everybody, about her having AIDS and harassing him and Rox. Angie explained that Tara was upset, because Coop chose her over Tara. As the police took them away, Rox could not help but flash her seven carats and say, "now hoe, it's official...yeah, dis is mine...I'm claiming mines...I'm Mrs. Walters, ya heard!" She flashed the ring all up in her face, as the police put her in the car.

Angie jumped in.

"Yeah, and you hoes better recognize that the dick is sowed up....dis my baby daddy dats right!" Angie stated while doing some kinda dance in front of the officer and Tara.

"Na...na, you my fiance' now!" Coop said, while kissing Angie.

The police took both of them away and charged them with vandalism and damage of personal property on a private residence. After all the commotion died down, and Angie and Rox convinced their parents that they would be okay, everyone left.

The next day, Mrs. Vicki and Mr. Howard called, to give their best wishes on their trip. Angie and Coop brought over the last of their personal items.

The second AIDS test came back, and of course, it was negative. All the shots they had to take to get to Africa, made them feel a little uneasy. They finally landed in the motherland and was greeted with great respect.

After making it to their hotel room, Rox was ready to get busy. She took a shower and came out in her red teddy, sex toys, garter belt and handcuffs. Brian stood butt ass naked, with his dick at full attention.

"You ready baby?" She said, with batting eyes.

"Like never before, my lovely Water." They freaked the night away. Rox made him come at least ten times, to make up for lost time.

"Oh...I'm sleepy W-a-t-e-r."

"Nah, you're mine's now, so you have to make up for lost time." He sat up and told her, "I guess da hood does make fresh water."

She smiled. "You damn right it does."

The End

Cast of Characters

Victoria Adams - Mom a.k.a. Vicki

Monique - St. Paul homegirl/1 year older

Angie - Childhood friend with issues/2 years older

Darlene - Hater friend that's good for a fight, but jealous of others/3 years older.

Carl - Football star boyfriend/ Senior

Terrance - Her undercover lover

Lynett Renea Adams - a.k.a. Lili/pill poppin sister/hater

Howard Davis - a.k.a. Mr. D/Step dad

Denise - Her man Carl's under cover girl

Mr. Erickson - Gym teacher

Aunt Judy - Track star/Lawyer

Kane - Cousin in Jail

Aunt Donna - Terrance's Aunt/God fearing

Angie Mackman - has a black mom and white dad, Mr. Mackman.

Darlene Longtongue - has a native american mom, black dad.

Monique Cherry - black

Roxane Adams - black

Terry - Drill team leader

Mrs. Ann - She owns the soul food restaurant

Tobby - Darlene's heroin hustler boyfriend.

Dr. Snatchout - The abortion doctor

Latasha - Her step sister

Brian Walters - Baller that she met at the wing shop.

Jay Hustle - Monique's boyfriend

Tara - girl from work

Coop - Angie's boyfriend

Leanna - Brian's old girlfriend

Uncle Tate - Brian's uncle

Acknowledgements

Vivian Heard (Mom), Eric Heard (Dad), Eugene S. (Rock) White Sr. (Grandpa),
Edna Mae Collier (Grandma), S.L. Ulmer (Grandpa),
Karl F. Marshall (Dad) and last but not least, my birth father
Darnell T. White…

To my daughters Tomeisha, Culizahnae and Jalena- always know you guys are my heart and you motivate me more than you'll ever know…

At the time in my life when I wrote this book, I have to thank the people that kept me straight and encouraged me to do something positive:
Rachelle, Roshae, LaShawn, Karla, Devienya, Lemarc, Dominique, and Kierra- thank you all for never giving up on me and looking out for my girls when I couldn't!!!

My peoples on lock down: Jermaine (Chat), Darnell (Nigga D), David (Lil Dave), Ronald(Ronnie) , Jerome (Noodles), Nunn, Frederick (Freddie), Rafael (Felly), Juwan (Doe Boy), Lemarc (Uzi), Derrick (D-Astro), Tammy, Denise, Yolanda (YoYo), Tiffany (Tif), Diana, Eva, and Lamont (Monty).

To the people that opened my eyes and kept it positive and loved my heart and kindness: Desiree, Kim, Kequina, Keisha, Darnell (Nelly), Donya ("D"), Danarious (Bonk), Asa, Gretchen, Larry, Travis ("T"), Mike, Kathy, Rashane (Ray Ray), Nina (Yellow), Big Keisha, B-Outlaw, Nanna, Tina, Chandra, Barb, Nicole, Kina, Yolanda, Pam, Chara (Tink), Valerie, Emily, Sandra, Joanne (Ms. Joe), Iresha (Icey), Donnella, Nicole (Nicky), Demetrius (Nicki), Twin, Tonya, Cynthia, Candace, Alice J., Denise (D-Nice), Dayna, Missy, Shonna, Shandel, Stephanie, Shaneeka, Ace, Tonya (Tiny), Tawanna (T-Momma), Mike, Keisha, Tone, Kim, Pie, Barb, Terrell, Britney, Moo, Marlin, Ronald, Kristen.
Special thanks to my elders that gave me strength when I didn't know I had it:
Pam J., Charlnetta (Chi), Sis Johnson, Bonnie, Rochelle, Pearline, Auntie Barb, Viola, Georgia, Uncle Sam, Eugene and Buchie.

Thanks Thomas for Tomeisha- she is the inspiration I needed at 16...

Thanks Dominique for Culizah and Jalena- I appreciate the two blessings that you helped me receive...

Thanks to my nephews Larry and Jabar and my God kids Clyde and Kye- since I couldn't make boys, I'll try my best with yall!

My two sisters Karla and Kellen and my brother Darnell- thanks for your positive influence!

George, Kani, Marcus, Ebony J. and Big Dave – thanks for being real!

Roy, Mack, LaSalle, Contact, Pam L, Brandy, Chuck and Henry for always speaking on me in a positive way no matter if I'm right or wrong and never hating when I'm not looking...

Thank you Jermaine for pushing me to do this and making me feel myself again...

Thank you GOD for Psalm 27: 1-5!

Thank you Mom, I hope I made you proud!

To the Senator and next President of the United States- Barak Obama for making it this far and encouraging me to do the unthinkable...

PEACE OUT-